Don —
Your friendship is God's gift and blessing to me —
  Peace,
  [signature]

The Lemon Drop Didn't Melt

A Tricia Gleason Novel

Mark Henry Miller

authorHOUSE®

AuthorHouse™
1663 Liberty Drive
Bloomington, IN 47403
www.authorhouse.com
Phone: 1 (800) 839-8640

© 2016 Mark Henry Miller. All rights reserved.

No part of this book may be reproduced, stored in a retrieval system, or transmitted by any means without the written permission of the author.

Published by AuthorHouse   03/29/2016

ISBN: 978-1-5049-8716-5 (sc)
ISBN: 978-1-5049-8715-8 (e)

Print information available on the last page.

Any people depicted in stock imagery provided by Thinkstock are models, and such images are being used for illustrative purposes only. Certain stock imagery © Thinkstock.

This book is printed on acid-free paper.

Because of the dynamic nature of the Internet, any web addresses or links contained in this book may have changed since publication and may no longer be valid. The views expressed in this work are solely those of the author and do not necessarily reflect the views of the publisher, and the publisher hereby disclaims any responsibility for them.

Acknowledgements

No, the novel title isn't a prompter for cinema. Not even close. It came to me while casting for winter steelhead on the Calawah River out of Forks, Washington. I knew that Tricia Gleason would have trouble to an exponential extreme. I then heard "Somewhere Over The Rainbow," the particular notion that "troubles melt like lemon drops…" And it hit me: trouble abounded for Tricia, so the lemon drop didn't melt.

In writing to my heart's content, I didn't have either a mask or silver bullet. And to even think I know how to ride a horse…well, you wouldn't even ask. No Lone Ranger I.

Which means I am more than indebted to many, each of whom helped craft this Tricia Gleason adventure. Editors that make me proud to be a writer.…Al Day, James Thayer and Slim Randles. Al Day who knows more about verb structure than most English teachers. Jim Thayer's a professor who knows three things: how to affirm, how to edit and how to be irenic in any circumstance, simply by offering, "You may be right."

Slim deserves his own paragraph. A writer of no little regard, Slim writes neighborhood newspaper articles for over 350 newspapers. I figured he would know a few things about verbs and how often one word gets used too much. He has helped the novel considerably, especially in making sure Tricia isn't completely overwhelmed with the silent and shadowed foe. Slim's my favorite cowboy out of Albuquerque. But now he's the one who has helped considerably with how lemon drops might melt. He's got a terrific podcast, slang and all: http:homecountry.podbean.com. Give him an ear or two; you'll be glad you did. I know that I am.

But this novel particularly tips a fishing rod to crime authorities—in detection not function. Forensic and DNA expertise happened because of the following: My dear friend, Chase Stapp, came through again. It doesn't hurt he's the Police Chief with the San Marcos, Texas, Police Department. And criminal investigations procedures from Jeffrey Hayes, Assistant Chief at the Leander, Texas Police Department, Eric Elletson, Washington State Police and Sean Absher, Snoqualmie, Washington Police Department gave the novel forensic verity.

More information than I could have ever googled when it comes to possible causes for miscarriages was shared by Dr. Karen Jones, Seattle, Washington Obstetrician. Other input on infant crises helped considerably. In addition, these two wonderful friends kept me from wandering. Gratitude on counseling content to Dr. Carol Stanley, therapist in North Carolina and Dr. Bryan Austill, therapist and clergy buddy in Dillon, Colorado.

Perhaps most critical to the novel's final destination I tip my hat to John and Dawn Koenig. Am proud they invited me to officiate their wedding. But even more gratitude for their helping Purple Heart Veterans through the WWIA. In Rockport, Washington, they've built a bunkhouse next to their log cabin home and more than a few times each year host the WWIA veterans and take them either fishing or hunting. You will note John and Dawn are scripted in the novel [aka Jon and Heather]. But in real life they are my heroes, not just because John knows where the 95% holes on the Skagit River are for either Coho salmon or winter steelhead, but because how much he and Dawn care for those wounded in defending our country. Check them out at: www.johns-guide-service.com and the WWIA at: www.wwiaf.org

Finally, everything happens, the long nights and short mornings, with focus and energy and ideas, because of the best friend in the world, my wife, Diane. Diane? Thank you for your support and suggestions on how the plot might morph into something interesting. Hopefully the read is more than that.

However, in it all truth is transparent, my mea culpa. Where there are mistakes, where the segues seem beyond remote, that's on me. Please be gentle and understanding. So hopefully when you and Tricia learn how the lemon drop does melt, it will be a good place… for you…and for her.

Chapter 1

She never planned for the grocery shopping to lead to surprise, embarrassment and mystery. All at the same time. Ordinary shopping is checking off the list, maybe seeing a nice price on chips. But this time was more.

She'd been in town only a week, yet the cashier looked at her, "Reverend Gleason," she said, waving for Tricia to come to the #7 check-out. Tricia kept her brow smooth although her curiosity lurked, *Why does she know me? This is my first time here.*

She saw the nametag, "Montina," which could have been last, first or even her middle name. Montina removed the puzzlement, "You don't know me yet, but I recognize you. You are the first woman pastor we've ever had."

"I like that name…Montina. I assume that's you…that you didn't switch nametags."

Montina pointed and smiled, "That's good. Quick and good. Nope, my nametag. Don't know of any other Montina…do you?"

"Not in a blink. Easy to remember."

Montina put her hand to her mouth as if to be quiet, "Oh, I should tell you. I saw your picture in the neighborhood paper and then in our church newsletter. You're even prettier than the picture…and the picture is great."

Extended her hand, "I'm Montina Creek, a member of your new church. Oh, I mean you are our new pastor at our old church. Welcome to our community. We're happy to have you on board. We can really use a good pastor. We've been without a steady pastor for over a year."

Tricia shook the hand of a new parishioner, leaned down to unload the cart. She figured she had everything on her list and then a good 2 for 1 price on the Doritos. Another clerk, a young man in his late teens smiled, "May I help you?" He didn't wait for an answer, emptying the cart on to the belt. He then snickered.

He placed an item on the middle of the conveyer belt. This certainly was not on her list… but part of her groceries…not part of her selections…but it was there anyway.

She didn't know what to do…embarrassment took charge. Tricia tried her cool world thinking Montina River or Creek or Whatever wouldn't notice. But she did, lifting the package of Trojan Lubricated Condoms, coughing for effect, and continuing. Not pausing a breath Montina simply offered, as naturally as possible… "Guess you're a scout—always be prepared."

Tricia said, "Oh, this is a mistake. Please take that off my bill…I didn't put them in my cart."

Truth was truth. But Montina wondered…if her new pastor used embarrassment to hide dishonesty. Said nothing more, collected the money, handed the receipt, "Have a good day, Pastor Gleason…I'll look forward to your first sermon in a few days."

Before Tricia could respond, Montina greeted the next customer. Tricia did her best wave, "Good-bye!" but the clerk, a parishioner she'd see on Sunday, had no response. As if they hadn't met…even worse coursing through Tricia's mind. She didn't matter. She swung at the first pitch and missed. *What in the world is this…lubricated condoms???*

What Tricia didn't see as she left for her car was the man standing by the pharmacy in "family planning," section, smiling. More than an attitude, it was a smirk. "Got you, bitch. Maybe it should be, got you, Pastor Bitch."

Other shoppers hadn't paid attention to him for the last hour. A busy Friday afternoon was great for his game plan. Most of the carts were in use. Wandering—giving casual its best impression—up one aisle then the other, carefully dropping items in shopping carts, especially those with infants in their car seats…items the hapless mothers would refuse when checking out. He wasn't invisible, but to them he was unnoticeable. Clever. Crafty. And with one real purpose…achieved. The rest was child stuff.

Just another day at the office he thought. But he knew. It was the first paragraph in a long story to unfold, one that would make sure his favorite pastor would never make it as a pastor…or worse.
A good start? You bet.

And he was pleased…the beard was natural, as if his own. It didn't slip. Masked his identity…she surely would know him. Couldn't risk that. Life wasn't life without surprise…and demise. The game plan.

He couldn't wait until her first office counseling meeting, especially if a church member's confidentiality centered the visit. Couldn't wait. He figured she would promise confidentiality, which he would make sure never was kept. He was good at transcribing the conversations… and then…oh, what is life without surprises and demolishing? Tick. Tick. Tick.

Chapter 2

Tricia liked the Yogi Berra quote about when you come to a fork in the road…take it. She looked back on her summer in Colorado, a summer internship. She had been surprised that her summer ministry would mean she had to be "up" every Sunday, find a lost parishioner and solve what appeared to be a murder/suicide. All that in addition to some fly fishing in the mountains.

The fork appeared…not in a river but in her future. She had been expected to return for her second seminary year at Ocean Divinity School in Berkeley but accepted the call of this church instead. Something nagged at her though. The thought of returning to Tillamook to guide for salmon on Tillamook Bay and cast for steelhead in the Wilson, Nestucca and Trask Rivers was undeniable. It pushed and tugged. The question of *do I really want to be in ministry?* pushed her hard.

Instead of heading to Berkeley and a continuation of her seminary classes, she went to Portland and to visit with her best friend in the world, Creighton Yale. He had been a minister, recently retired as a conference minister and had encouraged Tricia to go to seminary. He was always her *go-to* guide, one whom she could trust…and her trust never faltered.

When she relayed her doubts, he came up with what he called a *healthy compromise*. "Tricia," as he tapped his knee, a habit of making sure he was taken seriously, "you don't have to make an either-or decision. Okay? I understand your options: return to seminary or return to your fishing guide world. Why not find a decision that includes both?"

She was clueless.

He continued, "I have a friend in Seattle, not the most reliable guy in the world, but he knows the pulses of our churches up there. Talked to him when you explained your quandary and he came up with the possibility of being a licensed minister for a year. He said there is a church in Snoqualmie, 25 miles east of Seattle, that has been somewhere near desperate for leadership, about to close down. They haven't been able to have a minister for over a year. They've stuck together---a good indication of the members' loyalty to the church. For Sunday worship—but nothing more—they bring in substitute preachers. No continuity. The need for steady leadership is large… make that enormous.

"I bragged about you. He said you could be there a year…nothing more or less…to see if you can teach them what Jesus told the disciples to do when their nets were empty, to throw their nets on the right side of the boat."

He smiled. She nodded…no frown. The fork in the road---okay, so it was three forks. What probably secured the option was the combination of ministry and fishing. For she knew…although

Tillamook Bay and the rivers flowing into it…not even to mention fishing the Columbia River in August…as good as it could be… Washington fishing…for trout, salmon and steelhead was better than best. Creighton even knew three guides who could show her the fishability.

She called Ocean Divinity School about a year's licensed ministry… to see if it was possible for her to return for her second year later. She didn't say "return" was tentative. They said it was fine…and pointed out one recent graduate serving a church as Rector on nearby Mercer Island in an Episcopal Church. Was clear Hannah Ball could be a good connector. Tricia would make sure that happened.

The talk with Micah Dimmock, the Seattle executive minister friend of Creighton's went well. She had stopped into his north Seattle office to learn more. He said Creighton's recommendation convinced him Tricia should do the licensed ministry position, He had visited with the moderator of St. Andrew's United Church of Christ in Snoqualmie. Her name is Sage Worthy, an attorney in Seattle and lifelong member of St. Andrew's. An interview had been set up with Sage and her committee of three. They wanted her. Most of their wanting was genuine, although with more than a twinge of concern for the future of the church. That was a strong undercurrent.

She signed a one-year licensed ministry contract. Her housing was covered…a church member had been assigned to London by Microsoft and donated her house for the year which was a new 3-bedroom ranch that provided good space. Only ten minutes from the church and less than thirty minutes to "anywhere," which meant city and trout streams. No pets. No fuss. A good deal. In the beginning. The clincher, although Tricia didn't have any other no-cost options was she could walk from her home to a small hill and look down in the valley and see the Snoqualmie River. It could be her nest.

Tricia thought of this as she left the grocery store. The mystery of the condoms dumped into her cart didn't linger. Probably something just stupid and accidental.

She had a good impression of Snoqualmie, a city that celebrated the old and historic—how impressed Tricia was with the old trains standing watch over history…engines and cars along the road to Snoqualmie, a sleepy village. An outside train museum. Old Snoqualmie reminded her of Garibaldi, Oregon, standing sentinel over Tillamook Bay.

However, her research indicated all the new housing…up on the hill over Snoqualmie…wasn't a favorite of the Chamber of Commerce. Sure. More tax revenue and good for business. But those who had settled recently in Snoqualmie, mostly executives with 2.5 kids and 1.5 dogs and 1 cat, did most of their shopping in Issaquah, five miles west. Or Bellevue or Seattle. Snoqualmie wasn't a retail center. But it was a great place for families.

Plus, Snoqualmie was not on anyone's list for "fine dining." An old hotel had a restaurant that featured prime rib on Tuesdays. Otherwise dining options were limited. Most new owners appreciated the housing costs that were considerably less than Issaquah. And one of the St. Andrew's committee members was brash, "Tricia, live in Snoqualmie. Issaquah's so pricey, even glitzy and try to find a parking place…in front of your house there. Honestly? It's become an ant hill. And who wants to live in a faux toney ant hill?"

Tricia loved that bordering the north side of Old Snoqualmie was the Snoqualmie River, with fir trees and blackberry tangles on both shores. She also thought that Snoqualmie Falls was impressive. More impressive, though, was her learning that winter steelhead could be caught downstream from the falls. It didn't occur to her that "falls" was water cascading down…or a time of year…less than it would become a theological condition. Made her almost feel she belonged with a view of the river from near her home and the river flowing behind the church. A good venue for home…and church.

Her new home was one of five in a cul-de-sac. She hadn't met any of the neighbors, although Sage had said two of the families were church members. They'd be high on her visiting list.

Unpacking her groceries, finding where food fit in the pantry, she went to her new home office. Lovely, large desk, open window to the street, an impressive view of the mountains beyond the Snoqualmie River and lots of books. The homeowner kept it neat. Tricia would keep that going.

She noticed something, though. On the desk-pad a yellow sticky note. It hadn't been there that morning. Maybe she missed it when she put her books on the shelf. A note that simply said, "Reverend? Please call me. I'm hurting."

The number was local. Questions. And with that, concerns. Who is this? Who put the note here? Does someone have access to the house? Has the security failed? Tick. Tick. Tick.

CHAPTER 3

No name. Strange. Curious. Tricia dialed, not wanting to be unresponsive. Creighton had warned her the worst thing a minister could do was to ignore the pleas of members. He said he knew ministers who hated the hospital visiting, so they would be creative in excusing a no visit. He knew ministers, who when a church member was in depression, would mail them a book. They told Creighton, who had worked with ministers for over 30 years, "I cannot handle their depression; they need a therapist."

The ringing stopped, "Hello, this is Sage Worthy, may I help you?"

Tricia couldn't believe it. Sage? "Hi, Sage, this is Tricia Gleason. You wanted me to call?"

Silence. "I'm sorry, Tricia. I didn't...."

More silence.

Tricia was puzzled, "I just came home and saw your note on my home office desk, asking me to call. The note said, 'Pastor, please call me. I'm hurting." And left your number."

"Oh my, how strange. I didn't do that, Tricia. Yes, of course this is my number…are you sure you dialed it correctly? Maybe it is another number. Please check."

Tricia held the note…her hand shook…this is what the number is, Sage…"

Repeated it.

"Yes, that's my home number…I just happened to be home. I am glad I answered it. But no, I never left a note. Did you say the note was on your home office desk? How long has it been there?"

Tricia furrowed her brow, "No, I'm sure it wasn't here this morning. I saw it when I returned from shopping at the grocery store in Snoqualmie. I have no idea who put it there. Besides, whoever did this either had to have a key…or maybe…although I try hard to not do this…I left the front door unlocked. Makes no sense. Other than you didn't leave the note and I dialed the correct number. Not sure what to do."

"Okay, Tricia, now the attorney in me is taking over…is the note hand-written?"

"No, it's printed in cursive, small font, hard to read. Hand-written in calligraphy."

"Just the note…nothing else?"

"Yes, that's it."

Silence.

Certainly not a good start for Tricia…a new item in her shopping cart, meeting Montina and explaining why the condom package wasn't hers…and now this note. Tricia then spoke, taking the high road, "Oh, this probably means nothing, Sage. I'm glad I called. We may never know what this is about."

"Yes, you're right, Tricia. Some things we cannot know. But I know one thing. About you. Your references were right, especially what your mentor, Creighton Yale said."

"He said something that relates to this?"

"Yes, oh my, yes. He said you were very committed to connecting with people…that you were gifted in recognizing and reducing human needs…and then he said this…you will respond yesterday if it will help someone. This to me, Tricia, is an example of a yesterday response. You didn't hesitate. Reverend Yale also said you had the most important gift of a minister…you are a pastoral presence. We can count on you to care for us… and never from a distance. Thank you for that, even though this note and how it got into your home is strange. But I guess not everything makes sense…right?"

Tricia took a deep breath, exhaled and for reasons she couldn't identity, she felt better, "Well, thanks, Sage. For the compliment… making lemonade out of a mysterious lemon. Don't think anything of this…too much else to do. I won't worry about it."

Tick. Tick. Tick.

CHAPTER 4

⁂

Three. There were three standing on her porch, faces pushed up against her front door. Looked like children, although blurry. Through the smoky glass she saw only images. Then a tap. Tricia was curious... she had a hunch but only that. She had been told two church families lived on her street. She had met the young couple next door, recently married, six months into a new pregnancy, both employed. She forgot their names, but thought it was Bradley and Sarah Murdough. They knew they were having a girl, and had already picked out the name. Tricia, though not a parent, must be old school. She wouldn't want to know gender...believed in surprises. She appreciated that one worked for Verizon and the other Amazon. Reputable companies and good jobs. The wife worked for Verizon...they had a great maternity policy. A good thing.

The three visitors backed off, distancing themselves. *Were they afraid? Just wanted to meet her?*

Before she got to the door, a slight tap...she could see the taller one had reached up for the knocker. Then the doorbell. Tricia didn't want to open immediately, it could scare them. So she paused, counting to herself up to 12. A good number she had learned very early when living in the Seattle area. The number 12 was the "mantra number" for every Seattle Seahawk fan, to at least emotionally be part of the football team. She opened the door.

There weren't three. Yes, three children, but back on the sidewalk were two adults. All were beaming. The mother, "Okay everybody, on cue, 1, 2, 3…"

"WELCOME, REVEREND GLEASON. WELCOME TO OUR NEIGHBORHOOD!"

How incredibly cool for Tricia! A welcoming committee, welcoming her to the neighborhood. She was tempted to ask if they were sent by Mr. Rogers, but the kids were too young to know about the television program, "Mister Rogers' Neighborhood." Nothing like untimely humor to ruin a good visit.

"Oh my, how thoughtful! So very thoughtful."

She opened the door wide, stepped back with her best smile, "Come on in. I'd love to meet you."

She noticed each of the kids, probably 6 and 4 and maybe 3, had their hands behind their back. It was hard for them to walk, but their parents helped them.

Tricia walked ahead of them, turned back, "Why don't we come to the TV room. Sorry, I don't have any games."

The mother nodded, "That's a good thing. We're glad you are home. And you will learn this, Reverend Gleason. You are OUR pastor."

As if on cue, the kids responded, "YEAH!"

The mother then said, "I'd like you to meet our family…"

Before she added a name the taller boy jumped in, "Mom? We know our names. We want to tell Reverend Gleason who we are!"

The mother smiled, "You are right, Quentin…absolutely. Guess it is time for introductions. Go for it, buddy."

He didn't smile, he beamed…on the stage in the moment, "Reverend Gleason," his hands still behind his back, "I'm Quentin Gladstone, but my friends and my family call me Scooter. Except when I'm in trouble at home; then it's the full name, Quentin Harper Gladstone."

Tricia had been placed on top of the world by a little child. She wanted to hug him, but arms behind the back made that awkward. "Hello, Quentin, may I call you Scooter?"

He nodded, "Sure!" The mother tapped the daughter on the shoulder, but Quentin interrupted, "Mom? Not finished."

"Oops…great call Scooter…sorry to interrupt."

Scooter then showed his hands. They weren't empty.

Tricia wasn't sure what he held, but it was definitely hand-crafted. As if he'd practiced it for weeks, Scooter explained, holding up his gift.

"Reverend Gleason, glad you are our new pastor."

He pointed to her, "You? Fishing guide? Good fishing here. Big salmon. Not caught yet. Oh, we have a kid's fishing pond. Right here. You can come."

Quite a mouthful, but he came to his main point, holding up his gift. "Help you with fishing…I made you a fishing pole." He handed it to her.

Tricia teared up, without embarrassment, only with gratitude. "Oh, Scooter, can I hug you? This is so special…gosh, my own fishing pole."

He still wasn't finished, "Okay. I'll explain……the pole is a popsicle stick, the reel is the spool of thread, the line is some yarn from my mother and the hook is a paper clip. Great fishing pole only for you."

"How special, Scooter…and thoughtful. Thank you."

"I'm next!" the daughter explained, holding up a police badge; it was plastic. "Reverend Gleason, my name is Cynthia," as she pointed next to her, "My twin brother, Charles."

Charles, not to be upstaged, "Cynthy, go ahead. Can introduce myself."

"Okay, younger twin brother. My turn…explain my gift," holding up her gift, "Reverend Gleason, Mom and Dad told us you a detective… they said the kind of detective but I forgot…Hommy or something like that. Wanted to give you this…some of your past. Think that's real cool…do you ever watch 'Blue Bloods?' We cannot see it…our parents say a cool detective in the show."

Another warm moment, but not without an inner twinge. For yes, Tricia had been a homicide detective for the Oregon State Police. She was removed from her position when she blundered in a search of a warehouse. She and her partner thought the robber had gone into the warehouse. Tricia checked it out, thought the robber had escaped and told her partner that. She was wrong. And in a moment she'll never forget, the robber killed her partner. Horrific.

She still smiled, though, for the gift was more important than the memory.

The third child, Tricia picked up he was the *younger twin.* Said, "Hi, I may be the youngest, fifteen minutes younger than my sister—she beat me. Doesn't mean I don't count. Oh, I can count days and weeks and months and how old I am. Happy you our new minister. What I give…my father…made it…said you knew how to fly fish…could use this for…"

He paused and looked at his father.

"Indicator" his father explained.

"Yes, an indicator—guess you can make it smaller so it will float on the river and when it sinks that means there's a fish on the line. So here," he handed Tricia a foot-long piece of yarn…chartreuse in color. "Dad said this color—chawtoose…seen all kinds of weather. Always floats."

He then winced, "Oh! Forgot. I'm Charles…friends call me Chip. You can call me Chip. Okay?"

Tricia, often accused of being a wordsmith, was speechless. She had to say something, sighed, exhaled fully, 'Oh my goodness. I've never had a better welcoming committee. How great!"

She then held up the gifts, "And," pointing to each of the kids, "Know these are the best gifts in the world. I'll put them on my desk to remind me of where I've been."

Pointing to the yarn, "This will always float. Hey, maybe that can be a children's sermon. What do you think?"

Scooter didn't hesitate, "I bet you can figure out something about my fishing pole!"

Cynthia joined in, "And, for sure we need police and detectives. Hey, guess we've already started to help you being a minister. Maybe… ideas for children's sermons."

"Kids?", Tricia's eyes wet but sparkling through, "For sure. You are now part of my ministry."

Scooter then looked at his parents, "Mom and Dad? You're next."

They explained they had lived in Snoqualmie for 2 years…when their house was built. They were Andrew and Abby Gladstone, and had lived in the Northwest all their lives. Before her first child, Abby worked for an auto-repair shop in Issaquah and Andrew and his father ran a plumbing company out of North Bend. They both were University of Washington graduates, had dated since high school, and were very pleased to live in their home country.

Tricia looked at the clock on the fireplace mantel, saw it was close to 5 p.m. She wanted to ask Andrew and Abby about "their" church, but could do that later.

Abby also saw the time, "Oh, we've taken too much of your day. Guess your personal welcoming committee will be on our way.

Reverend Gleason? Please know we are delighted that you are our neighbor. And, no less, that you are our new pastor. Welcome to our community and our church."

On the way to the front door, Tricia said, "Might you wait a minute? Kids? Why don't you help me before you leave?"
She walked to her home office and waved them in, "Please come here a minute."

She pointed to her desk. "This is my desk…you each choose where I should put your gift…want to see them every day…and keep each of you in my thoughts."

They didn't hesitate…decisions made quickly. Everyone was pleased. Especially Tricia.

They stood on the porch.

Andrew paused, "Oh we didn't realize you had a plumbing problem. Please know the next time you need some plumbing done, let me know. We can help."

Piqued curiosity for Tricia, "Plumbing problem? What do you mean? I am not aware of a plumbing problem."

Abby didn't hesitate, "Yes, I told Andrew that a plumbing truck parked in front of your house earlier this afternoon. I figured you had called for some help. He stayed about 30 minutes, then left."

A complete surprise to Tricia. She had no plumbing problem. What is this all about? But, rather than share that, she smiled and lied, "Well, guess the owner of the house had called…he's in London…

must have been something he didn't take care of before he left. I'll have to ask him."

Tricia closed the door. *Plumbing problem? Plumber came to her house?* She then thought of the note on her desk. *What in the world?*

Tick. Tick. Tick.

Chapter 5

Not a good night. Not by any measure. Tricia gave "Sleepless in Seattle" a vivid footnote. The "plumbing situation" bothered her. She *knew* Clark hadn't ordered a plumber for the house. Before he left he told Tricia, "Everything's in good shape, Tricia. If you have any problems, here is the list of go-to-companies," handing her twenty names that could cover every imaginable problem…from stopped sinks to water leaks to electrical issues to landscaping.

So she knew. Because he hadn't called about any needed repairs, the plumber's visit was not Clark's call. Tricia had to know more.

Abby hadn't given her their phone number, but she found it on the new church directory. Didn't think 8:30 a.m. on Saturday was too early, so called.

The answer came quickly, "Good morning, Reverend Gleason. Can we help you with anything?"

"Oh. Good morning. Guess there are no secrets—you know my number."

"Oh yes, our church sent it to all of us and said you wouldn't mind if we called you…but it had to be important. That's why your number registered…you are on our quick-dial list. What can I do for you?"

"Forgot to ask a couple of questions before you and the family left. And. Before I say anything more, please know your children's gifts took my breath. They have won my heart!"

"We are more than happy about that…and know, if there's anything we can do to help—other than, I might add, to write any sermons—please let us know. But. About your call."

"Yes," Tricia said, "I wanted to follow-up on the plumber's visit. I checked with Clark and he said he didn't call a plumber. Abby? Do you remember which plumber it was? I'm certain it wasn't from Andrew's company or you would have known that."

"Oh," Abby responded, "Yes, it's our biggest competitor. You know the giant out to subdue David? It's Mountain Plumbing…they have a Snoqualmie address…here, we have it. They're on Main Street; here's their phone number."

"Thanks, Abby. Did you happen to see the driver? Or anything that got your attention?"

"No I didn't. I was coming home from shopping and saw the truck parked in front of your house. But I didn't see anything unusual. Just figured a repair was in order. Sorry I cannot be of more help."

"Oh, not to worry. I appreciate the company name and number. Hope your day goes well."

The Lemon Drop Didn't Melt

"Know we all look forward to being in church Sunday…I bet you're excited about your first sermon. The kids will look forward to the children's sermon. I guess you have to choose between a fishing pole, some yarn and a detective badge…right?"

Tricia, still bothered by the bogus plumber's visit barely heard that, but responded safely, "Yes, I hope Sunday goes well. Gotta be on my way…take care Abby."

It was Saturday, but Tricia figured since Mountain Plumbing was large, they'd answer.

"Thank you for calling Mountain Plumbing. This is Katherine, how may I help you?"

"Hello, Katherine. My name is Tricia Gleason. I'm staying in the home of Clark Hudson. He's in London for the year for Microsoft. The reason I'm calling is I wanted to know who called one of your plumbers to come to my house yesterday. Might you have that information? Here's the address…and the owner's name, again, is Clark Hudson."

No response. Silence. Tricia could hear Katherine clear her throat. A quieter voice…the greeting pleasantry all but gone, "Oh. Let me transfer you to our dispatcher. Maybe she can help you…"
Quickly another voice, "Hello, this is the dispatcher. How can I help?"

Tricia figured the dispatcher, for whatever reason, had been clued in by Katherine. Tricia explained anyway.

The dispatcher then said, "We need to contact Mr. Hudson, ma'am. He owns the house and we have done service calls for him before. However...."

The hesitation was not accidental. Something was up.

Tricia didn't wait, "Oh, I called him and he said he hadn't notified you. I was told by my neighbor your plumbing truck was at my house yesterday. I asked for more information from my neighbor and she only knew it was your truck. She never saw the driver."

"Well, I need to call our Snoqualmie Police about this."

Saying nothing more Tricia said, "The police? Please tell me what's wrong."

"Well, I'm really not at liberty, ma'am. Other than a detective from the county will be in touch with you…for more information."

"I'm sorry, but I don't have anything more than what I told you. I wasn't here and my neighbor said she saw the truck, but nothing else."

Tricia then decided to push, "Please tell me. I'm the new minister in town at St. Andrew's Church in Snoqualmie and in a previous life was a detective for the Oregon State Police. That may mean nothing, but a word or two of clarification from you would help."

The dispatcher responded with information that was brief, "I'll give you four words. How's that? Here they are. Our. Truck. Was. Stolen."

"Oh my," Tricia offered. "I'll look for the detective's visit and will help if at all possible…but honestly I am nothing more than a blank sheet of paper. Did you find the truck?"

Click.

Plumbing Truck. Stolen. Detective visit.

Not realizing she did this, Tricia looked at her hand…she had reached up from her desk chair and grabbed the yarn. Crazy.

Chapter 6

Tricia opened the garage door. Before she got in her car she looked up. Standing in her driveway were Bradley and Sarah Gladstone.

"Good morning, Tricia…we were just coming over with some blueberry muffins…thought they'd be good for your breakfast."

Tricia nodded, "How thoughtful." She didn't look at her watch…knew to do that was always the body language of *I don't have time*. She hedged the truth, "I'm not in a rush to get to my office…why don't you come in?" as she waved them in through the garage.

Tricia didn't have coffee made, but had some apple cider. Bradley and Sarah declined.

Moving beyond the *hello and how are you and fine thanks* Sarah looked at Bradley, almost for permission.

Bradley said, "Sarah, go ahead. Tricia needs to know."

For a flash Tricia thought maybe they knew something about the plumbing truck. She waited.

Sarah looked at Tricia, "Bradley and I have talked long and deep about this, Tricia. We don't want you to be thinking we are snoops. Or we are bringing trouble…."

She stopped without looking up. Bradley reached for Sarah's arm… "It's okay, Sarah. Tricia will find out sooner or later. In this instance I think sooner trumps later."

Sarah looked up. "Guess I better do this," as she looked at Tricia, "Tricia we hate to tell you this but Nurse Ratchet's a member of your church."

Tricia was clueless, "I'm sorry? Nurse Ratchet was not a good nurse… in the movie with Jack Nicholson. I think his name was Randle Patrick McMurphy. I loved the film but found the personality of Nurse Ratchet to be something more than unpleasant. But," as Tricia raised her hand welcoming a response, "A member of my church?"

"Yes," Sarah answered. "Let me explain. Actually we would normally attend your church…and we'd love for you to baptize our new baby. But we cannot. Because of Nurse Ratchet."

Sarah took a deep breath, covered a cough and continued. "Bradley and I have mentioned that I work for Amazon. I work in their largest office in downtown Seattle. I'm a project manager in Intelligent Technology. Margaret Tweety is my boss. She's also a member of your church. Have you met her yet?"

Tricia wasn't sure where this was going, but simply shook her head, "No, have only met the committee that called me, I will meet most of the members tomorrow…it will be my first sermon and worship service. But please go ahead…I'm curious…really curious."

Sarah didn't smile, "Well, this is the situation. I would quit Amazon in a heartbeat but my salary's very generous and they have an excellent health plan with exceptional maternity benefits. Plus, I received a $20,000 bonus which will be paid in two installments. I have received the first but this year's the second. If I leave before this year's up I have to give up $10,000.

"Margaret—the staff calls her Peggy—is my boss. She has an hour's performance review of me every Thursday. Probably the most not-looked-forward-to-hour each week. It is punishing and discouraging. That's the best description."

Still unclear where this was headed, Tricia nodded, "Sounds like the review is tough. Every time. It gives Thursday a horrible anticipation for you."

"Ah," Sarah, responded, "An understatement. Each Thursday, almost like a demeaning opening salvo Peggy says to me, 'Sarah? Goddammit. When are you going to stop fucking up? Your work is dreadful. And besides, you weren't in the office last Friday, worth a demerit.' Tricia, that was a lie. I had written permission to miss last Friday for an appointment with our obstetrician. Had it in writing. But Peggy ripped it up."

Sarah teared up, took a handkerchief from her purse, wiped her cheeks, "Sorry, Tricia, but I need you to know this. Margaret is Nurse Ratchet. Plus. She's a member of your church. Andrew and I talked at great length whether or not we should bury this…and we decided it would be better for you to be given a heads-up."

Sarah took a deep breath, "In case you're wondering, I did take this to Amazon's HR department…they ignored it and said I was doing

The Lemon Drop Didn't Melt

good work; that should count. I was horrified, but as I said, I am keeping my employment, at least until our daughter's born. Bradley's checking out employment options with Verizon for me. But for now, this is our situation."

Bradley held Sarah's hands, "Tricia, this has taken lots of courage for Sarah. But we believe it is important for you to know about Margaret Tweety's behavior and approach, so you won't be blindsided by her in some church situation."

Blindsided? Yes Tricia was, to hear about one of her church members who had damaged, apparently even pummeled, her neighbor. She at least will be alert for Nurse Rachet behavior.

Still, Tricia did appreciate the caring concerns…so she would be on alert. Tricia had seen "Cuckoo's Nest," one of her favorite movies. And she did find Nurse Ratchet to be unpleasant. One of her seminary friends, when they saw the movie on an old theatre station said that Nurse Ratchet was the classic definition of bitch. Even more, Tricia knew a couple of ministers who had that personality. She didn't have a strategy for how this might unload itself on her at St. Andrew's, but she'd be on the alert.

She got up, "I do thank you both. Yes, it took courage. Of course I hope that Margaret doesn't think she's my boss. But if so I can give my best Jack Nicholson impersonation. I remember in the movie Nicholson always gave Nurse Ratchet a bad time, but he knew she was not a helper to the other patients in the psyche ward. I promise you, Sarah, I will now be aware. That's a helpful warning sign. In the very least I promise you that. In part here is who I am. I'm a sponge in terms of learning but never a pin cushion in how people relate to me. When I meet her I'll look for a pin…or two."

They walked back through the front door.

Now on to the home office to go over her first sermon outline. She was tempted to shift to one's personality or visiting with neighbors, but no. She would go with the fishing story…about coming up with empty nets. She had preached it in Palo Alto and in Breckenridge and felt…really *felt*…it would hit home in Snoqualmie.

Chapter 7

"What do you want? Is there something you don't have or cannot get?"

One more time, "What in God's name do you need?"

She answered, "Don't bring God into this...you couldn't care less about God. In fact, you only care about yourself. Period. Stop. No more sentences, let alone paragraphs. In truth and in my experiences with you, right now and unlimited, you treat me like shit. I'm your punching bag to vent your anger and your tunnel to oblige your libido. In fact, why don't you say *choo, choo* before your sex invasion. I realize what's on your bucket list. Beyond humor when you said you want to be taken to the emergency room because your erection has lasted more than four hours. And I know how you judge women. You give them a grade, from an A to an F. And that's not about their anticipated performance; that's about their breast measurement. Yeah, I knew I was an A minus and you made sure the implant surgery realized a B plus grade. How sick is that?"

She pointed at him, "Get it? More to hear, although I think you are deaf in your heart and only responsive to your ego. You live as if you are taking a selfie with each breath. In fact, I don't think you can see anything in your rear-view mirror and your windshield's covered with mud. You think providing things is verification of love and marriage."

"Whoa, woman! Stop right there. YOU...the very YOU I'm married to have gotten everything you want. YOU wanted to move to Snoqualmie and live in the best house. I gave in. I wanted to live in Issaquah on top...of the hill and in the best house...but you couldn't park your car where you wanted...even said it would be living on an ant hill...and since you are anything but a Queen Ant..."

He didn't finish because it happened every time...no, it worked every time...her anger was the best blue pill in the world...Viagra amazed him...as one of his buddies offered, "It's always a help to rise to the occasion." And always welcomed...her anger meant sex was on the way. When words moved to deeds...and only her silence and groans were the result. That helped him. To shift from her finger pointing to his finger probing.

She started to unbutton her blouse, knowing the "next step" had nothing to do with whether or not she was a queen ant and everything to do with her ability to satisfy...and it was ALWAYS his choice... his flavor...his decision. Should she stand or bend or get mouthy... that is, mouthy without words?

More pleasured than exhausted, they were silent. He was satisfied. The only goal. The anger had gone downstream, the satisfaction in the function—he always called it the *natural function* and not sexual communication—was beyond measure. To the good…never to the bad.

In a somewhat normal voice…was curious to him how normal was the norm after sex…he said, "Courtney, tell me you don't have what you want and what you need. Tell me I'm not a good lawyer. Tell me I didn't win a liability case that brought you $1,000 a week for the rest of your life. Tell me you didn't win the lottery with me…even more personal than the Washington lottery. Tell me there's not one thing you don't have…or I cannot provide. Tell me that I'm not misnamed, Rider Samson…that's Samson as in conqueror. Tell me that you aren't provided the best stud service that money can buy…and you don't even have to open, let alone empty, your purse."

He whispered, "Tell me you aren't happy, really deep down…and excuse the reference, deep in."

She knew. Courtney Halverson Samson knew it wasn't a question. It was a threat. And if she told the truth, if she told him that sex was not the avenue to better health and a relationship that brought so much more joy, even ecstasy, than an orgasm, he would explode. And somehow she buried her true feelings. Because…and she'd never admit this even under oath, she did enjoy the material matters, and somehow being satisfied with things was always stronger, at least emotionally, than being okay in her heart, her being. She had no idea where her soul was. No idea.

She turned and embraced him…because she felt a physical action could mute a broken heart…and she was grateful the day would be chilly, because she could never wear a sleeveless blouse in public, not even when visiting her neighbors…the other rich ones who seemed to have better relationships. Down deep she was miserable. But even deeper she was fearful, not wanting the life she experienced—endured was more apt—to be taken away from her.

He was fast asleep—she thought. She knew he got what he wanted. Rider Samson, her husband of ten years. Willing to accept they couldn't have children, her cancer of the uterus ruled that out. But she was alive. And yes. He had provided the best medical care…even combined visits to get help—one to the Mayo Clinic and the other to M.D. Anderson. She really appreciated her family doctor in Issaquah, though, for he was gentle and kind and knew almost everything about treating her cancer.

And she survived. That was what kept her breathing. She was alive. Maybe not emotionally but certainly physically. Plus, she knew with his various trips, Rider, her husband who publicly was very touching and supporting and courting, never gave a clue that he was really mean and vindictive and destructive. More than that he was clever and knew how to keep her close. Knew that money would remain on the throne and love on the scaffold. That's what she read somewhere about controlling men in a marriage.

With the hug she whispered, "Let's go to church tomorrow. Haven't been in over a year. But you know that. I read we have a new minister…and you will be pleased…she's a she. And you'll be pleased even more, she's not married, and has been a detective and fishing guide…all the ways in which your testosterone will perk up. And I imagine other places will perk up. So, let's go to church tomorrow. And who knows? Maybe something good will happen…and we'll reach a new level of caring. And who knows, maybe even that thing called love will make an appearance…and it will have nothing to do with an erection. Okay?"

The snore was her answer. He didn't give a damn…unless it worked for him. He didn't give a damn…unless he was in charge. And even worse, he was never wrong…and with his own admission that was the most necessary ammunition for an attorney. Never wrong. Always right. And always…a thousand always never lose or be defeated or lose a judgment. He was always judge and jury and executioner.

She shook her head and wondered. Why didn't she just leave? Why? A thousands why's. She reached for her cheeks—they were wet…with tears…sleep finally took over…but the depression and exhaustion and emptiness wouldn't leave. Not sure they ever would.

CHAPTER 8

About to go to sleep, Tricia knew the number…she'd never forget the number of her favorite person…ever and always…her mentor, Creighton Yale. He had gotten older but somehow knew where to drink from a youth fountain. He considered his white hair a verification of wisdom and never age. He had helped her in her application for the Ocean Divinity School. Had supported her in her decision to shift from fishing guide to preacher. They had met when she chased down a double-homicide killer…helping her along, appreciating how her fishing guide expertise partnered her homicide detective experiences…to solve the murder.

More, she loved his counsel about the basics in ministry and what to develop as a student-minister in a Palo Alto church. He told her that Stanford students were bright…but never better than students from Cal…or anywhere else. He also thought spending the summer as an intern in Colorado would be good….that it could provide healthy highs and that had more to do with ministry than elevation. He comforted her when the resident minister announced he and his wife would be gone all summer…that she could do ministry even though she hadn't had a preaching class. Somehow that worked.

And he understood. She loved that about him more than anything. Most people she met—whether or not they were ministers—were more into judgment than understanding. Not Creighton Yale. He lived his mantra that good communication requires that you never forget you have two ears and one mouth. Always remember that.

She also hoped he'd never change his cellular number…it blinked on her I-Phone screen. As she picked up her phone…and it was his custom to call her Saturday night to see about her sermon…she smiled. He was the only person she knew who still had a flip-phone. He maintained he didn't need the internet or texting, saying once, "I'd be tempted to text while driving…and…do you know how many deaths happen while texting and driving?"

Ah, Creighton Yale. He was checking in.

"Hello, my white-haired mentor. How are you this Saturday night?"

"Greetings, Tricia. Just checking in. I cannot let the night pass without wishing you blessings and good luck tomorrow. Everything okay?"

She never lied to him. But, there were occasions when the truth wasn't fully unpacked. This was one of those times. She didn't think it relevant to talk about the mishaps…with the condoms, the note, the missing plumber's truck. She did, though, think it was more than important to follow up to her, *Fine, thanks.*

"Yep, Creighton, everything's just fine. Guess we'll really find out about tomorrow's sermon…my first…and as you've said, it's somewhere beyond important."

"Hey, preacher. Stay away from the hindering. No negative thoughts allowed…because they'll sneak in to your sermon speak…and worse than words, your body language."

"You are right. I do want to share one thing, though. A visit yesterday… almost like the three kings, although it was two kings and a queen. And, I'm not Jesus…not even a close impersonation, but let me tell you."

Tricia explained about the three kids…about the fishing pole, the detective badge and the chartreuse indicator yarn.

He responded quickly, "Tricia, each of those can be symbols for you…perhaps most of all the yarn. Never lose it…because literally within your grasp, you can hold the yarn as a way to keep from sinking."

She loved Creighton…better than a father…and he always could turn a metaphor into a working piece that never was forgotten or lost.

"Okay, Madam Preacher, how's your sermon looking?"

"Actually I am trying to decide. I don't think you've been here, but immediately behind the church is the Snoqualmie River. They haven't worried about flooding…the church used to be an Unitarian Church but they got too small and sold it to our United Church of Christ. I like that the river is next to us. And I saw on the Weather Channel that the sun will shine tomorrow in Snoqualmie…with a gentle breeze. I am tempted to show the congregation how to cast for winter steelhead. But I know. That wouldn't be worth a snicker to those in the church who know the steelhead cannot jump over Snoqualmie Falls, which is downstream. I'll explain the reason the steelhead, spawned upstream in the fresh water, after a couple of years in the ocean, return to that same river, yes even to the same place on the river where they were born…to die

"It's a lovely facility—small classrooms in one building and a very lovely sanctuary and fellowship room in the other. They have folding chairs which is great. Makes it possible to rotate the seating for worship. No pews that are wooden and permanent and fixed. I sure don't want the people to be that way."

"So," Creighton responded, "I'm hearing good words, Reverend Preacher. Even more I'm feeling confidence and not arrogance, wisdom and not guessing…"

She interrupted, "Come on, Creighton, stop the wordsmithing."

He laughed, "Ah, got me. More, though, I hope you *get me* in that I'm your biggest fan…and will always clap and cheer….and even though I'm in Beaverton, I will be there in Snoqualmie in spirt tomorrow."

Silence. With Creighton that was always a good thing…never followed with a warning. Always positive…he was her most positive friend in the world. She was right.

"Ooops, Tricia, see it's late…so will be over and out, or something like that. Grace and peace and light…and don't forget about the yarn…never know when it's needed. And remember. I'm with you, woman, no matter what. And. That's for starters. Peace."

How graceful and helpful. Blurred all the stuff from the day. Focus for the next morning was completely clear. She then looked on her desk shelf and saw the yarn. Thought she might take it with her. Decided not. She'd be just fine. Just fine. And the sermon was already marinating and the good weather would make it possible for her *body language* words to work. Leave the yarn. She'd be fine. She was wrong.

CHAPTER 9

The Weather Channel was spot on. This day, fresh and alive on a Sunday morning for the first sermon, much different from the "normal" for the Northwest. It was sunny, mild breeze, a counter measure to how often it rained, to the point the Seattle Chamber of Commerce made it clear, *In Seattle you don't tan; you rust.* Somehow typical weather was a favor to Seattle…just like in earlier time because Oregon residents were tired of Californians moving to their Rose City of Portland. They had on the border along Interstate 5, "Don't Cali-i-fornicate Oregon.

None of that mattered. What mattered was the new day was glorious in weather, so no one could use that as an excuse for staying home. Besides the Seattle Seahawks' game was a Sunday night game.

Sage Worthy, that was the moderator's name but as Tricia would learn, Sage was creative, "Tricia, here's an idea, especially because this is your first Sunday. As you can see, there's just one door to our Fellowship Hall and Sanctuary…why don't we stand outside and greet each person? Besides, the nametags are inside, so I can help be your official introducer. No commentary, only names."

Tricia was pleased, "Great idea...thanks for being my concierge director."

Sage added, "We can be here until about five minutes before worship...that's when Gloria begins the prelude. She told me she wants to play the "up" hymn softly, "Morning Has Broken," an excellent way to start worship. Besides, I am a Cat Stevens fan...so the song has more than hymn value."

Tricia came out of the minister school NOT to tell the organist—and in this case the church had only a piano—what to play. She even told the music director—and with St. Andrew's Gloria, who also directed their choir—what the worship theme was and asked for Gloria to pick the hymns.

Tricia was ready...as ready as she could be. The conversation last night with Creighton got her in the best frame of mind...so she was ready. She knew Creighton would be proud of her...and that was important...because she no longer had a sermon manuscript from which she read. He said more than often, "Tricia, don't read from a sheet of paper when you preach. Have a focus, be okay with yourself to slip once in a while, but keep eye contact...because your eyes are the avenue to your heart. And what most ministers don't realize—often because they think they write better than Hemingway, is that those who worship often get lost in the rhetoric and the absence of non-eye-contact. Which means the sermon is often a cure for their insomnia or the start of a new grocery list.

"Don't be the reader—share the voice of your heart. Got it?"

Tricia got it...and to make sure, she left her notes on her home office desk. Not that she exuded confidence, but she did trust in her thoughts...and most of all in *her creative walking design* for her first sermon. One thought would lead to another. She learned, though, when preaching during her summer intern ministry in Colorado, there would be times when a new thought would come to her. She needed the freedom to not shut the new from the planned.

She hoped her gifting two Kings and one Queen would be there with their parents. And certainly she was ready for Nurse Ratchet. She hadn't said anything to Sage about any of them...didn't want to pre-empt the greeting. And she wondered if Nurse Ratchet might have another persona.

Sage knew everyone's name, except for one couple. They said they were members but had not been active, what Sage termed the "CE" members, which means Christmas and Easter worshippers. Gave their names as Samson...she forgot their first names...but she did notice the wife looked down, even when Tricia shook her hand. The husband used both hands. Tricia guessed he was the warm one. She also noticed in the introduction, the husband called the shots, "Hello, Pastor. My name is Ryder Sampson and this is my wife, Courtney." The intro took away warmth...at least that impression wasn't ambiguous. A passing thought.

She did see a very tall woman, at least six feet tall, wearing heels and a very colorful scarf. The sweater and pants were black, but the attention went to the scarf. Gave *kaleidoscope* a classic definition. She beat Worthy to the introduction, "Tricia? I hope I can call you that...I'm Margaret Tweety. My friends call me Peggy; please use that."

Tricia smiled with an inner thought, *She's direct, but very nice. Don't slip up and call her Nurse Rachet.* "Thanks for being here, Peggy… and Tricia works just find. Please don't call me Reverend. The sound reminds me of a car motor getting started…and I don't want to be a motor that makes noise."

Tricia was so pleased…the usher had to set up more chairs for the service. She smiled…because when she was at the church in Palo Alto she had met a minister from San Jose who ALWAYS set up fewer chairs at the last minute than the number expected for a meeting. Which meant he always had to set up more chairs…the, what he called "living symbol" that the meeting—and no less the minister—were successful.

Worship began. Tricia noted, although there were white hairs in the group, that no one had a cane…and no one had a wheel chair let alone crutches. Her idea would work. She trusted that.

As she stood for her first sermon she could see who were at least emotionally "her kids," sitting in the front row with their parents, each of them beyond a smile. Beaming children's faces were right there.

She first said, "Something happened last night—a visit from a dear clergy friend…and actually my mentor—that encouraged me to change my sermon today. You can see the sermon title is 'Living With Empty Nets,' and I think it could work. But my wonderful friend, Creighton Yale, in his encouragement, brought another possible sermon to mind…one I will now craft.

As Tricia lifted her hand, "That doesn't mean this is being built while on the fly, but it does mean the flow will be like the river behind our church…and it will have a flow. Which sparks an idea…that I now invite you to do…"

Tricia, not divulging the sermon's new topic, 'Let's Be A Salt Water Church,' walked to the front door of the church, stood under the Exit sign, and said, "Would you come outside with me for a few minutes. And if anyone needs help, raise your hand and I am sure one of our members will help you…trust me, this will be okay."

Tricia gulped, smiled and waved an inviting hand. To her surprise the congregation got up…no one showed any resistance…she could see no furrowed brows or people holding back. They all came to the back of the church with her and stood with her facing the Snoqualmie River, flowing smoothly with a tint of green, indicating that fishing visibility was good.

She then preached, advising that she never gave long sermons and she hoped, "My sermons will not cure your insomnia." She loved that "Yale phrase." She then said the new sermon title was "Let's Be a Salt Water Church," read the scripture about Jesus helping people think better of themselves and not to be blind to their value.

Then the crunch point as she looked at the Snoqualmie River, "You all know the Snoqualmie River better than I. I think most of you know that in a former life I was a fishing guide out of Tillamook, Oregon. I loved guiding on the rivers that flowed into Tillamook Bay, especially the Wilson and Trask and Nestucca Rivers. My favorite fish is the winter steelhead. They come up to the place in the river where they began life. They've been in the ocean somewhere—we really don't know exactly where—for two years, some three years.

"Well, this is what happens…they come in the river—some of the steelhead are native and some are hatchery raised. But they each come back to where they began their life. They then spawn and die. Before they die they change their color—from chrome bright to splotchy and black…very tattered as they end their life."

Tricia saw nods…and believed not all the nods were from experienced fishermen or as she never forgot, fisherwomen—that some already figured out this was a metaphor. A good thing.

Tricia then raised her hand for emphasis…always an open hand, never a closed fist. A good body pose to speak, "But, for some of these spawned out, ready-to-die steelhead something happens. They don't die. Instead they retrace their way down the river to be in the ocean again.

"Then, amazing and part of the creation…the minute they hit the salt water they become renewed. They become strengthened. They gain the weight they've lost in their journey upriver. They return to their chrome brightness, to live and to be."

Silence. No one was restless…but no one moved. One of the kids… her personal King, asked, "Is there something more?"

The nodding smiles had the same question.

"Scooter? I know his name because Scooter and his family is my new neighbor. Yes, there is something more…I am your new pastor. We need to spend time with each other. And if you're like me…and like church members of churches I have served, there are times when you feel splotchy and changed, but not permanently. That could be for many of you. My hope for us at St. Andrew's…is that we become a

Salt Water Church…so when people come here, no matter how they are mentally or where they are emotionally…they can be renewed and strengthened…so despair and doubt and fear will never prevail…."

Tricia clapped her hands, "Okay, time to return to our sanctuary…and see if we now see our church in a new way. Thanks for listening…and my promise to you…I'll do my best to be a pastor who knows, perhaps even a little drop or two, about salt water."

It couldn't have gone better. Not for a breath.

As church ended, Sage came up to her, "Tricia, I have a surprise for you. There was an old man, dark, long hair. I don't know his name; he's not a member. I haven't seen him before. He had a scraggly beard, almost like it was pasted on."

Tricia has seen him during her sermon. He had been standing in the back of the group, behind Peggy Tweety.

She then saw his eyes…and almost fainted.

"What?" she exclaimed, "Are you kidding me?"

Tricia saw his eyes water up. Then the smile. Ever the smile.

Sage figured it out, beamed, "Tricia, I thought your mentor, no matter how he looked, had to be here. He and I had this all worked out. I didn't tell you—of course I didn't, because he said I was to deceive you for your own good!"

Tricia started to cry and gave Creighton a hug…the best hug she could muster, "Creighton…when were you ever a master of deception?!" He smiled, "Guess there's always a first time."

The members picked up on that…they greeted Creighton, the unkempt one, but obviously the closest friend in the world to their new pastor…

What a day…what a start…would it continue?

Tricia never thought it wouldn't. But she knew there'd be another sermon and another shopping cart and another plumber. Maybe. If only it were maybe. If only.

Tick. Tick. Tick.

Chapter 10

Time to relax. Tricia never liked the "chill" word. No reason, other than it could be literal, no warmth. She had no meetings Sunday night. The morning, as her new neighbor, Andrew, coined it, "How about this, Tricia, on a 1-10 for our church today? It was a 14 and that's perhaps understated. When the service was over, Scooter nailed it when he said you nailed it…and he loved that you mentioned him during the sermon. Wow, he's on fire. Plus, I heard one of the other members say—don't remember her name but she wore that black jacket with sparkles—she said that it was fabulous to experience Easter in October. All good."

Better than good that she and Creighton could have lunch together. He had made reservations…had done some research…they should *do it right*, so lunch was at the Salish Lodge, overlooking Snoqualmie Falls. He even knew that below the falls—they walked out to see it from a well-railed porch—later in November, maybe starting with Thanksgiving, "Trish…to illustrate your sermon today, there'll be winter steelhead starting…and maybe you can land one, unless, of course, it's headed back for salt water to live another year."

She and Creighton didn't plunge deep—not necessary, because the starting sparks—both bright and unsettling were in her rear-view mirror. She learned that technique from Creighton who said more than once, "Tricia, a lesson for ministry. Encourage your members not to focus on their rear-view mirrors. You cannot drive without one, so you don't turn across a lane and hit someone. But the key is to look through the windshield. A workable metaphor."

Their windshield conversation had to do with how Tricia could meet the members on their terms. The roster had 70 names, but not all attended regularly. Nor would they. Still, setting up more chairs was something that hadn't happened. According to Sage, they didn't have to set them up last Easter, when you'd expect that to happen.

The question for Creighton, "How can I meet the people on a more personal basis? Too much on Sunday morning is surface-stuff, what can be called social amenities. Hardly ever is there a deeper conversation. I could, I guess, have small group meetings…you think?"

He waited, which Tricia always appreciated. To think, to reflect and as he often said, to marinate. He took a sip of his iced tea and then said, "Here's my hunch, Tricia. You know you don't have to get anything done…for apparently no immediate agenda is facing you. Unless, of course, someone has an emergency or personal need that must be brought to you. Plus, think in terms of one full year…at least through next summer, the term of your licensed ministry contract. So, why don't you make the time to do this. I saw about 30 people today who might be retired—that's common for most churches today. So, set sign-ups for people to meet you individually, or as couples or families at time during the day and evening, for those who work.

"I've seen that done effectively…and when you meet with them, give them four questions about the church, but that will give them a chance to tell you about themselves…their informal church autobiography. But, make the questions more about church and not too personal. That will be an invitation they can accept."

Creighton paused. "Got a thought?"

She didn't hesitate, "Yes, good thoughts…the visits should happen… they can be in their homes which I would prefer, but also at the church, which may be their preference, especially if they aren't the tidiest. What questions would you recommend?"

He put up his hand like a stop sign, "Nope, that's for you…what comes to your mind? Even more, to your heart; what do you want to learn from your members?"

Tricia rubbed her teeth with her tongue, her habit when pondering, which to her was more than thinking. "Okay, I'd like to know their history with the church, what they see as the church's strengths, where the church needs to get stronger, maybe a new program they'd like to see and maybe give them something open-ended like asking if they have any questions of her."

"Hey, preacher woman, that's good. I'd only add one more thing so you're not off target in your sermons…ask them for a sermon they need to have preached. They'll love that and know you include their thinking. Think about your new buddy, Scooter. I bet he went sky-high when you named him in your sermon."

Tricia nodded gently, "Yes, his father said that Scooter was over the moon that he was included."

"Ah, such an important point for your visits. And, whatever you do, don't call them interviews. Because all the professional business people have had interviews, pardon the fishing image, but up to the gills."

They both laughed.

Tricia recalled that lunch and visit with Creighton...such a special friend. He was *there* for her. No other place he'd be. Best friend in the world. She'd always been able to call him...rain or shine...and hopefully it wouldn't reflect Northwest weather's abundance of rain.

A tap on the door...and she saw three munchkins standing there. Looked at her watch, was 7 p.m., not too late. She opened the door and there they were...two Kings and a Queen, each holding a small paper plate on which was a cupcake. Andrew and Abby stood on the sidewalk. Scooter was designated spokesman, "Can we call you Tricia?"

She smiled, 'Yep, you can do that in our neighborhood, but maybe Pastor Tricia will work at church. That okay?"

Cynthy protested, "Oh, we cannot remember two names...I vote for Pastor Tricia...even on your front porch." Two other sets of heads nodded their approval.

Chip then spoke, handing his cupcake to Tricia, "Pastor Tricia, we had such a great time today. We had an anonymous vote...we all agreed to make you—and each of us made our own for you—a cupcake. You don't have to eat them all at once...but maybe you can start with mine."

Ah, how precious, Tricia thought. She accepted the gift from royalty and set them on a table by the front door, turned and hugged each of the most beautiful kids in the world. Looked to Andrew and Abby, gave two thumbs-up.

She then sent them on their way, "Have a great day, kids. You've made mine very special."

"Pastor Tricia?" Scooter corrected, "We did have a great day, but now it's night…so we'll have a great night."

They all laughed, beaming like all was right with the world.

Tricia closed the door.

She loved the misuse of "anonymous" for "unanimous." She thought of putting that in a sermon…to quote the kids and say that even though the church's executive committee all voted to invite her to be their licensed minister, in a real sense it could be considered an anonymous vote, for they needed to each learn more about her and she about them. Felt good to mix the word…anonymous would work.

Her cellphone # rang, a number she didn't recognize.

"Pastor Tricia Gleason, please."

"Yes, this is she; who's calling please?"

"Pastor, this is Jordon Valentine, I'm a detective from the Summit County Police Department. I wonder if I could drop by tomorrow morning to visit with you about the stolen plumbing company truck?"

She knew this might happen…in fact, welcomed it. Maybe it would lead her to the note about calling Sage, "Did you have a time in mind, detective? I need to be in my new church office at 9 a.m. Could we meet at 8:30 a.m.? I can come to your office if you'll give me directions."

No hesitation, he had it all planned, "Oh, no, I don't want to have you do that. I have your address, and can make 8:30 tomorrow morning. See you then. Have a good evening."

She hung up and couldn't explain why the Easter day had a jostle to it…maybe even a tempering of the good vibes. Just a feeling. Faint but evident. Hopefully, even though she knew nothing, she could mention the unwelcomed note and that could lead to something.

Nowhere in her imagination could she guess where the detective's visit would lead.

Chapter 11

Making eye contact when meeting was always a strength for Tricia. Where someone wore their name tag, its location said, at least to her, how connecting a person could be you shook their hand. If worn on the left side, you had to turn to see the name. If on the right side, you could see the name. That worked especially with new church members…Tricia's less than scientific and maybe even a little eccentric way to judge a person when first meeting them.

That meant that Detective Jordon Valentine got off to a good start… nametag in its best place…on the right side. He didn't hesitate, "Reverend Gleason, I'm Jordon Valentine. I realize this situation may be somewhat trivial—a plumber stopped at your house—but honestly this gives me a good chance to meet you."

Candor returned, "I'm sorry?" Tricia asked. "Why would you want to meet me? I'm just a new preacher-type. A real newbie. You probably need to meet someone more qualified…that comes from a higher pay grade."

He laughed. She saw the laugh as genuine, not forced or stiff, "Good one! Assume the higher pay grade is from a heavenly distributor."

"Goodness, what a start…that's a new name for God…*heavenly distributor*…can I steal that for a sermon?"

"Sure. I heard it said once before, actually by my pastor, whose sense of humor is greater than his preaching—but don't tell him that. His opinion is that no plagiarism makes for dull sermons."

Another laugh. A good start.

"Okay," Valentine said, "My answer to why to meet you." He held his hands up for full disclosure.

Tricia interrupted him, realizing time was fleeting and she had promised Ethel to be in the office at 9 a.m., "Why don't you come in so this is not a stand-up conversation?"

He smiled again, put his hat in his hands, "Sure."

"Care for any coffee?"

"No, thanks."

He sat in the living room chair, a rather large leather chair that Clark Hudson, the owner, probably loved. Tricia saw that the detective filled it nicely…probably about 6 feet two inches and 220 pounds. She wondered if he ever played tight end.

Tricia pointed to him, "Okay, two points on our agenda. Let curiosity start…why would you want to meet me?"

"I read our Snoqualmie neighborhood weekly and one of our office staff attends your church. I found it a leap that you used to be a homicide detective for the Oregon State Police, gave that up to be a fishing guide, solved a snarly double homicide in Tillamook and then went to divinity school. My interest is that I want take at least the first step in your progression; namely I want to become a homicide detective here in Washington."

"Well, that's a worthy goal, Detective. Good luck in your efforts."

"Thanks," he responded, "But I have to assume it takes more than luck; I simply need to be alert and apply when the timing works…."

Tricia then did what she actually abhorred when meeting with people…but it was probably her safest way to move things along. She looked at her watch and doubled the effort by looking at the clock on the fireplace mantel.

He got it, "Oops, I forgot, you have a meeting at 9 a.m. Gotta get to why I'm here…at least the official part. About the plumbing truck."

He reached in his coat pocket for a pad, opened it, looked for a moment, closed it, looked at Tricia…again such good eye contact. "We found the truck, parked in the Target lot in Issaquah. We went over it for prints but there were none. The guy must have used gloves. At least we assume it was a guy. Please tell us what happened here."

Tricia said her neighbors asked her about a plumbing problem. She explained she didn't own the house, the owner was in London and said he would advise her if any repairs were needed. He felt he had covered all the bases. Besides the house was less than two years old. She hadn't called him—truth pushing for Tricia—but would. She knew the note wasn't on her desk when she left earlier in the day, when she had gone to the Safeway grocery store in North Bend…

"I called the number. It was for the moderator of my church and she knew nothing about the note."

Tricia hunched her shoulders and nodded, "That's all, folks…my story and as Willie offers, I'm sticking to it."

He didn't hesitate, "Ah, Willie Nelson strikes again. Love it."

He then asked for the note. Tricia still had it on her desk, retrieved it and gave it to him.

He looked, "Well, are plumbers ever women?," raised his hand, "please don't consider that sexist—but I wonder about gender."

"Why would that be an issue?"

"Because the handwriting is obviously from someone who knows calligraphy…and my persuasion is that's more of a woman thing. Ya' think?"

"I never considered that, but it could be. All I know is that the note wasn't there when I left, the plumbing truck was at my house for 30 minutes and the note was there when I returned from Safeway, and the person whose number was on the note—happened to be my church moderator, knew nothing about it. I don't think for a minute the note was a mistake. I was supposed to call the moderator. I was led in a wrong direction."

Silence.

The Lemon Drop Didn't Melt

But Tricia could see his mind buzzing…the eyes blinked a lot. He then spoke, "Did you say the truck was here for 30 minutes; that's what your neighbor said? And she was sure it was a Mountain Plumbing truck?"

Tricia nodded. She didn't look at her watch, but she knew time was shortening.

"Let me ask this. Did anything else happen to you recently that was not normal?"

She had almost forgotten it, but his question put the Safeway experience front and center. Tricia said, "Now that you ask… something did happen when I shopped at Safeway, but I doubt it has any relationship to the note or the plumbing truck. When I unloaded my cart, much to my surprise was something in my cart that I hadn't put there. It caused me some embarrassment with the check-out clerk who is a member of our church and like you, knew me from the newspaper article and the church newsletter."

"You said it was embarrassing. Might I ask why?"

"Yes, maybe not for many people, given how life is lived today. But in the cart was a package of Trojan Lubricated Condoms."

He didn't know how to respond, didn't want to push the personal button.

Tricia sensed that, "Let me say that it embarrassed me only because the cashier was a church member and I'm not married, nor am I dating and I didn't want her…to be blunt…to think I was unattached but a sexually active person and that might somehow influence my ministry."

He smiled, "Hey, I can understand…and the point is not about your personal life, the point is someone put that package in your cart. Do you think that was accidental? Or on purpose? We've had no complaints from Safeway that someone is cart-stuffing, but I'll check with the manager."

He looked at the mantel clock, "Time's up for me. Hope you can get to your office before 9."

He smiled, gave her his business card after writing something on the back.

She put it on the foyer table as she opened the door. "Thanks for being here, it is good to meet you. And I hope your goal of being a homicide detective is realized…oh, I forgot, but my detective voice is speaking…can I ask you to see if there are any prints on this yellow sticky note? Plus, please check again for prints on the plumbing truck…can never be too thorough."

He nodded, "Really good to meet you, too…can I call you Tricia? And if that works, should you have any more *occurrences*, please give me a holler.…I mean, give me a call. Although I like the Texas slang of hollering…my brother is a detective in Austin…which is why I loved your Willie quote. I'll get back to you with any updated information…and please do the same. And, I know. I gotta get out of your way, but are you interested in any fishing places in your new stream? If so, lemme know. I have great guide contacts and pretty soon, steelhead will around here…and if you're looking for a really challenging time I can give you a guide contact for the Klickitat River…in eastern Washington. Fly-fishing at its best.…"

She reached her hand out to shake his. "Yes, do call me Tricia…and I hope Jordon becomes Detective Valentine…that's much better than, *hey you*."

He walked down the steps, turned and said, "Have a great day. You didn't state it as such, the possibility the condom package in your shopping cart and this note have any link. But, honestly? I am hard to convince this is inconsequential. But, only my speculating. Probably no link at all."

He was wrong. Wronger than wrong.

Tick. Tick. Tick.

Chapter 12

Tricia arrived a minute early, which for her was better than a minute late. She never knew why but she felt that being late was insulting. That's the way it was.

The church secretary, Melita Coster, actually a church member—that wasn't always the best situation Creighton had mentioned—didn't greet Tricia with a smile. There was no *Good morning*. Rather a stark, "Tricia, we've got a problem."

Before Tricia could take off her coat, Melita pointed to the office front door. "It was open—wide open when I got here this morning. I cannot imagine, because I helped lock up the church yesterday—and by the way, not to escape in my concern, yesterday was great. You could not have begun with more fire and excitement and energy. Great for you…and for us…"

She stopped, almost mid-sentence, pointed to the door, the small glass window gone, "In the mix of such a good day yesterday morning, we have a problem this morning. Someone broke in. Couldn't have been a robbery because there's no cash here…our treasurer deposits the money in the bank—and I don't see anything amiss in my work area. I went into the sanctuary and found this note on the pulpit. Just a yellow sticky note."

She handed the note to Tricia. She looked at it. It was text language, U R NXT. Was clueless...nothing more.

But. It was the same calligraphy.

Melita said, "This has never happened before. This is a quiet town and we are a quiet church...never...and Cheyenne—he's my husband and I have been here for15 years...never has this happened before to our church. I wonder what it means?"

Tricia was moving past being clueless, but didn't offer her thoughts.

Melita continued, "Since the note was on the pulpit I wonder if it was for you? That message...sounds ominous. Doesn't seem to mean something positive. Oh sure *being next* could be you're next to win the lottery. But I doubt it. I hate to say this, but it's not like the note welcomes you or wishes you a pleasant day and successful ministry. Oh…"

Tricia raised her hand, "Melita, I honestly don't know what this is about. But, we need to do three things…first walk around with me to check on each room…and that will be good for me to start learning what the rooms are used for…two, I have a favor, I want to send an e-mail to each member with a questionnaire and invitation…and three, call this number and ask for Jordon Valentine…he the Kind County Detective…call the number by his name on the front. My neighborhood's had some problems with home damage so he stopped by this morning to ask some questions. Then, please give me the card back."

Melita nodded, "Will do…oh, before I forget, there's a message for you on the church voice mail…I took the name and number, but it sounds personal…sorry, I didn't want to meddle but it was on the church voice mail. Here," as she handed Tricia the note, "You might want to call her…she sounded very positive. So this can be an offsetting note, right? I still cannot imagine what is *next* in terms of this note."

They walked through the two church buildings…according to Melita everything was in good order. She heard Melita calling Jordon… and thought that something mysterious was at hand. She kept to herself that maybe…a maybe that could be shifting to definitely… these incidents were related and she was a center point. Dread seeped in…with puzzlement.

She looked at the voice mail note, then listened to the message. Very cheerful and welcoming. "Hi, this is Hannah Ball; I'm the Rector at St. Stephen's Episcopal Church in Mercer Island. We haven't met but I took classes at Ocean Divinity School…last year when you were an intern in Colorado. I'm new this year and thought it would be good for us to have lunch…please give me a call…here's the number."

Melita had put the information on the note. It was a simple thing, but the number Hannah gave on the voice message was different from what Melita had written down. She'd go with Hannah's own voice. Might have been a silly mistake…we all make them, Tricia thought. But, maybe not. She'd keep that in mind in case Melita was dyslexic. She would try to remember to ask Sage.

The Lemon Drop Didn't Melt

Tricia went to her new office…it was nice…not next to the church office, so private conversations could be held. That gave her some privacy…and she was sure people visiting her, especially with anything serious and confidential, would feel more comfortable and trusting.

She called Hannah, "Hello, Hannah, this is Tricia Gleason, I'm the new kid on the block."

"Oh, great…thanks for getting back to me…and so soon. I know what it's like being new…however, wondered if we might lunch it… and I know this may be pushing, but if you have time today, I know a wonderful restaurant in Issaquah…the Issaquah Café. It serves breakfast all day and they have Reuben sandwiches to die for. Could we have lunch today?"

It was not as if Tricia was overbooked and she thought it would be more than helpful to visit with a new clergy colleague, "I'd love that, Hannah. Thanks for your hospitality…see you at noon."

"Oh, great. Could we meet at 1 p.m.? I have a church meeting that is scheduled for an hour, to begin at 11 a.m. But, either you know or you will find out, rare is the church meeting that ends on time. It could last 'til 12:30 but can make it to Issaquah from Mercer Island in 30 minutes. Here's where the Issaquah Café is."

She gave the address and closed, "I look to see you…and, please, this is my welcoming treat."

Tricia smiled, "I appreciate it…I'll get the next one."

Tricia started with her invitation message to the membership and listed the questions she'd like them to respond to on a separate sheet. Then she walked back to Melita's desk, handed it to her and explained her game plan for her first steps in this ministry.

Melita scanned the questions, nodded, looked up with appreciation, "Oh, how creative…we've never done that before…I bet the members will love it. Is it only for members? I ask because we have five families or individuals who get our communications and attend a worship occasionally. And, before I forget, I left a message for Detective Valentine and asked him to call me back."

A twinge flittering for Tricia. She really wanted to show Jordon the note…primarily because the note appeared to be the same calligraphy to the one found in her home office.

She said, "Thanks, Melita. If he calls back see if he can make it before 12:30…I called the new Episcopal Rector, Hannah Ball, and she's invited me to lunch at the Issaquah Café. Been there?"

"Oh! My husband and I love it…any time…not a slick place but as homey as you'll ever find. And I'm gonna tell you…when you leave there you could never give a speech on world hunger."

Tricia went back to her office and thought about what next Sunday's worship service should include, especially the scripture and sermon. There's was a calendar for each Sunday of scripture lessons, called the lectionary. Listed on it would be four Bible passages, one from the Old Testament, one from the Psalms, one from Paul's epistles in the New Testament and one from one of the four gospels, Matthew, Mark, Luke and John. Tricia had some good scripture references and a national mailing where ministers commented upon each of the four lessons. For the most part, the four passages related to each other. Although she hadn't preached that often—the previous summer in Colorado were the most Sundays she had preached, Tricia leaned most often the gospel lesson.

Creighton had told her that preaching on a lectionary passage was best, since he believed a minister really, when it came down to it, only had three sermon themes. Using the lectionary would bring diversity and keep a good distance from *here he goes again* in the sermon. Tricia was pleased the scripture was about Jesus telling the disciples to go back to fishing again...even though they'd fished all night and had empty nets. Jesus told them to go back again and throw the nets to the other side of the boat. The result was empty nets.

What Tricia didn't know...because the notes and the Safeway cart began unrelated...where all this would lead. Something...or probably, someone...was lurking. Which meant she was clueless...not a good place to be.

What she didn't know...the wait wouldn't be long....she would need to hold on to the yarn. Because the yarn, more metaphor to Tricia than anything else, didn't sink. She liked that part of the gift...what it meant. Maybe she'd need it. Of course she couldn't say for sure, but Creighton had told her she had *an inner trouble GPS* when something untoward seemed to approach.

Chapter 13

If Tricia were to write a first-impression paragraph about the Issaquah Café it would start with the word *nondescript*. A strip mall with all the usuals…a dog food store, a bank, a telephone company store, an Enterprise car rental office, a Thai restaurant that she would not be sampling, a grocery store, a cleaners. And there on the window, "Issaquah Cafe," with fading letters. Maybe tired and worn…maybe not popular.

As she opened the front door she saw there were no empty tables… and it was 1 p.m. on a Monday. Surprising. Before she could look around inside, "Tricia?"

The smile was great—Tricia's first impression of Hannah Ball was that she was the "real deal." Tall, maybe even six feet, a few inches taller than Tricia, not thin or bulky. And hair? Hannah gave it her best Little Orphan Annie impression…curls everywhere. Absolutely everywhere.

The Lemon Drop Didn't Melt

The hug was natural, then Tricia, always a smart-ass [Creighton's favorite description of her] said, "I'm sorry. Have we met? Tricia? You are looking for Tricia?"

Hannah dropped her arms, "Oh my, what a colossal screw-up. I thought I recognized you from the picture in your church newsletter. Am I wrong? Do you have a twin sister?"

Tricia laughed, pointed her finger, even waggled it, "Got ya! Yep, I'm Tricia Gleason. I have been called worse but that never made it to my profile."

She reached for another hug.

Hannah couldn't resist, "Okay, you got me…but I won't keep score. Unless you do."

"Nah, Hannah, scorekeeping is for Pharisees and I ain't one. Am not interested in keeping track or indicting anyone."

"Me neither, Tricia."

The hostess held the menus and cleared her throat, "Sorry, ladies, but social hour is over. I have been saving a table for you two…so let's kick some butt and get going."

"Whoa, what kind of restaurant is this? Sounds like something from Texas…and I bet with that you are locked and loaded," remarked Tricia.

Hannah smiled, "Hey, Great Lady," winking at the hostess, "This is working out better than you and I planned."

She turned to Tricia, "Ah, got you back."

Tricia loved the start…and already felt good about Hannah…no nonsense and probably if Tricia ever had some problems, Hannah would be one to help her avoid taking any prisoners. A great start.

Hannah held the menus, nodded to Tricia, "Of course I can hand you a menu…that would be proper…but I've been here before and Great Lady is a church member, and she said I should recommend one of two options…what this Café does the best. So I will not let Great Lady—oh, she also goes as Melanie Crawford—be disappointed. I suggest either Swedish pancakes or fabulous meat loaf. But, I wouldn't mix them…

"And," Hannah continued, holding out the menu to Tricia, "Of course I honor freedom of choice…so here, the other choices."

Tricia smiled, held up both hands as if it were a robbery, "Nope…I'd love the pancakes…my mouth's watering already. Besides it's always a good thing to suck up to church members."

Another laugh…felt so good to Tricia…her snarkyness wouldn't be offensive. Well, maybe not endearing, but at least, effective.

Hannah went the meat loaf route—and it did look really good to Tricia. But the pancakes produced a review of the restaurant, at least from her stomach and heart, that would never use the words nondescript or ordinary. Not for a breath or bite of food.

Hannah wiped her mouth as the waitress left the check. She grabbed it…"My treat, Tricia. Have a few more minutes?"

"Sure," Tricia responded, "I'd love to visit some more."

The Lemon Drop Didn't Melt

Hannah looked outside, "Hey, this is a great day—let's go outside, a nice bench in that tree grove…and that bench needs occupants."

Tricia tapped her temple, "Ah, I bet that bench will appreciate two pastors…you think?"

Hannah didn't hesitate, "Love it! Bet you already know a minister loses survivor grip without a sense of humor."

Tricia and Hannah walked to the bench, sat and were quiet.

Hannah waved her hand to the sky, "Look up, Tricia. And realize more blue than clouds up there. Makes the day worth enjoying."

Tricia smiled and asked Hannah, "Tell me, Hannah, about your ministry…at lunch we did the family stuff and fishing interests, the common ground. By the way, I will want the name of your guide out of Rockport. I've heard the Skagit River's the read deal for Coho and once in a while a Chum—maybe the hardest fishing salmon there is—can spool you."

Hannah raised a hand, "Oh! How could I forget. This is October—and some preacher-types, which would include us, consider October for World Wide Communion Sunday and Reformation Sunday—but I don't. Don't tell my Bishop but I consider October as Coho Time…and I forgot…next week, Thursday, I'm going with a couple from the church—they're buddies who fish often with a great Skagit River guide, Jon Thorsen, and we have one more seat available. It's casting and retrieving jigs…but since you have been a fishing guide you can probably teach us a few things.

"I've fished with the couple in the church and Jon before. I had a funny experience last week. And don't know why I said it because I really know little about fishing but he anchored what seemed pretty close to shore—the Skagit River is large…wide and smooth…but for over 20 years Jon knows exactly where the fish are. Anyway. I thought he was too close so I asked him about it. No sooner did I get the question out than he set the hook, handed me his pole. Fish on! I couldn't believe it. We brought the Coho in, beautiful 12 pounds, chrome bright. He smiled and looked at me and said he had a new name for me. Said my new name was GIT."

Tricia looked with curiosity, furrowed brow, "GIT?"

"Yes, Guide-in-Training."

More laughter. Such goodness.

"One other thing about Jon and his wife, Heather. Really more important than fishing. First, Jon took ten years to build a log-cabin home. Wait 'til you see it…it'll take your breath away. More, though, they support the Wounded Warriors in Action, our soldiers who have earned Purple Heart, being wounded in combat. Jon and his community buddies have built a bunk house next to their log home. Each quarter they host four wounded veterans and take them hunting and or fishing. So incredible what Jon and Heather do. No fanfare, no trumpets, but the caring from their heart leads to something. You'll be impressed…I know I am. Plus, I've read the guest book in the bunk house, comments from the veterans. You should read it…what benefit the veterans realize. One even wrote that Jon and Heather and the time casting for Coho gave him both success and peace. That's what I would call a real ministry."

Tricia was impressed, "That's great to hear, Hannah. The thought of doing something to help...your Mercer Island Church have any mission projects? I've always felt, as my mentor, Creighton Yale, often reminds me, that churches who amputate the Gospel deny being the church. We should remember the cross is both vertical and horizontal. Any suggestions, because I don't think St. Andrew's does much reaching out to help others. At least not that I've been told."

"Good question and I'm guessing you and your congregation have some things going. But, let me tell you about our church—about 7 church members and I, one Sunday a month, drive into downtown Seattle to the First Methodist Church. They feed the homeless—about 250 each day. On our Sunday we help them serve. We also bring food...like Cheerios...nothing fancy. I can send you the information on it."

"What a great idea—do send me what you can on that...sounds workable and possible," said Tricia.

"But, Tricia, back to the fishing option—how about taking next Thursday to go find some sermon illustrations? You have to do that."

"Well, I think it's pretty clear," then she smiled and admitted, "But now, I could fish every day next week...no schedule yet. But Thursday is now taken...for sermon illustrations."

"Good. Really good. We'll love it. And something with that...I assume where you're staying, the church member's home, has a freezer."

"Yes, but why do you ask?"

"Well, I assume we'll catch Coho…three for each of us and the couple joining us really prefers to catch and not eat the fish, so they always share. After we fish Jon will fillet them, cut them into pieces that can feed 2 people, then vacuum-packs them. I put them in the freezer and when a church member invites me for dinner…look at it this way, a Coho salmon fillet…lot more impressive and memorable than candy or wine or flowers. And what I've found, even though illustrations are less than frequent in my sermons, because they may not like my stories…but," raising her finger for emphasis, "They never complain about my salmon!"

Hannah paused, looked serious at Tricia, "Okay, our future is fastened down. Tricia, I hope we have a few minutes…please tell me about how you are…down deep, if you trust to share…and what you are experiencing, even in the first week."

It was honest and genuine and anything but negative. Trust. Respect. That's what Tricia held inviolate in any good relationship. In fact, she thought of Creighton who said that any viable relationship would have trust and respect and be covenantal. He described covenant as a relationship between at least two people they promised to give their fullest for the good of the relationship.

Tricia felt that in the moment. So. She tried to not overstate how well last Sunday went…never wanted to be indicted for her ego dwarfing her heart. And then explained, details by detail about the two sticky notes, about the condom package in the cart, the detective's visit…

Hannah was a good listener, which meant the world to Tricia, "Tell me, Tricia, does any of this have a background? Maybe something causing the mishaps…that's what I will call them. Anyone who would

The Lemon Drop Didn't Melt

want to be trouble for you? As you've stated, you were a homicide detective, a fishing guide and you had a student ministry at the Congregational Church both in Palo Alto and in Colorado. And you did have homicides to solve as fishing guide, as student minister, as summer intern. Anyone in that cloudy time really mad at you?"

Tricia was blank, although it was a great question she hadn't even considered. More thought was in order.

Hannah's question about anger triggered Tricia's own question, "Hannah? Something I need to work on. I'm not sure you do any counseling. Personally, counseling people, who've come to me with really serious personal issues...I struggle with what to do. Creighton said as ministers we should not be all things to all people. He said what had worked for him in the fifty years he served churches or was an executive minister who worked primarily with clergy, he knew his limits as a therapist. He said what he did when he came to a new community he learned who the best therapists were, contacted them asking their permission for referencing. I wonder. Do you have any go-to therapists? Are there some you'd recommend?"

Hannah said, "What a great question. Tricia, let me check the specific information I have about therapists who've helped me. To be honest, bailed me out of really onerous struggles for some church members. I'll do that right away.

"However, there is a member of our church who is a most competent therapist. She's also a good friend. I even know her cell phone number. Let me contact her for permission so you can call her as your counseling helper, should the need arise. Your mentor, Creighton, seems like a man with great experience, matched by his wisdom. A great combination. I believe, always have, that we are not all things to all people. I'll check with my therapist member. I'm sure she'll be pleased to help you. Her name is Dr. Lynne Walters. Will get her contact information once I check with her. That can be a start."

Tricia looked at her watch, "Oops, I need to scoot. Thanks, Hannah, for your inviting me to lunch. And for your mention of Dr. Carlton. Hope she's willing to be on my speed dial. I cannot thank you enough. I'll think about your question. But with that I will look forward to casting jigs for Coho. That will be a treat. Let me know where I need to be when next week Thursday morning. And I will think about your question, if someone's really mad at me."

They stood and walked back to their cars…in the small lot in front of the Issaquah Cafe. Hannah reached her car first…clicked the doors open, turned and hugged Tricia. "Be good to yourself, Tricia…and know I'm here as friend. Truth friend. I look at you the same. Got it?"

Tricia smiled, "Back at you. Keep me aware of any way I can support you."

She smiled as Hannah turned on the ignition and backed out. Hannah waved and smiled.

Tricia smiled back, then turned and went to her car.

Something was wrong. The car tilted. Out of balance. She then looked. The two tires…right side…front and back tires…were flat as her Swedish pancakes. Then she saw the slash marks. She didn't think of pancakes.

Tick. Tick. Tick.

Chapter 14

The silence got louder.

With some relief the next few days were normal. That means nothing extraordinary or irksome or surprising jolted Tricia. She was particularly happy Hannah called to say her therapist member, Lynne Walters, would be pleased to help, whenever necessary. Gave Tricia Lynne's number

But the silence she needed never came. She was back in her quiet house. The visit with Jordon was not necessarily helpful. But his efforts were not under appreciated. Melita had given him the *U R NXT* note. He had taken the two slashed tires. A pleasant visit, but very routine. He said no prints on the notes and no one saw the tires slashed—he had checked with each shop manager--and there were no prints to be found on the plumbing truck.

As a detective, Tricia always worried about the routine. In fact, Creighton once told her the essence of ministry—she always appreciated his wisdom and creative mind—was to *redeem the routine*. That meant to her that all of life's events may not have a reason, but they could have a purpose. Jordon asked about a purpose, "Tricia, why would someone do this to you? Is there someone who really hates you with a perfect hatred…or even an imperfect snarl?"

She liked Jordon's images but she had no answer. She had gone over the possible hit list and came up blank. The homicides happened. In each instance, though, the ones who did the killing were either dead or locked away where they could walk only six feet in any direction, and for one the six foot walk would become six feet deep.

Jordon asked her for names of past fishing clients who might be threatening…and she could only think of one pair—two brothers who had never fished before. They came to her sled boat drunk. Well against her better judgment, she let them on board. Then, as she told Creighton about it, "They went from worse to worser. In fact, one had a salmon clobber his spinner, he jerked, the fish jerked…snapped the pole right out of his hand. We raced back to that part of Tillamook Bay and let out 4 lines, bouncing the bottom, trying to snag the line. We then saw the salmon surface…but it was in the mouth of a sea lion…the sea lion tearing the fish apart, shook the carcass so violently we could see the spinner pop out. In that moment I told the two guys we were heading back to my dock…along the south shore of the bay…got out of the boat with them sitting there. Reached for all 4 rods and walked away. They hollered something about coming back. I only pointed to their car."

She could remember their names and knew they were friends of her ex-husband. But she also knew they couldn't be the bad guy---or guys if her troubles came from more than one—because one was pencil thin and had rheumatoid arthritis and was in a nursing home. The other brother had died in an apparent suicide.

She couldn't think of anyone, at least not now, beyond these two.

Tricia thought about the past few days. She wanted more focus. She sat at her office desk and tried to figure out what was happening. Actually she began to feel worse, that the mystery man would win. She hated losing. It was worse than anything she could think of. She knew people who had physical or mental reasons to feel horribly. But for Tricia, sitting alone in her home office?

The silence. The thoughts. The quiet. How to turn down the volume?

The question Jordon hadn't asked occurred to Tricia. She asked her own question, out loud, so maybe the broken silence wouldn't perturb her, "Why was the plumber in my house for 30 minutes…or at least more than simply to leave a note? Why would someone break into the church to leave another note? How did the threat—she called it a threat, a way to keep it inhuman and more an object…objects didn't breathe—know she was headed to the Issaquah Café?"

All that was key, a key she didn't hold. Would she ever find out? She had better. Because the one gift of being a minister Tricia had, she didn't know how to get; she couldn't compartmentalize. No matter who she talked with, no matter. She couldn't partition the troubles in their own place. The swirl of everything never isolated to themselves. It bugged her. Worse than that. Much worse.

Back to the unquiet silence.

She almost didn't hear it…but the noise was not in her mind. Someone was at the door. Knocking…and then stronger.

She opened the door and looked at the distress on the face. She recognized the woman but couldn't remember her name. Tried. Failed.

The bail-out came, "Pastor Tricia. I need help. I tried at your office but Melita said you were home. She gave me your address and your cell number. I couldn't call though. I was afraid I couldn't complete a sentence. I know. This is sudden. This is rude. But the truth is…"

She stopped. A new silence. Except for the whimpering.

Tricia stepped back, motioned for the visitor to step in and pointed to her office. She then pointed to the chair for the burdened woman.

Tricia sat in her office chair. She didn't say a word. She figured the silence now could help. It did.

"Thank you for letting me in. I'm afraid to even ask if you have time, because I cannot accept another rejection. You may not remember my name. We met last Sunday after worship. My husband and I thanked you for the sermon, such a memorable metaphor of going outside and pointing to the river. I appreciated it but my husband only says things he knows the person wants to hear. He's consistent that way. It all revolves around the truth; he's a total asshole."

Tricia still didn't know her name. Which was okay. Because what Tricia needed was a few paragraphs from her to understand. And in a flash, as the visitor spoke, nothing else mattered to Tricia. It only mattered that she listened, for she knew that a good minister was into understanding and not judgment. It was time to put understanding to work.

Tricia nodded and was about to ask the visitor's name.

But the visitor raised her hand, "Please let me explain. Oh. I forgot to tell you my name. How rude of me. My name is Courtney Halvorson Samson. I give all names because my maiden name, Halvorson, is more important to me than my married name. My husband's name is Rider. He is not misnamed, Rider. For he rides everyone he can, in his law practice and in our marriage. But I need to speak about why I'm here."

Courtney swallowed and then coughed.

Tricia asked, "Courtney? Can I get you something to drink? Water maybe?"

Courtney gave a hint of a smile, the intensity of her eyes—they glared, and with a furrowed brow only spelled *trouble*. That body language became softer, "Yes, that would be nice."

When Tricia returned, Courtney had uncrossed her legs, and her hands were no longer fisted. It was not that she was relaxed, but she was better. At least Tricia thought Courtney was less tense. And as Courtney spoke it was clear that the water helped, but the reality could be somewhere beyond harsh.

In the next 30 minutes Courtney, in an even stream of words, explained how miserable she was in her marriage, how she had been abused, how Rider bruised her sexually, how his wealth was his power, how she had been to counseling but the counselor said she should leave the marriage. Courtney felt that was probably right, but she so feared Rider. She feared if she left the marriage she would end up being cast out by their friends. He had endeared himself to their friends, none of whom knew his brutality.

She then said, "Can I trust you? I've already believed I can or I wouldn't tell you so much. But I have to ask…can I trust you?"

Tricia nodded and then spoke, "Yes, Courtney, you can. I hear you. I understand you. I will not write notes after you leave…and we are not recording this. The question is, what can you do? How can the horrifying experience in your marriage—and I choose horrifying with what I'm hearing—be resolved. I have a couple of questions. Would that be all right?"

"Yes, ask me anything. I feel better already because I see that you listen."

Tricia said, "I have just a couple of questions. Has your husband ever gone to counseling with you? You said you had surgery for uterine cancer. Had you and your husband wanted children? Ever thought about adoption?"

Courtney said, "Yes, Rider did go a couple of times with me to our marriage therapist. But, the truth is he's such a velvet-smooth-liar, and he said that I'm making it all up," as her fingers indicated quotation marks.

"I had thought of wearing a low-cut blouse and maybe even a sleeveless blouse to the counseling sessions to show my bruises but he forbade it. And when I met with the counselor alone I simply couldn't describe the abuse. I don't think Rider ever wanted children, so if I did—which I really did—it wouldn't be happening. Because,

The Lemon Drop Didn't Melt

the truth is our bitter marriage would be the worst place for a child. The worst. What can I do? What can I do? Can you help me?"

Tricia knew to give an answer would serve two bad purposes…one, it might not be true because she didn't know in that moment exactly what Courtney should do…but, two, if she had a recommendation, and if Courtney followed it…at least short of visiting personally with her husband, it could be disaster for Courtney.

That meant…not to answer, but to ask a question that would keep the conversation open, "I'm not sure what help I can provide, Courtney. Please know I'm not trained in counseling. I do listen as well as I can. What I do is to see about another marriage counselor, since you don't seem pleased with your current counseling situation. But I wonder…as maybe a next check-it-out-step, do you think your husband would visit with me? Not that I have answers, but maybe I can learn more. And if that works, maybe a next step…in some attempt to find reconciliation could happen."

Courtney looked shocked. She certainly wasn't pleased, "Oh, I don't think for a minute my husband would want you to know about our situation. He's too self-centered, and, to be honest, his reaction last Sunday wasn't…."

Courtney stopped. Put her hand to her mouth, then said, "I'm sorry I shouldn't have said that."

Tricia knew that Rider Samson didn't share his wife's affirmation of Tricia. That was okay.

She said, "Courtney, don't worry. My theory is if he has some comments about me, then, he should say them to me personally. You don't have to be his messenger."

Courtney smiled, "Oh, thanks, I'm glad you understand. Well, I think I've over-filled your ears today." She sighed, put the empty glass of water on the side table, "This has been helpful. I guess to share my hurt with you—and even stronger—my depression, makes me feel better. At least I know now your caring is real. And I understand and accept that you aren't trained as a counselor…but," Courtney raised a finger, "I bet you are trained in prayer."

Tricia stood when Courtney leaned forward and walked to Courtney, "Can we share a prayer?"

Courtney started to cry again as she got up.

Tricia reached for some Kleenex, handed them to Courtney.

Tricia reached out and grasped Courtney's hands. Courtney took a deep breath, exhaled and blinked away a few more tears, "Thanks, a prayer is my best medicine."

"Dear God, thank you for being with us. Please let Courtney know she isn't a stranger. May she know that your promise always to be with her will always be kept. Please assure her of your love and caring, that your blessings upon her will be forever. No less, dear God, we pray for Rider, that he is aware, somehow, of your presence. We ask all this in the name of Jesus Christ, who is our Lord, Amen."

Courtney didn't smile, but she reached up for Tricia, and hugged her. "Gosh, I haven't felt this good in a long time. Thanks for your prayer.

Even more, thanks that you opened the door to my fear…some of it escaped. In short, I accuse you [*she pointed and smiled*] of helping me feel better."

Tricia said, "Wow, Courtney, that's the best accusation I've ever received. Thank you. And remember, you can re-name our conversation *Las Vegas*…what happens here stays here.

"And," as she opened the door, "Courtney, we mentioned perhaps a new counselor, here, here is a card I have for a counselor. My clergy colleague on Mercer Island recommended this counselor, her name is Lynne Walters. Hannah, my clergy friend said I can recommend her. Why don't you set up an appointment? I'm hoping it will help. Certainly worth a try."

Courtney took the card, sighed, hugged Tricia again, "Oh, my. You are such a caring pastor. Thanks for what you're doing…for our congregation…and yes, especially for me. I'm so glad I can trust you…that what we shared will stay here."

Stays here? Not for a breath.

Tick. Tick. Tick.

Chapter 15

Courtney got in her car, waved to Tricia, drove to their very luxurious Snoqualmie home. Started to code in the gate. Didn't.

She was so positive about her visit with Tricia…and the recommendation of a new therapist. She picked up her cell phone and dialed.

To her pleasant surprise the call was answered. Not a secretary or a recorded voice mail, "Hello, this is Dr. Lynn Walters, how may I help you?"

"Oh, you answered. Thank you. Dr. Walters, my name is Courtney Samson. I have your name from my Snoqualmie pastor, Reverend Tricia Gleason. She got your card from your Mercer Island pastor, Reverend Hannah Ball. I was just visiting with Reverend Gleason and she said I should call you. I realize you don't know me. But I really need help. May I set an appointment?"

No hesitation, 'Thank you for calling Courtney, your timing is perfect. Will tomorrow morning work? I just had a cancellation."

"Oh yes, guess my call's great timing. That's the second best thing to happen today. Visiting with our new pastor was the first. Thanks, I'll be in tomorrow."

Chapter 16

Lynne Walters put her briefcase on her desk as she turned on the lights in her therapy room. As she looked out her window she saw the gray and drippy weather, so typical of Seattle and the Eastside of Lake Washington. She then looked around her room and was satisfied with what she saw. The walls were a soft white and her couch and chairs were a light blue and very comfortable to sit on, as well as warming as a color scheme. She had several pictures of places she had visited over the years hanging on her walls. She enjoyed remembering her trips to interesting countries like Turkey, China, Israel, India and even Afghanistan. Her patients often had questions about the countries she had visited. "Dr. Lynne, weren't you frightened to visit India?" Or even, "Were the people in Afghanistan threatening to you?" Sharing her experience of the beauty of people all around the world brought pleasure to Lynne. She was pleased that sharing these experiences helped her patients appreciate the wonderful quality of life they experienced in Washington as well as realizing people around the world were really more alike than different.

Lynne loved meeting new people and learning about the things that made them happy as well as what caused them distress. Today had a new patient. The patient was intriguing for Lynne. She was a married woman who lived in a new and expensive subdivision in Snoqualmie with her husband. This was the newest area on the Eastside of Seattle that had been developed. The homes were owned by the "new" wealthy people. Many people who lived there were recent transplants to Washington State and were doctors, accountants and attorneys. Microsoft had a large presence in the neighborhood also as many of their employees lived there. Several of these people had large mortgages as well as outlandish student loans. Over the past few years Lynne had heard many stories from very unhappy people who lived there and were barely getting by financially. Her new patient's name was Courtney Samson. Courtney's pastor, Tricia Gleason, had referred her to Lynne. Tricia had gotten Lynne's name from a Mercer Island Episcopal Priest, Hannah Ball. The priest was someone Lynne had done a fair amount of collaborative work with over the years.

Lynne was impressed with Pastor Gleason when she called about Courtney. She seemed to know the limits of how pastors could effectively interact with parishioners and the daily problems they faced. She also seemed acutely aware of how pastors could harm parishioners by being "too friendly" with them during their "times of trouble". It was refreshing to hear Pastor Gleason articulate awareness of potential pitfalls her parishioner could face by simply talking to her pastor. She very clearly wanted to connect Courtney with someone who could help her.

"Dr. Walters", Tricia said, "I am quite worried about Courtney's safety and well being. Courtney reported to me some serious control issues her husband Rider exerts over her with money and sex. He also limits her ability to develop friendships and interact with her family. I can tell this situation is clearly over my head and one I am not trained for. Would you help her? And please call me Tricia."

Tricia continued, "Courtney is right here. May I have her talk with you now?"

"Yes, by all means…by all means," Lynne responded.

Courtney talked about her troubled marriage and her hesitance to get a divorce. She didn't know what to do. But it was clear she needed help.

Lynne understood, "Courtney, let's go ahead and make an appointment. It is difficult to go in to too many details over the phone and there are a lot of things we need to cover when we do meet. Please go to my website for there are forms that you need to complete and bring in on your first visit as well as information about me. I also am going to need insurance information so my bookkeeper can bill your insurance."

"Dr. Lynne, I do not want my insurance billed. I will pay cash. I do not want my husband to know I am seeing you at all. He thinks that I am in a Bible Study when I meet with Pastor Gleason and if he knew I was talking about him to other people……"

Courtney's voice faded as she began to refer to her husband. Lynne could sense the deep fear Courtney lived under and knew that this could be a very difficult and sensitive situation.

Chapter 17

Courtney arrived 10 minutes early for her appointment and helped herself to coffee. She was dressed stylishly in designer jeans and a matching blouse. She also wore an imported wool sweater from Ireland. Courtney wondered if this would be another waste of her time and this would become one more example of not getting the help she needed. *How did her life get so messed up?*

"Good morning Courtney. I am Dr. Lynne and it is good to meet you. You sounded a bit nervous yesterday so I am glad you found my office without any problem. I understand you do NOT want to use your insurance, so the paperwork won't take too long. You seemed to have a lot of questions about confidentiality when we talked on the phone, so let's start there."

"Thank you Dr. Lynne. It is true I do not want my husband to know I am seeing you. And if he were to discover I am seeing you, I do not want him to know what we talk about." Lynne knew this was a tricky question, especially when she was most likely going to hear information that would reflect some abusive behavior on Mr. Samson's part. Lynne also knew that if Courtney became more agitated or upset and had any self-harm inclinations, Lynne would have to take action to protect Courtney from Courtney. This would likely void the confidentiality that Courtney so keenly wanted. Lynne knew that she needed to "tell it straight" to Courtney. Lynne then explored Courtney's history, family and individual, about addictions, self-harm, suicide attempts and depressive episodes. Overall Courtney reported some healthy coping patterns. She did have a prior history of self-harming when she was in late adolescence.

"Courtney, you have done such a thorough job with your paperwork that there is just a little bit I need to review with you. But let's start with confidentiality since that seems very important for you to know it is in place. Since you are paying for therapy yourself, I do not have to report anything to your doctor or insurance company. You are not responsible for any children or vulnerable adults so it is unlikely I need to report anything in that area. I am a mandated reporter in Washington. This means if you tell me of any children or vulnerable adults being abused or harmed in any way, I have to report the abuse to the State of Washington. You are no longer protected by any confidentiality in that situation. Do you understand about losing your confidentiality in that case?"

"Yes Dr. Lynne. I actually lived next door to a couple who had their children removed by Child Protective Services (CPS) due to the father's drug involvement. The children lived with the Grandparents for a while and then returned home after the Dad went to treatment. I understand and am not concerned about that at all."

Lynne was hesitant now. She figured that what she brought up next was going to be a very sensitive topic for Courtney. She knew that how she handled it would help build trust for their future work together, or create a barrier to the future work they would work on. "Courtney," Dr. Lynne continued, "it seems like in your last two years of high school and first year of college you went through a really tough time. This was the time period when you reported harming yourself by cutting your wrists as well as one suicide attempt. What can you tell me about that time period?"

"Dr. Lynne, it was an awful time in my life. My parents got divorced because my Dad was having an affair with my Aunt Jennifer, my mom's sister. He is now married to Aunt Jennifer and all of us feel awkward about the situation. My cousins feel terrible and I just try to stay away. Frankly, I think that was one reason I was in such a hurry to marry Rider. I was so unhappy at home and there was no one who cared about me."

Courtney lifted her face up and looked directly in Dr. Lynne's eyes for the first time in the session.

"Courtney, I am so glad you can see that so clearly! When you realize that type of connection then you are very close to NOT repeating the mistakes you made before. This is the area I wanted to talk to you about as it relates to confidentiality. IF, and it is a big if, I am aware you are suicidal and that you are planning something to significantly harm you, I am required by law to take action to protect you-from yourself. This means I will call anyone I can think of to help you."

Lynne realized she had just opened up a large vulnerable area for Courtney and was curious as to how Courtney would handle it.

Courtney was sitting in the chair crying, not sobbing, but just a soft cry. After a few minutes Lynne inquired as to how she could help.

Courtney, through her tears said, "you just have. I have never known anyone would care enough about me to protect me from harm. Even as a child I saw myself as all alone in the world. Then after Dad married Aunt Jennifer, my Mom just retreated into her world and did not even notice me at all. We hardly even talk at all any more. And my Dad and Aunt Jennifer just ignored me-and still do. I do not have any family, except for Rider and he is always either hurting me physically or controlling everything I say or do."

"Courtney, I'd like to move on into what is bothering you today-what brings you in to see me? Pastor Gleason seems like a very caring woman who has also been very helpful to you. I would certainly like to help you put together a plan to move you beyond your pain. If you want to do so too, then let's get to work."

Chapter 18

"Dr. Lynne, I am so glad we can talk and I hope you can help me. I am so unhappy and I feel trapped in my marriage. Rider calls all the shots. He tells me when we eat and when we don't. He tells me when we have sex and where. He has actually pretended to pick me up in a bar, and had me pretend to be a prostitute. He has threatened to 'pass me around' and share me with random guys so he can watch them have sex with me. When we have sex at home, he sometimes bites me so hard, he draws blood. If I cry, he hits me with his fist and even leaves bruises-but not where anyone can see them. I have begged him to treat me nice and he tells me he gives me everything I can possibly want so to stop complaining.

"I tell him I want to get a divorce and he takes me to his gun safe and just points to his gun and then laughs. I don't know what to do. He is an attorney and knows all the judges and law enforcement people in the Seattle area. When we are in public he pretends to treat me nicely, but he is secretly doing something to hurt me. An example would be holding my hand, but he really has a nail in his hand that he squeezes into the palm of my hand until it bleeds. He did this last night while we were out for dinner with his partner. Then when we got home he started ripping my clothes off me and threw them away calling me a 'stupid bitch'. He then took his shoe off and starting hitting my ear with it until it bled. You can still see the blood that dried for where he cut it."

At this time Lynne took her camera phone and took some close up pictures.

Lynne asked Courtney if she had any other pictures of his abuse from earlier times. Courtney said she once had pictures but Rider found them on her iPhone and destroyed her iPhone. She only has a simple phone now that is linked to Rider's account and he has access to her records.

Lynne asked if Courtney had ever consulted an attorney. Courtney just grunted in a bitter way. It was clear that Courtney believed that the entire legal community was in the palm of Rider's hand. Courtney had very little money of her own and nothing was in her name. The house, the cars, the boat, the vacation home in the San Juan's and all of the investments were in Rider's name alone. Courtney said she was paying for the session by writing a check for groceries that was more than the grocery bill. She had been saving that money up and had $1450.00 saved up. Courtney also said she still loved Rider and just wished he would treat her nicely, like he does every so often. Courtney was not ready for a divorce at all. She also reported she had no resources to support herself and did not have friends to help her either.

Lynne told Courtney about Lifewire, which is a Domestic Violence Victim resource center in Bellevue, a neighboring community.

Courtney was afraid to even call for information as her husband knew everyone in the legal community. She knows he did some pro bono work for the legal clinic affiliated with the <u>Lifewire</u> facility. Lynne then talked about DAWN (Domestic Abuse Women's Network) in Tukwila, a South King County facility. They also provide legal help, support groups and transitional housing for women who need help. She gave Courtney the numbers.

Courtney then asked, "Dr. Lynne what do I do? I am scared to do anything. I am afraid he might even kill me if he finds out I am talking to you. I also don't think I can support myself at all."

Lynne noticed the tears started again. This was a woman who had been so isolated that she no longer had any friends, except the few she was beginning to cultivate at church. Lynne was also curious about Courtney's cousin. They once had been close and perhaps they could be close again. But safety had to come first.

"Courtney, there are a few things to do. <u>Lifewire</u> might be too close to your husband's professional network. We cannot take that chance. Please call <u>DAWN</u> and arrange to see an 'exit' counselor there. That person will help you plan carefully your leaving. It is important that you realize that right now you are at the highest risk for being killed or severely injured by your husband. This is because when an abused wife makes plans to leave the abuser, his anxiety increases and he wants to control her even more.

"So everything you do from now on needs to be done carefully. Please buy a 'cash as you go' phone and use a false name. Ask Pastor Gleason if you can keep the phone at the church somewhere where you can easily access it. Continue trying to save up money for right now. Also do consult with DAWN's attorney to help you begin to set up your finances the way they need to be for the future.

"For our work together in the future, we need to help you establish a resource network of friends. I think there are more in your life than you realize. Please go to the library and check out a book by Alice Miller called <u>Drama of the Gifted Child</u>. Please read very carefully about people she names 'enlightened witnesses'. These are the folk we are going to identify together who will become 'Courtney's Collection of Enlightened Witnesses'. They will be your companions for the journey. After you have connected with <u>DAWN</u> and feel safe to do so, please call me and we can start the other work-but that might be months away. In the meantime, let your Pastor know what is going on. Your most important connection for now is <u>DAWN</u>. Good luck Courtney. Please be safe."

As Courtney left the office, Lynne hoped she would take seriously her safety warning and instructions. She also hoped that Tricia Gleason would provide the spiritual support over the next few months that Courtney needed. Somehow Lynne thought she would be working with Courtney in the near future.

CHAPTER 19

Tricia never liked Saturdays. It was more than her new preaching world. Since her sermon, as Creighton would have it, was *in heart ready to go*, she never rehearsed it. She did know ministers who did. That rehearse, rehearse, rehearse mantra describes a couple of her student buddies at Ocean Divinity School. One was even honest enough—he was a licensed minister in addition to taking his seminary classes—to admit he fell asleep one night practicing his sermon in the sanctuary pulpit. She guessed with a tap on his shoulder, "Well, Herb, guess you cannot say your sermons are a cure for insomnia!" He didn't hit her back, their friendship brought a smile and nod.

The other reason she disliked Saturdays came from her back story. She actually hated Saturdays, a feeling that pushed toward anger. Because Saturday was always combat fishing. No matter when or where for her. During Fall Chinook season on Tillamook Bay the boats were more numerous than the seagulls and the guides knew the better trolling water. Rookies weren't stupid. Even if they came for one day—it was always Saturday. They considered Tricia their

Pied Piper…as one guide buddy said, "Well, Gleason, how's it feel to be a Pied Piperette?" She disliked it no less during winter steelhead fishing, especially if heavy rains came before any Saturday—and you could stretch that from Thanksgiving to Tax Day—because the rivers were often too high or the visibility was less than one foot… so the possible fishing water was somewhere between slim and none. Which meant she often had to be on the river at O-Dark-Thirty. She remembered one time she had to navigate through some rocks and logs at four in the morning to reach a place she called her "95% Fall Chinook Bobbing Hole." Fortunately, her clients trusted her. But no fish that day…it was no fun having the hole be on the 5% side.

All that flowed through her. She was told it was too soon to cast into the Snoqualmie River for steelhead. After she got her slashed tires replaced, she went to the strip mall fly fishing shop and got a map of the Snoqualmie River. The owner was there to help. When she mentioned she was a fishing guide he gave her special attention. In fact, he leaned a little too close after he came around from behind the counter. She slid sideways as he showed her with a red pen where the better wadeable holes were. She still had all her fishing gear in her storage locker in Tillamook. Which meant she needed to retrieve it before she and the winter steelhead introduced themselves to each other. She smiled at that since one of her favorite clients had given her a t-shirt that brought laughs if not the truth, *When the steelhead hear my name, they tremble.*

She did need more groceries and thought maybe Montina was working at the North Bend Safeway.

Bingo. Montina saw her enter, waved at her and said rather publicly, "Hi, Pastor Gleason. I look forward to your sermon tomorrow!"

Lots of glances her way. Tricia was better than good in pretending she didn't hear and looked at her grocery list. Trojan Lubricated Condoms weren't on the list. But visiting with Montina was. Tricia had one question to ask.

As she started up the dairy section she heard footsteps. It was Montina. "Pastor? Got a minute. I'm sorry if I embarrassed you. I hope you didn't mind."

Tricia hadn't really, although she didn't need to be identified as the pastor. Things happen. "No, Montina. No harm, no foul."

Montina looked past Tricia, "Well, we are alone here. I wanted to tell you something. You sure have a handsome friend."

"Pardon me? A handsome friend?"

Montina smiled, "Yes, yesterday someone asked to speak with me. He had gone to the manager. She came to introduce him. I wasn't that comfortable because my manager looked like this was serious business. She then introduced him…a great name…Mr. Valentine. He said he was a King County Detective and he had a question for me. He said he had asked the manager and she didn't think so."

Curiosity pushed, "A question?"

Montina said, "Yes, he wanted to know if any customers had had trouble with items in their shopping carts they hadn't put there."

That was the exact question Tricia wanted to ask. But she waited for Montina to continue.

"I told him that happened one day…when five shoppers told me an item or two shouldn't have been in their cart. Don't know why but for some reason I didn't mention that to you. He thanked me and then left. Wow, what a good looking guy. Do you know who he is?"

A dilemma. Truth or not? Since Tricia always felt the truth should trump any distorted version—which she found for those she interviewed as a homicide detective, the ones who lied always forgot what they had said—she answered, "Yes, I have talked with him. Nothing major, he was investigating some other matter in Snoqualmie. He didn't tell me any details. He saw me because he wondered if anything similar had happened to any of our members. I told him I was the new kid on the block. That's all."

Montina smiled, "Well, good, I'm glad I didn't tell him your name. Guess it was someone else who talked to him about shopping here and having more in their cart than they planned. Hey, no harm, no foul, right? Oh, I meant it what I said. I do plan to be in church tomorrow. One of your church members, Hattie McCay is a friend of mine. She was there last Sunday…and I think your challenge will be to have two Easter services in a row. That's how she described what she called 'your sermon by the river.' Sounded great. Hope for the same tomorrow."

Tricia spoke graciously, "Thanks, Montina. It is wonderful to hear that response. So, we'll see about tomorrow; I will give it my best cast."

Montina laughed. "That's great…besides I like casting better than shooting. See you tomorrow."

The Lemon Drop Didn't Melt

Tricia now could only remember to get some bread and milk and had forgotten the rest. She wondered, though, Jordon hadn't mentioned anything about his visit when they last met about her slashed tires. But she thought Montina said he was in yesterday. So maybe the next visit he will share it. But, maybe not. For she knew—very well—that a good detective doesn't tell all he knows.

In any case it was better shopping at Safeway this time. It was more positive than her first time. Nice to have nice.

She got in her car, and before she could start her car her cell phone rang. She recognized the number…it was her neighbors, either Bradley or Sarah Murdough. She had given them her number.

"Hi there, this is Tricia."

Silence.

"Hello?", she repeated.

She could hear a speaker in the background, something about visiting time was over. What in the world was this all about?

Then a halting whisper, "Tricia? This…..is….Bradley…we need you….Sarah has had some serious trouble. Our obstetrician is with her now. I'm at the Emergency Room. Doesn't look good for our new daughter….could be real bad. Can you come to be with us? We're at Swedish Hospital in Issaquah."

"Oh my, Bradley. Thanks for calling. I'm on it right now. I am in North Bend Safeway. Will jump on I-90 and get there promptly. Oh my. Please tell Sarah you've called me…I'll be there. And know…I'll do whatever I can for you. May God be with you all."

"Oh, thanks, Tricia. We know we don't come to your church, but we know in our heart you can still be our pastor and a trusted friend. Both sets of parents aren't in the area, so we will be very grateful for your being with us. Thanks."

Click.

Oh my goodness, Tricia thought. They have to be scared, even terrified. Gotta get there a few minutes ago.
Tricia didn't really care about speed limits. Fortunately, it was Saturday afternoon and traffic was slight. She thought the University of Washington had a home football game, which meant that the Snoqualmie and Issaquah fans would already be at the game.

Tricia couldn't help herself. It was vivid. Sarah's sharing about being mistreated by Peggy Tweety. Tricia wondered if the verbal abuse had somehow impacted the pregnancy. Of course that probably had nothing to do with it. Tricia didn't find anything unusual about Peggy after worship. She was pleasant and even said a few nice words about how much she enjoyed the service. Still, emotional fracturing in the work place is hard to keep isolated.

But. Sarah's workplace could have nothing to do with her current medical crisis. Tricia hoped beyond hope that everything would be okay. Before she accepted the new ministry position she was told that the Swedish Hospital system was excellent, that they had a lovely hospital in Issaquah and a very highly regarded medical clinic and offices in Snoqualmie. In fact, she remembered seeing it when driving to her church office. She made a mental note to check it out for herself.

She saw the hospital sign and went to the Emergency Room entrance. Fortunately, there was parking space. As the sliding door opened Tricia hoped she wouldn't see a Nurse Ratchet. She didn't.

Before she could get into the lobby Bradley came rushing to her. He hugged her. Tricia had learned not to speak…but to let the hurt one unload, to get the information and learn where they were emotionally. Bradley looked at her, "We are so glad you are here, Tricia. Our daughter is fussing a bit…but still refuses to make her entry. That means maybe we'll be okay. You're here. That means everything to us. Let me check to see if we can see Sarah. Our obstetrician is with us. You'll love her. We are lucky…she was in the hospital seeing another patient. Her name is Claire Nelson."

He sighed, took a deep breath, exhaled and said to her, his eyes watering, "I feel better already. It's good to not be alone."

Tricia smiled, "Come on, fella; let's check on your bride."

"Bride?" he asked. "I like that…keeps the marriage fresh."

All Tricia could think of was *Oh boy, I hope it's more than a word that will keep the marriage fresh. But for now that was a non-issue. The mother and the child. Front and Center.*

Chapter 20

Tricia liked her already. That didn't come from any class...was what Creighton once told her, "Tricia, you are blessed. You have an inner gyroscope that intuits the situation...whether fear runs things or not."

Fear wasn't running anything. Immediately. Tricia liked the obstetrician. Because she wasn't standing over Sarah; was sitting next to her bed. Although virtually a newbie in ministry, Tricia had learned when visiting someone in the hospital, ALWAYS find a chair. Otherwise, the patient would think you are there for the "hello, how's things," and then gone. The patient would think you had more important items on your agenda.

It was very clear Claire Nelson had only one game plan...to take care of her patient.

Dr. Nelson saw Tricia, stood up and said, "Hello. Bradley said you would be coming, that you are their neighbor. He said that also you are a pastor. Good of you to be here. Sarah and Bradley said it is okay for you to be updated. I'm glad to do that. Let's get another chair for our visit."

The Lemon Drop Didn't Melt

The handshake was firm but not pressing and anything but limp. The handshake always made an impression on Tricia. Even more, though, Dr. Nelson had good eye contact...looking at Tricia, "I'm Dr. Nelson; thanks for being here." Dr. Nelson was tall, neither pencil thin or what might be *Goodyear Blimp*. Her hair flowed gently to her shoulders, her complexion clear. First impression? Favorable. Very favorable.

Dr. Nelson looked at Sarah, "Sarah? You can remain in bed. No walking around. And for sure, you'll have to cancel your volleyball game this weekend."

Tricia loved it. A sense of humor. That said this situation must not be literally a life and death situation. Perish the thought.

"My thanks to you, Dr. Nelson. Bradley explained how grateful they are. Thanks for letting me be part of the seminar."

They all smiled...Bradley got the third chair. They sat.

Dr. Nelson wanted to bring them up to date.

"Okay, I believe we'll be just fine. Certainly this is scary. When I learned Sarah had come in to the ER I checked on things right away. Now, what I say...you don't need to take notes. There is some information I need to get," as she looked at Sarah, then glanced Bradley's way, "But not now. I want to give you what we are dealing with."

Dr. Nelson then explained, since Sarah's term was at six months, the chances of a miscarriage were unlikely. Not definitely unlikely, but some tests taken already verified that Sarah was not having a miscarriage. That mostly happened before 20 week's pregnancy.

The most likely emergency that would rush her to the hospital is possible premature labor. Premature labor is going into labor [having contractions] before 37 weeks along. The other obstetrical emergency that can occur at that time is a weak cervix. However, that was also not the case for Sarah. The other set of symptoms Sarah could notice is pelvic pressure, like a weight or heavy feeling in her pelvis…or cramping.

A negative evaluation, that is, no premature labor or weak cervix, would be fewer than four contractions an hour, the ultrasound showing a normal length of her cervix. That was the case for Sarah…a negative evaluation.

Dr. Nelson raised her hand, "Perhaps this evaluation is too much… but I want you to know we've done all the tests, your daughter is just fine…even has a thumb in her mouth..but there appears to be nothing medically involved."

Sarah looked puzzled, "Nothing medical? I did have what appeared to be cramping…felt very tight in my lower stomach. That worried me."

Dr. Nelson nodded, "Sarah, I can appreciate the cramping. However, everything, at least for this moment is positive. No miscarriage is about to happen. Your child isn't asking for delivery. Let's have you rest here and I'll check later this afternoon. Perhaps then we can have you return home."

"Dr. Nelson?," Bradley inquired, a worried look bouncing off his brow, "If everything's okay physically—and we are so relieved to hear this. Is this all phantom discomfort? Well, it seemed more than that for Sarah. And, for me?"

The Lemon Drop Didn't Melt

He raised his hands as if he was surrendering, or as Tricia read it, asking for more. It wasn't an inquiry as much as a pleading for something more.

Dr. Nelson understood. She didn't know how to broach *the other subject*, but knew both Sarah and Bradley wanted something more. So, she guessed, "Sarah? You haven't offered much with me about your work. Sometimes what causes difficulty in pregnancy is if the mother stands a lot. That could be what we're dealing with."

Sarah shook her head, "No, Dr. Nelson, I'm hardly ever standing; I work at a desk."

"You work at Amazon in an executive position; didn't you tell me that, Sarah?" Dr. Nelson inquired.

There was silence. Sarah looked down. Was an awkward silence. Not calm but uneasy is how Tricia sensed it.

Tricia sensed it immediately, *There's something else going on here.*

Trusting her inner gyroscope, Tricia asked, "Dr. Nelson? Can this difficult time for Sarah be triggered by anything else? I could be wrong and perhaps this is not anything I should ask. But, when a mother believes she and her unborn child are in danger…could there be emotional factors? You did say the child's breathing was normal… and no medical problems were revealed in the tests. That is assuring. But, anything we haven't covered?"

Tricia was careful not to use the P word—*psychological.*

Dr. Nelson nodded, "Well, there can be other factors. For instance, Sarah, do you work more than forty hours each week? Do you drink enough water? Because dehydration can bring on contractions. Are you getting enough rest? Is there stress you're aware of? Because stress, being on your feet too much, working long hours can cause what you're experiencing. I simply know from the medical information, neither you nor your daughter are in trouble. You are doing fine…very fine.

"You've mentioned that you work at Amazon and I bet working forty hours per week…well, that may be fanciful. I'd be willing to wager a 40-hour workweek never happens. Maybe you'd be delighted if forty hours was the maximum. So, if the work time is extensive, maybe you should take off a few days…to get some rest. Would that work?"

Sarah squeezed her eyes shut, shook her head, took a breath, "Dr. Nelson, yes the Amazon position is demanding. But I knew that when I began. I'm now in my second year with them…." [She didn't want to say the financial impact…that if she left Amazon her two-year bonus, totaling thousands of dollars, would be lost. Plus, the medical insurance was most helpful.]

She didn't continue…kept looking down…a tear started down her cheek.

Dr. Nelson sensed what was really happening…it was the stress of her job. What she didn't know it wasn't a *something* issue; it was a *someone* issue.

Tricia looked at Bradley as he got up, grabbed a tissue and handed it to Sarah. The moment was awkward. Bradley looked at Tricia and rolled his eyes. She knew exactly what was in play. How to deal with this?

Tricia said to Dr. Nelson, "Dr. Nelson, it may be for Sarah the work at Amazon pushes pretty hard. Hard to fasten that down. I'm very grateful for the good medical report. As for the workplace, that will be important for Sarah, and certainly with Bradley's help, love and support, to address. I certainly will be with them to do our best to see how Sarah cannot worry about full term for their baby."

Dr. Nelson pushed her glasses up, then took them off. She stood up, realizing the medical causes were absent. Also realized the psychological factors were center point on the stress target. She looked at Tricia.

"I think we've covered all the important bases. Thank you, Reverend Gleason, for being here," as she reached into her doctor's jacket pocket, pulled out a card and handed it to Tricia.

She continued, "Sarah is a very special lady. Clear to me she and Bradley are in great hands with you...as their neighbor and pastor. That's a wonderful combination. I'll do my best to bring their child into the world, healthy and strong and maybe even out of the gate, sucking her thumb. My cell phone number's on my card...please let me know in whatever way I can be helpful."

Dr. Nelson took Sarah's hand, "Sarah, I know in my heart, which is better quite honestly than any medical test...I know you'll be fine... my goodness, how special to have Bradley and Pastor Gleason in your corner...and know I'm there, too."

As she left, Tricia knew they all were in good shape. Dr. Nelson? What an impression. It was more than her well-focused eyes, her willingness not to stand over Sarah or Bradley or herself. Had to do with the gentle manner of her teaching...and the great combination of her kindness and competency. And the words of hope…perhaps the shortest sermon Tricia ever heard.

Tricia turned toward Sarah, then reached for Bradley, grasping their hands. "Can I offer a prayer?"

Sarah, dabbled her eyes, took Tricia's hand, "Yep," she smiled, "I believe a prayer is a visit with God…and you, Tricia. How special. The best combination."

She squeezed Tricia's hand, "What a gift you are. I'm already feeling better."

After the prayer, hugs to Sarah and Bradley, Tricia nodded to them, "I'm headed home…be good to yourselves. And know.…"

She didn't continue, but Sarah did, "Guess we know what we need to do."

Tricia didn't respond. Didn't have to. But she wondered if Sarah could manage the matter of work and stress and demands. Oh, if they only came from the work and not the supervisor's attitude. What a major issue to face.

CHAPTER 21

Some people rang the doorbell. Or, other versions. A tap slightly. A well-measured knock.

But, no.

Surprise was Tricia's response. For the pounding on the door was not an UPS driver…or the Gladstone children a few houses away. Not even close.

"I know you are in there!"

A man's voice. Stronger. A very mad man's voice. The tone offered no range between inquiry and statement.

Rather, as Tricia opened the front door, the face gave *menace and rage* a classic reality, *Tricia didn't hold her breath, because her breathing was important.* And the look, if it could kill, well…

"Why did you do this? Who in the hell do you think you are?" She looked at him, knew him, but had never talked to him. The words pierced, and in a mild understatement, gave her a thousand paper cuts. She didn't see foam in his mouth but she expected that would be next.

She did see his hands fisted. Didn't know if they would be sent her way. No guarantee they wouldn't.

What do do? What in the world is this? Guess my sermon last Sunday never reached him. Salt Water? He was nothing but acid...pure, pernicious, destroying acid.

Tricia thought she'd speak the first word. Not to answer him. Well, not directly, "I'm sorry. I was upstairs in my bedroom," she lied.

He knew it, "That's bullshit...and nothing less. You were in your office, right there!" He pointed to her left. He had seen her. From the front window. A clear message to Tricia: forget the lies.

"Okay, you're right. And obviously this isn't a visit," replied Tricia. "I'm not sure you should come in," pointing to his hands.

He took a step back. Tricia wished he'd turn and take more steps to the sidewalk and leave…leave….leave. She could offer to push him. But she knew the temptation…shouldn't be more than that.

Her hopes were dashed, "I insist you let me in. Don't think I won't come in whether I'm invited or not."

Patience fled. Understanding was long gone. Tricia spoke as evenly as she could, "I know you are Rider Samson and you are a church member."

She hoped that would bring him some civility. Wrong again.

"Well, that's right. But my reason for being here?" Samson pointed to her face. Tricia leaned back. He made it clear, "My reason for being here is you are wrong. So wrong. Worse than that. You have brought me...."

He stopped and used spit for the next sentence. Missed her but hit the door. Ah, how refreshing, Tricia's ironical thought punched, *He left his own DNA...in case anything needs to be done. Gotta keep my detective hat handy. Be direct, Tricia, she preached silently to herself, trying to not look upset.*

Tricia took the direct method, "Mr. Samson? I don't think I should call you Rider. I have no idea why you're here, but with your attitude, why don't you leave and come back when you can be more pleasant? Because now you are so raging and unpleasant—that's my best words—we should not be talking any more. Your attitude makes conversation not likely. Your attitude?"

She pointed over his shoulder.

He laughed. "Oh, being direct, right? Or, if not, trying to take the high road? Maybe they taught you that in seminary."

He laughed again as he clapped his hands. "Nice attempt. But," as he pointed to her, "I am not going. I need you to explain yourself. Because it better be good. For what I have learned will mean you won't be able to preach a second sermon in OUR church. Not YOUR church, but OUR church. Don't be on your high road, your innocent-as-can-be-road. Let's get to the road called reality...called disclosure, called integrity. Because you've done your best to nail me in a coffin in my neighborhood."

Tricia was completely puzzled. She had no idea what he meant. *What in the world did he learn? What was this all about?*

He continued, "Well, I can see hospitality is not going to happen. So, let's stand here...but I don't trust you, so your words—how do they say it when you call the Sears agent, something about being recorded for quality assurance?"

He pulled a small recorder out of his pocket, held it in her face, thought maybe he'd use it as a weapon.

"Okay, Reverend. You're on...please answer the questions..."

He then launched questions but gave his version of the answers.

"First, did my wife meet with you for counseling? I can answer for you. I know she did. I know what she said. That would be no mystery. She told you I was a tyrant, that I was a sexual deviate. That was for starters.

"Second. Did you tell her that you wanted to meet first with me? Did you tell her you weren't qualified to be a therapist but you could give her a name? Did you tell her something about a Lynne Walters? Of course you know what I'm saying. Of course. Shit. You are a miserable bitch."

Tricia had no idea where this was going. She figured that Courtney must have told him about the visit with her and he could only imagine what she had said. So, why is there trouble? Maybe because the great and famous [her cynicism triumphing her thoughts] attorney didn't want anyone to know. Let alone a minister newbie, whom he had only seen once.

"Well," Rider Samson continued, "I'm sure you think I learned all that from Courtney. Don't you!"

It wasn't a question; it was an indictment. Tricia felt it better she not be recorded. She didn't respond.

He picked up on his tirade, almost shouting, "Well! She, the snarly wife—oh, did she tell you I give her two thousand dollars each month for her personal expenses. Did she tell you about her, let me quote it this way, other sexual escapades? I would doubt that. Here's the truth—bitter and repulsive to me. Courtney never said one damn shit word to me about your visit. I learned it from you!"

Tricia was more stunned than surprised, and her surprise was higher than she could remember. She could be silent no longer, "What in the world? I'm trying to listen to you, Mr. Samson. But honestly, I don't know what you are talking about. You are accusing me of saying something about when I met with Courtney? That never happened."

Tricia's anger kicked into gear.

She continued, looked at the recorder in his hand, "I hope this is recorded. You are standing on my front porch in a rage, out of control. I am unsure if you won't hit me. Look, your hand is still fisted. And you spout off that I have messed you up. That's absurd. Get off my porch. Get a better attitude and return. You are not welcomed with such a toxic manner."

She thought he would walk away. She thought her words had sharpness and conviction. The thought evaporated on the spot as he nodded, reached into his pocket and pulled out a note. Thrust it at her, "Read this and then tell me that I'm off. Go ahead. Read it. And then….we'll see what follows."

The note was crumbled. Opened it up. Tricia looked at it. Felt sick. Felt worse than sick. She was pretty sure the blood left her face. What in the world?

"Your wife went to your new minister. She told the new minister you were a horrible person. The new minister revealed that to my neighbor. How can you trust a mouthy minister?"

Tricia held the note. Not sure why but she wanted to keep it. She didn't look up, which she simply couldn't do. Was like her eyes could only see her feet.

He didn't wait. "See? I got this note a few hours ago…was on my car window. How miserable you are. You talk about trust and confidence and respect? That's bullshit. You have betrayed me. To my neighborhood. But I wonder, maybe also to some of my clients. And even more…although I will make sure if she doesn't know this…to the moderator of the church. I bet Sage Worthy will find this note—oh, I Xeroxed it because I knew you would either tear it up, flush it or pee on it. Well, woman. What you have done is you have peed on my reputation. And I will make sure it doesn't stay quiet. It will be roared to your church leadership, starting with the head guy in Seattle. Oh," as he raised his finger, "I know who he is. And I know…"

He didn't finish.

Silence.

Although it took great strength, Tricia looked up, looked him in the eyes. She could see prison bars across his face—or maybe it was mirrored in what was across her face. She was devastated. Totally. Hope had fled for her. And she knew, at least in that heart-breaking moment, she might not be able to find any salt water.

She spoke, somehow firmly, "Mr. Samson. I have read the note. And yes, your wife met with me and yes, I had hoped to meet with you. And yes, I did give her the name of a therapist...."

She paused...not for effect, but wanting to measure the truth with as much strength as possible, "I have not spoken to anyone about my visit with your wife. No one. That note is a lie, a complete set-up. Nothing in it is true. I have not betrayed your wife; I have held my visit with her in complete confidence."

Tricia lifted the note, she crumbled it, "This note is a lie. A brutal lie. It is untrue. I am not the person this indicates. I never told anyone. End of conversation. And, I will tell you, if you decide—and you've already indicated you will do this—if you decide to take this to our church moderator and our church conference executive, you had better provide names of those indicting me. Because I doubt it will ever pass beyond anonymity. Someone's out to get me. I don't believe it's you. I don't believe it's your wife. But somebody's out to destroy me. And they are using you as my personal sodium pentothal."

He didn't smile. He smirked. Clicked off the recorder. Put it in his pocket. Said to her, "Words are cheap. And you've made them even cheaper. Of course I expected you to be in denial. That's one of the stages when someone dies. And then there's rejection and anger. Guess you've got a few stages to go through. Think you'll ever get to acceptance, which, of course, requires integrity. Are you ready to face the truth? And as you stated last Sunday, good luck in finding your own salt water. See? I listened. So bad that you speak but you don't listen. Not for a breath."

He turned and walked down her front steps, looked back at her as he opened the door of his Corvette, fluttered his fingers at her, "Twittle-dee."

And drove off.

She was glad she hadn't invited him into her office—it was right off the front door. She had thought of getting off the porch, to not have the visit be seen. She gambled no one would stop then to visit with her. She was glad she kept the front door open, and even though it didn't happen, was fully prepared to jump in the house and slam the door. She wondered what he'd do with the recording. But she didn't have anything to apologize for. Actually, a glimmer for her, even a slight smile. She was glad what she said. She never backed off the truth. But, the calm didn't remain.

Tricia stood as if she had become a mummy. How dreadful. She knew it was a lie. She knew she had held the confidence from her visit with Courtney. She also knew…as her mind raced to condoms, to sliced tires, to phony phone numbers. She knew…

Went in to her kitchen, uncrumbled the note, looked at it again.

Saw the script. It was calligraphy.

Tick. Tick. Tick.

Chapter 22

"Creighton, you are better than chartreuse yarn."

Tricia could begin any conversation off the charts. At least Creighton told her he loved her creativity, which he said was euphemistic for whacky. But, he loved whacky. Because as he said many times to her, especially when she preached, "Tricia you are special. You do so much more than live up to your minimum."

Was the reality of humor engaging humor? Would his comment, light and positive, help? Tricia wasn't sure.

Creighton could tell the tone of her voice. It wasn't exactly a trouble whisperer, but he could tell, especially with Tricia, when something wasn't right.

"Tricia? What's this about yarn."

She explained the gift from the neighbor girl and how she had it in her hand that very moment.

Creighton said, "Okay. I get it. Share. Vent. Obviously something's wrong…and you aren't going fishing right now so you won't need the yarn for an indicator drifting the river. What's going on?"

Tricia gave him, as he would say, even though Mexican food was not in his top ten meals, *the whole enchilada.*

"Oh my, Tricia. Trouble lurks…in so many ways. A couple of procedure questions. Have you mentioned the latest pissing tirade from the lawyer with the detective? He seems like a savvy guy who is reliable and as important, competent. Touched base with him?"

"I will, Creighton. But for starters, you're it. He just left an hour ago."

"What about your church moderator…did she tell me last Sunday she's an attorney? Maybe she knows Counsel Pisser and can let you know if this is his behavior mode…you know, if someone cannot support you get rid of them."

"Good point. I have good vibes about Sage. Yes, she's an attorney. And I should apprise her of my experiences. But, I sense you have another reason for that…and knowing you've worked as an executive minister in Oregon and I know you've had situations that on good terms were snarly, could this become one of those…snarly?"

"Well, Tricia, this is not a prediction, but for sure what you describe, especially the slashed tires and the ominous note, Mr. Samson…."

He paused which meant to Tricia, this would be a critical insight. She waited, because she knew Creighton would continue. She was on target.

The Lemon Drop Didn't Melt

"...because the accusing lawyer, if he didn't get your cooperation by admitting what obviously is not true—and you are not paid to lie—could press charges."

"Oh no," Tricia exclaimed, "You mean charges that could challenge my ministry? I know some of the rules, some of the ethics, when being ordained. But I'm not ordained yet. I have read the denomination's Manual On Ministry and do know there's a process in which a minister can be defrocked. Think it's called a Fitness Review."

"Yep," Creighton affirmed. "All he has to do is contact your moderator, plus your executive minister, Micah Dimmock, that you have betrayed him. He could show them the note and they couldn't care about the calligraphy...and because he wouldn't whisper his claim of your lack of fitness, they are obligated to do, as a lawyer would say, discovery."

"He could do that?"

"Tricia, you are good but that's naïve of you to ask. Yes. Make that double-yes, he could do that. In fact, I would bet he may have already thrown you under the bus. What I advise is, even though it's late, I would advise at least you call your moderator and tell her you need to talk with her. Plus, connect with your detective...didn't you say his name is Jordon Valentine? He needs to know that very apparently all the, let me say *events* are not coincidental. This could be the very least.

"I know...ominous...but still. A truth in ministry. You cannot be too careful, especially when someone confides in you. They are upset, they are at wit's end, and as I like to say they are reaching up to touch bottom, so they unload on you."

"Creighton? I'm sorry, but don't you believe me? Don't you believe that I didn't betray Courtney Samson? I didn't..."

Suddenly Tricia felt empty. She knew Creighton understood her. But what about support? Understanding and support weren't always connected. And of all things the emptiness wasn't academic. *Did Creighton not trust her? She couldn't stand not having him in her corner. It would be devastating.*

"No! Tricia. Hold on. Please listen to me. I trust you. I respect you. And I know. In my heart of hearts, you are trustworthy. Don't think for a breath that I believe you've made a blunder. What I believe..."

Another pause. Words being thought through.

"...what I believe is someone's out to get you, to make your life miserable. Which, of course, with all this happening, let me ask... because this pulses through every instance. Let's assume there is someone...this is not a collection of people trying to make your life one trouble after the other. One person. And to be honest, there is one person I can think of. It just popped into my head."

"One person? Tell me, Creighton. Who would that be? Who would do this? Who would be out to get me?"

"Hey, it just came to me. Assuming there's one person, the only person I know who cannot stand you, who spelled revenge big-time, is your ex-husband. He could do this. He really could."

"I hear you," Tricia responded. "But, Creighton he needs to be eliminated as candidate for harming me. Because we both know, even though he was six feet tall...the verb *was* operative here. You

The Lemon Drop Didn't Melt

were with me when he was shot dead. So now he's six feet under in the pauper's grave outside of Tillamook. How does that go? Ashes to ashes? He couldn't be the culprit because he's secured in an urn. Buried. And I try to bury all that he did to me…and to those others. So. He couldn't do it."

"Sure, but he's the only person I can think of. If we cannot think of someone, then the *why* question must be asked. What is the motivation here? Why is someone out to get you? For once you answer that, the calligrapher will be identified and your troubles will melt."

"Troubles will melt? Why use that phrase? Doesn't that come from the Rainbow song?"

"Yes, it does. The song, 'Somewhere Over The Rainbow' says that 'troubles melt like lemon drops.'"

"Good possibility, Creighton. Look. I've taken too much time. I'd better go over some sermon notes. But before I do that, will call Sage and Jordon and see when I can see them."

"Call Sage right away, Tricia. And tell her to call your executive minister. Better to give her a heads-up."

Creighton had another thought, "I have one more question. Am curious. Where did you have your counseling session with Courtney Samson? In your church office? And, second. Maybe she's the one who told a neighbor. Because I cannot imagine she's not complained about her husband to someone else. Could be more than one someone… maybe many someones."

Tricia said, not knowing why the question of where the visit with Courtney took place, "I don't know her, really. Creighton. If she tells others and maybe told someone she met with me. Where we met? She came to my house…we met right here."

"Well, just a curiosity. Hey, I'm with you, woman. Totally. And. I respect and trust you. Thanks for sharing. Keep me posted.

Creighton then asked, "Did you tell me you saved the note? So, you have it. I would imagine that Mr. Samson also has a copy…wouldn't be fit for an attorney to not have evidence in his folder."

"Yes," Tricia answered. She looked at the note on her table and felt both empty and sick. *Could this be more harmful than I think?* She shook her head, hoping the grim dread shook out.

Creighton said, "That's good. Keep the note. Not for a frame and not to be an insert in next Sunday's bulletin."

He laughed, "Oh, one more thing…guess I'm the questionnaire… fishing's always been your balm…hope you have some fishing on your calendar."

"Ah, so true, Creighton. Fishing's my balm. This good thing happened. I met the Episcopal minister…serving a parish on Mercer Island. Had a great lunch. She's invited me to join her and a couple from their church…actually next Thursday. Am set up to cast jigs for Coho salmon on the Skagit River. Evidently the guide's fished that river for over twenty years…and October is Coho time."

"Oh boy, Tricia. I wish that last statement was recorded. Some joy came through. I got a glimpse of it. Good! What a great way to end this visit. Remember…keep casting…don't lose your yarn…and know the value of lemon drops."

Tricia smiled…finally. "Later, wonderful friend."

Click.

Tricia picked up the phone. It was answered on the second ring, "Hi, Sage. Tricia calling. I know it's late…but I wonder if we might visit for a few minutes after worship tomorrow?"

"Sure, Tricia. Is there anything wrong?"

"Oh no," Tricia lied, "Just thought it would be good to visit about some ideas I have for getting to know the church members better. Plus, have an idea for a mission project."

Sage was encouraged, Tricia was relieved, "Will be good to learn your ideas, Tricia. I'm sorry, but I cannot be in church tomorrow. However, I talked to Melita yesterday and she gave me your sermon topic…love it, "Empty Nets." Guess you being a fishing guide impacts your thought…and your preaching. That's good. Take care…be sure you know I'm very grateful you're here. Good news."

When Tricia hung up she googled "Somewhere Over the Rainbow." Ah, how lovely…IZ sang it. She had read about him…how he struggled with obesity, sang this song…and then the horrible happened. He died at an early age.

She heard him sing, "Troubles Melt Like Lemon Drops."

Down deep Tricia ached. Really ached. She knew she needed to be proactive. With that she thought she should contact Hannah, her pastor buddy. Yes, she would do that. But not tonight.

She played the song again…and suddenly her eyes flooded with tears.

The thought hit her…and it wasn't a snowflake…rather, it avalanched. *I'm a lemon drop that doesn't melt.*

Tricia Gleason. Fishing guide. Homicide detective. Minister. And now, someone's enemy. Would the lemon drop ever melt?

She finally fell asleep, not realizing she was clutching the yarn.

Chapter 23

It wasn't that she didn't have enough to fuss over. When she arrived at church, Melita, the church secretary, met her. She looked over Tricia's shoulder, "Good, we are alone for a moment. Can we go to your office, Tricia? I'm glad you came early. I guessed right."

Tricia hunched her shoulders, squinted. *What is this? Something's obviously wrong with Melita. Ohmygod. Maybe Mr. Smash-Your-Mouth got to her?* She was glad Sage would be at worship this morning. That was good. She left a message for Jordon Valentine; he hadn't responded. Now. This.

Melita had the office door opened, walked ahead of Tricia. The worry look was like a cloud overhead that was about to burst. And still she needed to keep her sermon development in mind and in heart. She wondered what Melita had to share? Could it be Tricia's reputation took another hit? Could all this be circulating…how she had betrayed Courtney…and now it was common street talk? Tricia never thought she was, what Creighton called *the paranoia type*. But he commented once, "Tricia, just because someone's not paranoid doesn't mean no one's out to get him."

Melita looked at her, then suddenly didn't let Tricia sit down. Rather, she hugged Tricia. *What in the world? We have barely shaken hands.*

Melita stood tall, very rigid. She took a deep breath, exhaled, looked Tricia in the eye, her eyes teared, "This is terrible, Tricia, simply terrible. I learned it yesterday afternoon."

That was when piss and vinegar blasted Tricia…could Samson have given Melita a heads-up? Because Sage had given Tricia a warning about Melita. Her middle name would never be *confidentiality*. In fact, Sage referred to Melita as a *verbal newsletter*. Warned Tricia to not share any notions that might not happen, particularly any thoughts Tricia had about new programs at the church. If Samson had told Melita, then the whole congregation would know. Tricia's mind raced, *Not a good thing…to be in a church less than a month… and the church…*

But Tricia knew she hadn't revealed anything to Melita. She hadn't. Only talked with Melita about sending out the get-together idea and the questions. And THAT needed to be circulated far and wide. Still, what are these tears all about? What in the world could be "terrible, simply terrible?" Yes, Tricia could say that about all the non-coincidences but Melita knew nothing about them. And certainly Tricia had disclosed nothing personal…either about her or about anyone in the church, let alone a box of condoms in her shopping cart.

Melita blinked the tears away, "Wanted to share with you…I haven't told anyone else, Tricia. But, you are more than my boss; you are my pastor. And I don't believe what I just learned."

Here it comes! To say Tricia had alert buttons pushed…what an understatement. She even imagined Melita screeching what she was about to share. Could Tricia handle it? Once Creighton had said there would be "help, murder, police" moments. This was one of them. She thought of the trains parked along the road into Snoqualmie…*would one of them start up and come right at her?*

Melita looked down, stopped mid-sentence about Tricia being the first to be told.

She looked back up at Tricia, her make-up black meandering lines down her cheeks, "Please know I mean it. I've told no one. And for sure I cannot tell my husband. He'll go bezerk. He doesn't have the first clue…but honestly, about him," she shook her head, "no, I cannot tell you anything about him and how he will react to this."

Tricia thought she had patience. But the gripping possibility of what Melita would say…*give it up, Melita. Give it up. Hit me directly. I've got a sermon to preach."*

Fortunately, Tricia's thought was no more than that. No words. She put impatience aside…at least emotionally. She looked out the office window and saw members arriving.

Melita then spoke, haltingly, but it was clear, "Tricia, I learned yesterday afternoon I have breast cancer. There's no history of it in my family, but I had felt a lump so I went to our family doctor. He said it was unclear. Had the various tests, even a biopsy. Jacob doesn't know. Oh, he's my husband. He will freak out. I was sent to an oncologist and she said that they would do a lumpectomy. Will you be with me for that?"

Tricia wanted to roll her eyes, give the world's biggest sigh of relief and say…no shout out, THANK YOU, JESUS. But of course she didn't. Wanting her concern to trump her personal relief she held Melita's hands and said, softly, "Melita, I hear you and I share your concern. For what it's worth, I had the same diagnosis a few years ago. Had the lumpectomy and there were no traces, no lymph node involvement. I didn't need chemo, but some radiation. All worked out. Let's hope and pray you have nothing more than that."

Melita didn't smile, but she nodded, "Oh, thank you. Please know this is between us…as friends…well, from me a church member to you my pastor. I'll let you know once I'm ready to share with Jacob.. but not right now."

She looked over Tricia's shoulder to the wall clock, "Oh no! I better get in to help hand out bulletins. The Samsons offered to help, but called me earlier this morning and said they were having some problems, so couldn't be here. So, I'm your Girl Friday—I know that's so old school, but deal with it, okay? Lemme get to handing out bulletins… and see if your sermon can fill my personal empty net now. I liked the sermon title…will bet the sermon will be more than likable."

She gave Tricia a hug…"Go, Preacher Girl. Get those nets full."

Tricia went to her desk. For whatever reason—well, she knew the reason—she looked at her desk and wondered if Mr. Calligrapher had left a message. The desk was empty. Tricia couldn't focus well. That had to change. Part of her was concerned about Melita, because until more was known about the lump…that could be horrible and not even close to trouble. It could be well beyond that. But the other inner tug was about the Samsons. She wondered if Rider was riding

The Lemon Drop Didn't Melt

all over Courtney, or if he wouldn't ever show up at church again. It may have been wrong, but part of her…the largest part of her… wanted that to be true. Her want turned to hope.

To that Tricia remembered that Creighton had told her, "Tricia, know this about ministry. EVERY minister has, no matter how helpful the congregation is nor how competent the minister is…EVERY minister has at least three members the minister would most like to trade." Which meant that more than a suspicion, it was definite for Tricia, Rider Samson was her first name on the trading block. The thought for Rider to leave was not ambiguous. Absence in this case didn't make the heart grow fonder; more apt, something about out of sight and out of mind. But Tricia knew, or at least could make a case, Rider Samson didn't know calligraphy.

She saw many arriving, and to her surprise, there was the Safeway clerk, *condom lady* she might be called. Although Tricia wouldn't believe for a moment Montina—she thought that was her name—was a magician and had placed the condom package as a way to see how Tricia would respond. No. Forget that.

She also saw her personal two Kings and Queen…that gave her such a warm feeling. She hoped the warmth trumped all the cold, the wind and the rocky boat. She also hoped, as the scripture said, after having fished all night with no fish, the disciples wanted to go home. But the scripture said Jesus stood before them and told them to go back out in their boat…and to cast their nets to the other side of the boat.

Tricia's problem…what was the best side of the boat? Not a good question. But it was an important one.

She walked to the modest sanctuary, saw most chairs filled. Hopefully they were there to welcome and appreciate her. Not in any case to indict her. *Those are such horrible thoughts...thoughts? Scram!*

Tricia couldn't deny though, as Creighton said, "Tricia, you can win any worry-wart comment. You worry with the best of them. You need to quarantine the worrying."

The prelude ended, she hadn't paid attention. She didn't realize the pianist played "Somewhere Over The Rainbow." That was a good thing...because right now she felt two things: one, her lemon drop wouldn't melt. And two, would the nets stay empty?

"Good morning, everyone! This is the day the Lord has made; let us rejoice and be glad in it."

The response was like trumpets announcing good news...it caught her right where she needed...in her heart...and deeper, in her soul. Yep, Creighton was right...worship could be a good thing. And maybe...who knows? Maybe the preacher can hear her own sermon and cast nets in the right direction.

And then it hit her, *casting.* And in the blink of an eye, she thought beyond worship and all the terrible matters...and thought of fishing with Hannah next Thursday. The fishing? It brought a calm and comfort...and even peace and joy...for her soul...more, for her living.

She continued, "I'm so glad we can be together today. In fact, I hope you share the gladness. So. Hopefully as we share this worship, for you and for me, on a 1—10 it will be at least a 9."

Almost on cue, Scooter said…and it wasn't a whisper…'Yes! How about a 11?"

People laughed and some applauded…

She was tempted, spur of the moment, a flash of spontaneity, to say to Scooter, "Gosh, Scooter, that went better than we planned."

But she didn't. Because it would have been untrue…nothing but gimmick…and Tricia believed the gimmick didn't help. She wanted to help.

Worship started…and she felt better. Much better.

For the moment.

Only.

If only.

For more than a moment.

Little did she know what happened in her office didn't stay in her office. For after all she wasn't in Las Vegas. She was in Snoqualmie.

Tick. Tick. Tick.

Chapter 24

Life slogged along for Tricia. She wished she could push the clock at least to triple-time, then to have Thursday get locked in. But, alas.

Her hopes for the worship to go well were realized. At least, she mused, if someone said she looked calm and in control, if truth pushed, she would have said something about all they could see was the body of the duck moving across a lake; they couldn't see her feet [that is, her emotions] churning like mad.

She was able to get her message across, that in hope the nets can be filled. Although she wished it preached more to herself. It didn't.

But it did make connections. The people, no less this second Sunday, were affirming. One even said, "You don't know this, but your sermon, especially when the disciples were asked to think about the other side of the boat…caused me to think through my own situation. Gave me some thought about how I'm making decisions. I have never thought of the boat's other side. Thank you. You have ministered to me this morning in your sermon."

Tricia could only smile, because it was the reception line. She didn't know the person and he didn't have a nametag. She wanted to follow-up during the social hour but he had left. The comment, though, helped her feel better. That her sermon wasn't in vain, at least for one of them gathered.

But this Monday morning she was alone in her office. Melita asked for the day off, and since the office was only open each weekday from 9 a.m. to noon, and since nothing needed to be mailed from the church office, that was okay. Besides, that would mean she and Jordon could visit alone.

She hadn't told him when she reached him yesterday afternoon all the sordid details. Although she did say she had a new note and some heightened concerns.

She invited him into her office. His khaki pants were well creased and his sweater was what Tricia considered a splash of colors…maybe even kaleidoscopic. He even brushed the front of his sweater, "Hey, my theory is if you cannot be impressive, you can be colorful."

She smiled and thought *if only I can have a sense of humor.* The word *presumptive* never came to her about Jordon.

Tricia sat in front of her desk in a soft chair. Jordon sat in the other soft chair, a chair that swiveled. He commented, "I like this."

Tricia responded, "I'm sorry? You like this?"

He didn't hesitate, "Yes, you have good skills, no need to show your authority," as he pointed to her desk chair.

She furrowed her brow and raised her hands to eye level.

"Let me explain. Tricia, I like that you don't sit behind your desk. You are sitting in front with me. That says you don't have to be in charge. That says we can visit with no authority. And for sure, you aren't hammering a gavel."

She nodded, "Oh, I get it. I'm no judge. Which means you cannot be a jury. Right?"

He looked serious, like a switch had been flipped, "Okay, you mentioned another note…got it?"

Tricia said, "Yes, but first, let me explain how I was pissed on yesterday."

"Oh my," he responded, "Sounds like anything but pleasurable. Sure hope you weren't a sponge. That'd be ugly."

"Well, I'm not a sponge but it was ugly. Let me explain."

When she finished, almost a verbatim detailing, his eyes squinted, "This is not a good scene. You are accused of violating confidentiality…."

He steepled his hands and tapped his chin, "I'm not a jury, but I do believe…and maybe I'm wrong but I doubt it…I doubt it fully. It may be he's right…that you did in fact not keep Courtney Samson's session with you. But I won't go there. Not at all. I don't know your accuser, but my sense of this is, you weren't into betrayal, nor would you be.

"So, next step. What could be up? It could be that Courtney told some people and it got back to her husband. Did you say his name is Rider?"

The Lemon Drop Didn't Melt

Tricia nodded, "Yep. His name describes his modus operandi…at least that's what I experienced."

"Okay," Jordon said, "Or maybe she told her controlling husband… and with your account, that's what he seems to be, at least to you… and when he heard she had counseled with you he tried to figure out how to get you out of the picture."

Tricia cautioned him, "Jordon, let me respond. Of course I'm grateful you believe me. It is the truth. I never told a soul. And it could be he found out Courtney came to me. And your third, maybe Courtney told someone. But, honestly? None of that stands with viability. Because, this is what Rider Samson gave to me…"

He took the note. Read it. Pursed his lips, scowled. Shook his head sideways. Sighed. I have only one word, Tricia, only one word…."

He waited and then pierced the silence, with a sound well above a whisper, "Shit!"

Jordon continued, "I see how it is written. I'd like to take the note…"

She handed him the note, "Yes. Please take it. Do something with it. As you can see, it's the same calligraphy as the sticky-notes on my office desk and in our pulpit here at church. I need your crew to make sure it's the same writer. And then, if there are prints. Oh, I wasn't a good detective because I crumbled it and then flattened it out. But I will give you my fingerprints…and then see if there might be latent prints. Well, yes, there will be Rider's print. So this note will not be pure for prints of Mr. Do-Me-In."

"You bet. I'll make sure we do a full check on the note. But, deeper…"

She knew where this was headed, similar to her conversation Saturday with Creighton. She was right, for in so many words Jordon knew—not beyond reasonable doubt but with a strong sense of being correct, everything that happened to Tricia was well beyond coincidental.

Jordon then summarized, "Well, Tricia. This is really not good. Right now we don't have anything to go on. Let me ask…actually two questions…first, where did you visit with Courtney Samson? And. Has anyone else shared with you anything confidential or intimate that the person would be aghast if your vow of trust was broken?"

Tricia wasn't sure what to say. But she could keep it well contained, "Courtney came to my home. And, yes someone in addition—and it's not in any way related to Courtney—has shared with me something very personal and said I was the only one who has been told."

"See? People do trust you. But obviously there's someone who doesn't. Even worse, there's someone who wants you…I don't know what word to use here."

"I can say it, Jordon. Down deep I sense in my heart, pushing to my depth of soul, someone wants me dead, the inevitable of his version of a water torture. Drip. By drip. By drip."

"Okay, that may be. That doesn't mean, though, that this will continue. Not if I can help it. And I'm not one of these guys who has silver bullets and I don't wear a mask and I'm clumsy on a horse."

She smiled, "Okay, Tonto. We'll keep the horses out of this."

He said as he got up, "Let me take this note…will give you a report. Oh, one other thing, where were you when this other person revealed something personal? Did you say it happened at church?"

She got up, "I didn't say, but yes, it was at church. The person visited in my office. No one was around. At least not in the office or at the secretary's desk right next to my office. Why do you ask? Because Creighton asked the same thing…wondered where I met Courtney?"

He didn't say anything.

She leaned toward him and tapped him on the shoulder, "Hello? Earth to Jordon."

He smiled and then tapped his temple, "Just thinking about something. Want to marinate it a bit. Will let you know after I check with some of my buddies. Probably nothing. But, I've learned in the world of being more than Columbo, that nothing at times ends up being the turn key."

"Yes, maybe I should be more detective than pastor. But!"

She made the motion of casting a rod, "What I'm really looking forward to? Next Thursday I'm going to where I bet, not for a moment or forever, will there be a sticky-note. Nope, I'm going fishing! Yes!" She pumped her fist.

"Wow, look at you! A smile that beams. Wow. Fishing must mean everything….oh, I remember, you used to be a fishing guide. May I ask? Where you headed?"

"I've never been there before but a clergy buddy, she's the minister at the Episcopal Church on Mercer Island, fishes with a guide on the

Skagit River out of Rockport. We'll be fishing for Coho..and evidently it won't just be fishing."

"Not sure, Tricia, I understand. You said you were going fishing… will it be more than that?"

She didn't hesitate, "Oh yes, in addition to being peace to my soul… my friend said it's always more than fishing. She said there'll be lots of catching."

"By this way, Jordon," as they walked outside, "Do you happen to like salmon?"

He raised his eyebrows, "Hey, guess what? I love salmon. Please put me on your list, just in case you catch more than you can eat."

He reached out to shake her hand. She really wanted to give him a hug…but not now. A car drove up. Tricia didn't notice the driver.

Jordon said, "Thanks for this new evidence…will get back to you… probably on Friday, unless something happens before you get to the Skagit River. Take care of yourself."

He turned and went to his car, and waved before he opened his car door.

"Tricia? Got a minute?"

She looked and saw it was Sage Worthy. Tricia forgot she left a message for Sage, who wasn't in worship yesterday.

Sage got out and walked toward Tricia. She looked at the driver leaving, "Oh, don't recognize that man…a new church member?"

Tricia smiled, 'Not yet. But, let's go into my office; I can explain."

As they walked to her office, Sage said, "I'm sorry I missed yesterday. Haven't talked to anybody. I liked your sermon topic. Sure hope the worship filled their nets. Oh, I'm sure that's the case. People are talking about what a good preacher you are. I'm assuming you have more than two sermons?"

Tricia laughed with Sage.

Certainly Tricia hoped so, too. Well, she knew she had at least three sermons. For her sermon on "Bulletproof Faith" was her favorite. And that would be for next Sunday. She hoped.

That is, Tricia pondered, *If I'm still on board for the third sermon.*

Sage sat in the same chair Jordon sat in, "Oh, this is a warm seat. Must be your visitor sat here."

Tricia nodded, "Yes. Sage, thanks for being here. I have some information to share…and then need your advice."

Sage responded, "Glad to listen. I'm all ears and heart. Please share."

Tricia more than hoped Sage's intentions would hold. She'd soon find out.

Chapter 25

Tricia thought maybe this was sweater day; hadn't seen or heard that, but perhaps Snoqualmie had such a theme. Sage's sweater was as colorful as Jordon's, and her slacks matched the blue-theme perfectly. But, she knew they wouldn't be discussing their sartorial preferences. She only wished.

Tricia outlined the purpose of the visit, "Sage, I need to visit with you. I need to give you some, let me say, difficulties I'm having here in Snoqualmie…"

She could see that statement caused worry for Sage, who interrupted, holding up her hand, "Oh my, Tricia. This isn't sounding good. Maybe a bad novel with that statement about difficulties. Now, of course, you've only been here less than a month. And I'm sure you didn't rob a bank…that your name isn't Bonnie and you haven't met Clyde.

"Besides, I cannot imagine a pastor could get off to a better start. Two Sundays ago the service…and especially your sermon, plus the decision to take us outside. There were rave reviews. Last night a member called me to share her delight you were on board…asked if we could give you an extension with an undeclared date. Now, that's endorsement. No one has made one negative comment."

Sage paused, "But, I'm talking too much...you say you're having difficulties. Let me zip my lips and open my ears. Please share."

Tricia only wished her difficulties were not a big deal. She continued, "Let me start with a bottom line, Sage. I'm meeting with you for a couple of reasons. One, you are the moderator of our church, the person in charge of the business of the church. Well, there is more. You are the person who helps the congregation be strong when it comes to all operations. Plus, you are an attorney and in that vein you may be able to help me. Third, you know the executive minister, Micah Thorten, and he may be getting involved with my difficulties."

"What? Micah involved? That sounds ominous. Why would that be?"

Well, I know our denomination's protocol when it comes to a minister not being ethical. That reality may end up being my reality, and I know the role of the executive minister...to oversee misconduct reviews."

Sage responded, "Oh my. If that's your bottom line, Tricia? Please fill in some paragraphs of why you're thinking in these terms. I do hope you are not Bonnie."

"No, I'm not," Tricia responded. "It could be much worse. Much."

Sage put her hands together, folded as in prayer. She only nodded to Tricia, suddenly the look of fear.

Tricia then mentioned the paragraphs, wanting Sage to be fully on board.

"So, Sage, what I'm worried about is Rider galloping into Micah's office saying that I'm unfit, that I did not keep the confidences of his wife. That's not true, but the calligraphy note, with the others I've told you about, are hard to prove I was untrustworthy. And that could mean a horrible situation for me. But honestly, more so for you and the congregation…that their new pastor, the lady who tells fishing stories, cannot be trusted. I cannot think of anything more dreadful, even terminal, than a minister who violates confidences. I cannot prove it…simply my word against a calligraphy note. I do not betray confidences."

Sage said, "Tricia, first of all, I am grateful. I am grateful you have shared. I am now aware of the inner dynamic for you. And, yes, it may also be for us, but perhaps not remaining inner. Micah's a good friend. Yes, he's pushed and pulled in his work, helping almost 90 churches in Washington, Northern Idaho and now a couple of Samoan Churches in Anchorage, Alaska. But he is never too busy to not help a minister. Why don't you let me visit with him privately… simply as a heads-up. If you want to come along, that might be good.

"Oh, actually he did call me last Friday to ask how the first steps for you and us were. I told him you couldn't have started in a better fashion. I still believe that…good steps."

Tricia couldn't stop thinking, which became words, "I felt that, too, Sage. My first Sunday went better than I could have ever wished. Good steps. I felt that. But now I'm sensing my steps are stumbling. My dilemma? I cannot disprove what Rider says…well, more directly and factually, what the note says."

"Can I see the note, Tricia," Sage asked.

The Lemon Drop Didn't Melt

"No, I'm sorry. I've given it to Jordon Valentine, he is having it examined. Along with the two other sticky notes. Perhaps when they've done the testing, they'll give them back to me and certainly then I'll share. Absolutely."

"I have another thought, maybe a couple of them. Please listen," Sage advised. "First, I am in your corner. I do trust you. Okay, all reality needs to be in this. I may be wrong. But I don't believe I am. Secondly, it is good to include Micah in our situation. In case a charging Rider pounds on Micah's door. Rider may do that, but at least the pounding won't come as a surprise. Oh, by the way, I do know Rider. He's in a different law firm. But…"

She hesitated, "No, I cannot share any more. Just that I'm not surprised Rider went into an attack mode…it's happened before. Now I've never talked with Courtney about the marriage, but the few times they have been at church, I have sensed their relationship doesn't flow smoothly. In fact, now that I think about it, during our social fellowship hour after worship, they are never together. Of course that can mean nothing. But, nothing amiss I'm aware of."

Tricia felt better. Not vindicated, but Sage and she weren't in opposite corners. Good to have an attorney on her side. Just in case. She spoke, "Sage, thanks for your endorsement, your affirmation. And thanks for your plan to share with Micah. I feel better already."

Sage held up three fingers. "You got it. Here's a third…I haven't met Jordon Valentine…was it he who left when I got here? Hope he helps…and deeper, hope their forensics tests give you an identity… of, let's call this guy, the guy who makes it clear you are someone for whom he has only one purpose, destruction. Let's hope he gets identified, so we can get you taking only good steps…and let me be sharing what I hope for you and for us…dancing."

Tricia smiled with relief. It was so helpful to have Sage's support, "Well, Sage, I would never qualify for 'Dancing With The Stars,' and I couldn't be Bonnie and have a thing with banks. But I am an honest person. I am. Thanks, Sage, for listening. Please let me know if anything in this sordid mess comes your way."

"You can book that, Tricia. I am in your corner…oh…"

Tricia hoped the next words would be good. She wasn't disappointed.

"Just had a thought, Tricia. I do know your background. Maybe you will need to put on…but not forever…your detective hat. Maybe you can do some of your own work on this…at least the mental part. And, what I'm thinking…I'm gonna bet you are not doing enough casting. Got any fishing planned? Cannot imagine you haven't done research on fishing in Washington. Am I right?"

Tricia smiled, "You be right, Sage. In fact, I'm going to fish for the first time in Washington…casting for Cohos."

"That's great! Got it all planned?"

Tricia told her about next Thursday, "To be honest, Sage. Given all that I've offered about the bumps and the stumbling, next Thursday cannot get here soon enough. By the way, you like salmon?"

Sage licked her lips, "Hey, do I tell the truth? Yep. When I talk my nose doesn't grow. And I think the same is for you. I love salmon. And wouldn't be offended if one of your Coho has my name on it. Well, not the whole fish. But. How about a small fillet?"

"Ah," Tricia smiled, "Consider it done. Consider it done."

"I will, Tricia. Because I know two things about you, no…make that three. I know you know how to fish. I know you know how to preach. And. Drum-roll, please. I know you can be trusted. So, let's move on…with good steps. Stumbling not allowed."

They walked to Sage's car. She waved to Sage as Sage left the parking lot and said, "One salmon fillet coming up!"

It wasn't a whisper.

Tricia walked back to her office. Walked with a new resolve. Tricia was right. Thursday couldn't arrive too soon. With hopes that Tuesday and Wednesday would be good. No sticky notes. Some first visits with church members. She didn't mind praying for that. For days without calligraphy. And with the prayer, "Dear God, please don't consider me a stranger."

And yet. Something inside. Something way deep inside. Something was missing. She couldn't put her finger on it. It was a phrase…she thought. Slipped in when it was said…then fled.

Chapter 26

Tricia couldn't sleep. The three days had gone well; that wasn't the problem. Her visits with the church members, one retired couple, two widowers and a gay couple…had gone better than she'd anticipated. She learned their personal story. That new knowledge would help Tricia with at least these members. If they needed to get her attention, it wouldn't come from a voice of anonymity.

Even more helpful, she found out what they hoped for their church. One of the widowers said, "It's so good you are here. Just to have this kind of meeting with me. Shows you care. Shows you want to do good and do it well….see, I know my grammar…actually I was an English teacher at the high school. Please know this…it's makes so much difference for the good because you're reaching out to us, paying attention to us. When we call you for help, I know you won't send a book."

Tricia was curious to that, "Send a book? I'm not sure I understand."

"Oh yes," he said to Tricia, "The previous two ministers were into books. Whenever any of us identified a problem, they'd send a book that purported to solve the problem. What they didn't know is, how important it was to have them visit us, to be present with us. Well. That beats every book anyone ever wrote."

Still, Tricia couldn't sleep. The uncluttered and non-sticky-note days had helped. She was alert—didn't want to miss her alarm. Actually it wasn't necessary, for she got up in time. She met Hannah on Mercer Island. She looked forward to meeting the couple from Hannah's church. They weren't there.

Hannah explained, "The couple couldn't make it. The husband has a terrible cold and didn't want to bother us. So, maybe next time. However, that gives us a great chance to be together. Here's our game plan," as they drove away from the Mercer Island commuter parking lot. "We meet Jon at the boat launch, it's called Roger Miller Steelhead Park, at 7:00 a.m. It will take us about two hours to get there…up I-405, then on to I-5. We'll get off at Arlington and drive east about 45 minutes to Rockport. Meet Jon and then, it will be fishing time."

She glanced at Tricia, "I don't know how you are, but I don't want to be battling a salmon and have my cell phone bleep at me. So I keep it in my car. No news for me, at least while fishing, is always good news."

Tricia hadn't even thought of that. But she agreed, to be casting and not doing any church business? What a great idea.

Hannah talked some about Jon and Heather. "Tricia, you'll love them. Heather won't be fishing with us. She drives a school bus. Jon also helps at the high school when he's off the river. He coaches the wrestling teams—used to be a wrestler so he loves helping the youth with that. But what I think is most impressive about them…is their caring spirit.

"They are committed to helping veterans through the WWIA—the veterans support organization for our military who have earned the Purple Heart. Didn't I share some of this?"

Tricia nodded, "Yes, you did, but remind me."

"Okay," said Hannah.

She said that at least quarterly, Jon and Heather hosted the veterans. They, with community support, had built a bunkhouse. Jon would take the veterans fishing…and at times bear hunting. Even the ones who had no arms. It was incredible how the veterans were helped.

"You should read their journal," Hannah recommended. "Amazing affirmations from them. So impressive what Jon and Heather do."

Tricia listened to Hannah. Helpful. But, something else was happening. No words could describe. Well, maybe Sage's words on Monday were a prompter when she asked if Tricia had fishing planned.

Certainly Tricia felt better when Sage said she had talked to Micah and he hadn't heard from any church members with any complaints. Nor had he heard from anyone singing Tricia's praises. But that wasn't unusual. For as Sage offered, the executive minister mostly heard from church members wanting to know what they needed to do to get a new minister. So, Sage had it correctly. At least this time, no news was good news.

The deeper matter wasn't with her new ministry. It wasn't fussing over the sticky-notes. It wasn't about Rider's claims. It wasn't about her next sermon. It wasn't about thinking about a new mission project for her church.

No. Her feelings. It came upon Tricia with power. The joy inside. Part of her heart and part of her soul. The fishing. Absolutely the fishing. How she had missed it. How she needed to be fishing. Sure, the catching had helped and as a guide there was always enough catching for her clients to reserve dates a year in advance.

Tricia didn't have the words…but it was undeniable how much being a fishing guide meant to her. And more often than she'd ever admit to anyone, including Creighton, her mentor and best friend, her go-to guy with anything, that ministry was becoming more stress than satisfaction.

To a point deep inside Tricia, she could hardly wait until they reached the boat launch. What she didn't know was if this was simply a thought prompted by the rocky start in Snoqualmie. Or. Was it something more? In any case, Tricia thought, *focus on fishing, make that my mantra. Period. Nothing more. Nothing less.*

The trip went smoothly and as dawn broke, Tricia felt good about the weather. It was cloudy—more preferable to sunny and bright. Clouds, at least in fishing, were always a good thing. Nice to give "cloudy" a good take.

"There we be," Hannah proclaimed. As they drove over the bridge, Hannah stopped and said, "Look at that, Tricia. Look at that."

She pointed at the river…large and flat.

Tricia saw it…a reminder of Tillamook Bay and pointed upstream high above the river, "Look, Hannah, an eagle."

Hannah was curious, "I bet there's lots of eagles in Oregon, too. That's true isn't it?"

Tricia nodded, "Yes, when I was a fishing guide, my boat was docked on the south end of Tillamook Bay. When we fished for fall chinook salmon, mainly in September and October, you could set your clock to an eagle."

"Oh? How so?" Hannah asked.

"It was great," Tricia answered. "The eagle had a nest on top of one of the Douglas fir trees. At 7:35 each morning, off the eagle went to the north shore. The purpose was to get breakfast for the chicks. Seeing that eagle this morning…sweet. A memory returns. That is good. I love eagles. Totally."

"Oh yes," Hannah responded. "You should be here in February—eagles everywhere. Might even call it Eagle Central. More eagles than you can count. In fact, there are eagle-watching boat trips. Lots of bird lovers in Washington. Audubon is very popular."

She then pointed downstream. Tricia looked and knew it immediately. Her bones were alive; they even spoke to her. "Oh wow, Hannah, a sled boat. A sled boat."

Hannah was curious, "You sound excited. A sled boat? Yes, that's Jon waiting for us. His sled boat is 23 feet long. You can see he has a jet motor and a trolling motor. The jet motor gets us from point A to point B faster than fast. And the trolling motor, in case we would be drifting downstream, is used to barely give up ground to the current, while we are bouncing bait along the bottom....but we won't do that today. No, the trolling motor is used in a couple of months when it's steelhead fishing time.

"Today? We'll anchor and cast. And, be ready. For this is prime time for coho. Although there'll be other fish grabbing our jig. Mostly coho. But, there are Dolley Varden trout and although it's late for them, there could be some pinks...they come in every other year... this is the *other* year...in September, to be honest, and I had this happen a month ago, you can see if you can cast and NOT get a bite. How crazy is that? Then two other fish we may catch. One likely now. That will be the beast of salmon, the chum salmon. But one other, although this is early for them, still, we might get a winter steelhead. They aren't really here until after Thanksgiving. But then...."

Hannah looked in her rear-view mirror and saw lights coming, so she drove across the bridge, turned left for the parking lot at Howard Miller Steelhead Park. She finished the catching options, "As I mentioned we might also hook into a chum salmon. They are big and mean and ugly. Probably will snap the leader. For sure the chance of getting spooled is high. However, it's a great adventure. We only keep the Coho, the limit is four, two hatchery and two wild Coho. However, it's always fun to learn which fish you've hooked. The chum we toss back, as long as it hasn't pulled us in."

Hannah stopped, put her hand over her mouth, her eyes wide open. "Shame on Hannah! Shame on Hannah!"

Tricia was curious, "Pardon me, Hannah...What's there to be shamed about?"

"There I went," Hannah responded, "Telling *you, a fishing guide,* all about fishing on the Skagit River and describing the fish. Me! Telling a fishing guide. I'm sorry for that…hope you understand."

"Hey, Hannah, I haven't told you…I have two middles names…-*Understanding* and *Appreciative.* Both in high gear now. I am impressed, actually, at what you know. Most of my clients are clueless…and worse, they really couldn't care less. All they want is a fish in the boat. So, to know you and I are fishing today and each of us is aware of the catching options? It's all good. It's all good."

Tricia smiled. The voice of her bones, the joy in her heart…almost overwhelming. *Ah, she thought…so important and vital…no, make that vitalizing.*

Tricia wanted to run to the sled boat. But somehow she was restrained. She even felt like dancing but thought that was not a good move… didn't want to be too demonstrative about her joy. It was almost like she was okay…as Creighton had once told her, "Tricia, for you the song, 'It Is Well With My Soul' does happen when you are fishing."

He was right.

She and Hannah approached the sled boat. Tricia sighed. Deep. Very deep.

Jon helped them into his boat. A great smile, "Hi there, Hannah. Where's your church buddies?"

Hannah explained, pointed to Tricia, "Jon, say hello to Tricia Gleason; she's the new pastor in Snoqualmie."

Jon hugged her, "Hi, Tricia. I hope you don't mind the hug [he had already hugged Hannah] but I like to hug pastors. Brings me good luck…give me a touch of preacher's luck."

She laughed and pointed to him, "Got it."

She appreciated the candor and the warmth. She felt welcomed. Very welcomed. He was certainly physically in shape…must be the wrestling…tall, maybe six feet two, not flabby but she saw his face. Kindness from ear to ear.

She then looked at the three rods…she almost fainted. They were the same rods she used when fishing for salmon in the rivers that flowed into Tillamook Bay, especially her favorite river, the Wilson. The Loomis rods and the Shimano Symetre 3000FL spinning reels. And the threaded line. It was if he had taken them from her storage locker in Tillamook. Her eyes widened.

Jon noticed that, "You look surprised, Tricia. Is there something wrong?"

She couldn't hold it back, "No, a thousand times no. I'm so impressed… and even more…delighted. For this is like I'm about to fish the Wilson River in Oregon."

Hannah was puzzled, "What's this about? Wilson River?"

"I can explain."

She looked at Jon, "Jon, you have no idea. Maybe Hannah told you I used to be a fishing guide. What she didn't tell you, because she doesn't know, I have this exact sled boat and the exact jet and trolling motors and it's perfect, the same rods and reels and threaded line. How impressive. Over the moon."

Jon clapped his hands and looked at Hannah, "Well, Hannah, guess we'll have double luck today. Maybe even quadruple luck, the limit for coho. I'm blessed. Got the right boat and equipment for Tricia. Plus, we cannot miss. No, correct that. I cannot miss, having two preachers on board."

He looked to the sky, "Dear Lord, thank you. For two lady preachers. What a gift!"

Hannah looked at Jon, "Okay, Jon, enough of the applause. I never knew we could catch a fish sitting here at the launch and our poles standing in the corner of your boat. You think?"

He nodded, "Okay, you got me. Let's get to it," as he turned up the jet motor, pulled out into the river and headed downstream.

They went not quite a mile, then Jon anchored and pointed, "That river coming in is the Sauk River. Just below it there is my 95% hole. Here," as he handed Tricia a rod, "Lady fishing guide, make the first cast. Will more than guess that you've done this before."

Jon loved it, "Let's see if the combination of former fishing guide and preacher works. Remember, this is my 95% hole, which means there's a 5% chance we will get shut out."

Tricia nodded, "Yep, know all about the jigging. I'll cast to where you're pointing."
She cast about five feet from the bank, a two-second count, then lifted the pole once, reeled down and lifted again.

The Lemon Drop Didn't Melt

Tricia smiled, joy dancing inside. Yes, she knew how to cast. Jigging…as easy as riding a bicycle. The cast was perfect, she judged just right. Two seconds. Hannah had her mouth open, her eyes wide as saucers. Tricia tried to be cool, calm and collected, the image of a duck floating smoothly on the surface was her body language. She lifted the pole to raise the jig, then dipped the rod and reeled.

It was third time to lift the rod, but she couldn't raise it. She felt something solid, knew what it was, jerked on the rod and felt the thrust. Fish! Suddenly the water swirled and exploded. The bright and shiny Coho was dancing on the surface.

Jon whooped, "Ninety-five percent! Yes! This preacher can fish!"

Tricia knew just how to do it…lift the pole and reel down…bringing the fish to net. Jon was ready, net in hand. But, as soon as the fish came close, it ran away, plunging out of sight.

"Hey," Jon remarked, "You think Ms. Fish has something against preachers?"

The river splash was joy to Tricia…fishing, playing a salmon…the loudest YES in her heart. Finally, maybe five minutes in battle, the salmon was netted. High-fives. All around. Jon got the club, made sure the fish was ready for the fish box. Before, though, he asked Tricia to come to the side of the fish box. Pointed to the center post in his boat, "Hannah, please take our picture."

Standing there. Jon handed Tricia the coho, she noticed it had sea lice, had just come in from the ocean, fresh as fresh can be, believed her first Skagit River Coho was about twelve pounds. They stood there. The picture taken. Jon took the coho, put it in the fish box, looked at

Hannah, "Okay, Hannah, you're next," pointing to the mouth of the Sauk River, "Just like your preacher buddy. You can do it. Yep, off to a great start. You're next. We've got eleven to go. Should limit out. Hey, with preachers, it's always…"

Hannah made the cast. For her it was the second lift…a solid pull, she set the hook, the river was on fire. Well, not literally, but the boiling water was caused by the salmon. It wasn't quiet. It was exciting. The best kind of excitement in the world.

After netting the coho, Jon said, Looking at Hannah's coho, "Wow, an identical twin, Hannah, to Tricia's fish. How cool is that!"

Tricia took their picture. Jon put the coho in the box, picked up his spinning rod, "Okay, ladies. Your proud fishing guide's next. How about three for three?"

The day could not have gone better. Eleven coho in the boat. They had gone downstream and anchored across the river.

Jon anchored and pointed, "Preachers? We need only one more to reach twelve. Forgot to ask. Hannah, will this be like last year?

Hannah said, "Gosh, Jon, I haven't thought of that. I never told Tricia."

She turned to Tricia, "What Jon's saying is that last year, and our congregation is about the size of yours, Tricia, we had a special salmon bake. We had the bake as part of our stewardship campaign…a great way to bring the congregation together after they've made their financial pledge commitments to the church for this year. Don't know if you and St. Andrews have talked about a financial campaign, don't even know if you do your finance campaign in the fall, but maybe you can consider that. Jon contributed lots of coho, so we had more than enough. If you want to think about it, our church has a large freezer… we can store the salmon for you. Think about it."

Tricia didn't hesitate, "I've thought it through, Hannah." With a wink she continued, "That is exactly what we'll do at St. Andrew's. But. Will twelve coho be enough for 70 people?"

Jon laughed, "Ladies? I don't know the story that well, but it seems to me that Jesus fed thousands with fewer fish."

Tricia loved the idea and knew she could pull it off. Never for a moment thought it might not work. She couldn't imagine Sage and the church officers turning down a salmon fillet all-church dinner.

Jon spoke, "Tricia, let's catch our twelfth salmon…and then maybe you and Hannah can come back for a repeat next Thursday. I have a cancellation, so the sled boat's yours."

No way. No way in the world would Tricia refuse that invitation… nothing better than casting…and to think, their day today…every hole was 100% catching. Wonderful. "We reserve your boat, Jon," Tricia offered. Hannah said, "It's a deal," holding up her rod.

"Tricia, grab your rod…let's see which of you can win the last fish in the net contest. Maybe even a double, a photo-finish to the net. A great way to end the day."

They cast, about ten feet apart. Jon grabbed the net and said to them, "Don't want to put any pressure on you preachers…but I'm ready. I think…"

He never finished the sentence, "FISH!" yelled Hannah.

As Tricia started to reel in, to get out of the way she thought she was snagged on the bottom. Solid. No action.

She said, "Oh, Jon, I want to get out of the way, but I'm snagged," lifting her bent rod.

Before Jon could answer the snag moved. Fast and strong.

It was a double. Two fish at once…joy upon joy.

Jon, smiling, "Okay, we can only keep one, preachers. So, first come, first served."

Hannah brought her coho in quickly, not much of a fight. Fish netted and put in the fish box. How lucky for them…they needed a hatchery coho to complete their limit…and Hannah's fish was a chrome bright hatchery c oho hen.

Tricia hadn't seen her fish but knew it wasn't small. She saw the fish…gasped, "Jon? This could be the fish of the day…bigger than big."

As it came to the boat Jon laughed, "Hold on, Preacher Tricia!"

He pointed to the salmon, which saw the boat, did a 180 degree turn and took off, reel singing, Tricia holding on. And suddenly. Or as Jon would describe it, *sooner than fast,* she couldn't stop the fish from going downstream.

Jon laid the net down, rushed to lift the anchor, turned the boat around and headed downstream.

As Jon caught up with the fish he could see where the fish was headed. The hole was called the Cedar Hole, known for its sunken logs and limbs...you'd often lose the fish there. He didn't say that because he figured, at least they could see what he knew was pulling against Tricia. The chum surfaced...ugly and huge and most uncooperative. Had to be twenty pounds if it weighed an ounce. Which it did. The salmon hadn't spooled her; she had reeled in most of the line back. Otherwise, all the line would have been pulled from the reel... evidence of spooling...if Jon hadn't gone downstream after the fish.

The salmon plunged deeper than they could see. Then silence. Tricia felt emptiness. Her rod no longer bent, the line was slack. She knew.

Jon laid the net down and smiled. Nodded to Tricia, "Early release."

He looked at his watch, "Time to go. We have limited. Good for you... yes, good for all of us. Let's head back to our house. I will fillet the fish and vacuum-pack them. Bet your congregation will be pleased, Tricia, their preacher has filled their nets."

He had no idea how timely that was, changing the metaphor to reality of filling nets. Tricia beamed. She even thought about dancing.

Then a surprise. Jon had beached the boat by the launch and started to clean the salmon. Some had eggs which he put in a plastic bag.

Tricia knew the drill. That would be good steelhead bait in month or two. He threw the guts of the fish into the water. Then he whistled.

Tricia couldn't figure that out. Suddenly the whistle's purpose was clear. In swept a large osprey and started to grab some of the fish entrails out of the river.

Jon smiled, "Haven't named him yet. Or maybe she's a she. But this has gone on for over five years…my whistle might mean I'm an osprey whisperer. Not bad, eh?"

Jon put the cleaned salmon fillets into plastic bags, "Ladies, let me trailer the boat. Hannah, you know where Heather and I live. Think she's at home now…just about noon. Why don't you drive over…be with you in a bit."

As Hannah left the fishing adventure, aka Roger Miller Steelhead Park, "Now, Tricia. If you think this was an adventure. Just wait. Wait until you see Jon's log cabin…and the bunkhouse. That will be an adventure…and whenever I'm there all I think is…it's about healing. Something we all need."

Tricia could only hope Hannah spoke the truth.

When they drove into Jon's driveway, it caught her breath. Never. Not even close. How incredible the log home! And to think that Jon built it, with some friends, over ten years. As they parked Hannah pointed beyond their garage, "There's the bunkhouse for their visiting WWIA veterans. We'll look at it before we leave."

The Lemon Drop Didn't Melt

The world for Tricia was good and valued…and now, at least, in focus…maybe always. She didn't know. If only her hopes had a future.

Standing on the porch was Heather. Tricia noticed her smile and heard her enthusiasm which added to her welcoming, "Hello! Jon said you'd get here. I am so glad to welcome you. Understand you caught a few fish."

She came down the steps, hugged Hannah, "Glad you're here, Hannah."

She looked to Tricia, "You must be Tricia. Jon said you are a delight. He's biased about preacher ladies. Well, Hannah's the only one. But he did say something about a clone. That must be you. Glad you're here, have some sandwiches made, hope you're interested."

Tricia reached her hand, "Hello. I'm Tricia Gleason."

Heather smiled, "I'm Heather Thorsen. Great combination…that you are preacher and fishing guide…and Jon said…homicide detective. Guess we've got all the bases covered, but the detective role…won't need that."

Heather grasped Tricia's hand…firm and yet not forceful. And the smile. Genuine. Tricia could tell. She liked Heather already. She liked the eye contact and the hair reaching her shoulders. She also could see the Washington clothes…wool, knitted sweater, levis and boots up to her knees. Tricia sensed to visit would be good, as good as the fishing.

What Tricia didn't know the fishing would be second-place. She'd learn that. But not now.

Chapter 27

"This should be enough…you think?"

Jon held up a bag of the vacuum-packed salmon fillets and smiled, "Let's see, we got the fillets, each can feed two people, even if they're hungry, from each of your coho. If my math's correct twelve times six. That comes to 72. Heck, Tricia, you could feed most of Snoqualmie. With some left over. Do I remember something about twelve baskets left over?"

Tricia and Hannah could not be more pleased. They looked at Jon, who stood next to Heather, then burst out in applause. Smiles abounding.

Heather responded, "That's nice."

She looked to Tricia, "Yep, very nice to get applause, but honestly, that's for the stage. And we aren't on any stage."

Heather reached out her arms with an invitation, "But hugs are better."

The Lemon Drop Didn't Melt

Jon said, "Okay, ladies, quit gushing," as he lifted the two bags, "Can put this in your car, Hannah. But, before you leave, and speaking of applause and good news, let me show you our bunkhouse."

Tricia was amazed. The bunkhouse was behind their garage. It had been finished, maybe two years ago. The bunkhouse was where the wounded veterans stayed when they were cared for by Jon and Heather. There were four bunk beds, extra-large, so no one had to sleep on the floor. There were two full bathrooms, a stack of towels.

The word that came to Tricia was *neat*. But, even more than a description. She felt in her heart this was a healing and caring and loving bunkhouse. And who in the world could ever say that about a bunkhouse? For Tricia, and she'd seen one bunkhouse when in Colorado last summer, they had to do with dirt and grime and unclean windows and cowboy boots on the floor.

As Tricia looked at the bunk beds and the floor and the windows and the two bathrooms…she knew. She knew for sure, if she had a white glove? She could wipe everywhere and there'd be white gloves with no evidence of dust. She didn't have any pocket change, but she also knew if she had a dime and dropped it on one of the bunk beds, it would bounce. The dime, not the bed. She smiled to herself.

They were about to leave. Hannah walked over to the storage closet, reached up and picked up a book, showed it to Jon and Heather, "Do you guys mind if Tricia looks at this?"

They shook their heads in unison and said, almost on cue, "No. A thousand times no."

Hannah handed the book to Tricia.

Heather said to Tricia, pointing to the book, "This is a journal our veterans have written in, their comments about staying here...they call our place Camp Stillwater. Please take a moment and read it."

"I have an idea," Hannah chimed in.

Tricia didn't know what Hannah would say. But Tricia thought to herself that reading the journal might have a purpose, a deep purpose for Tricia. On the way up Tricia mentioned, only the Cliff-notes, a brief short version, of the sticky-notes and how irksome they were, how ruffled Tricia felt.

What Hannah then said...maybe it was instinct for Hannah. But, maybe it was inspired with Tricia in mind, "As I mentioned, I have an idea. The last time when I was up here I came into the bunkhouse alone. You had invited me to read the journal. I read it in here. By myself. Couldn't believe its power and value. Why don't we let you read this, Tricia? We'll be in their kitchen."

Tricia was quiet, knowing it would be helpful for Tricia to read the journal entries. She didn't know exactly why but she could read and react without an audience. And for sure, this wasn't theatre.

They left and closed the door. Tricia sat in a chair next to one of the beds, opened the journal and started to read. She got to about the third journal entry...and burst into tears.

Chapter 28

Although Tricia sputtered the words, wiping the tears with each paragraph, she read out loud. More for her to value the words, the thoughts, the affirmations.

"I have never felt so welcome at someone's home since I have been here. As I told you both. The period where I faced medical retirement from the military that I have spent the majority of my adult life and have grown to love. At times, this period of my life seems dark and helpless. But this trip has brought light and hope to me. You both have amazing hearts. Being here has warmed my heart knowing that there are people who care as much as you both. Thank you both for everything. I haven't caught so many fish in my lifetime." It was signed Craig.

Tricia smiled, she could identify with catching so many fish…wasn't a good day. Today was a great day.

She spoke the second entry, "I truly want to thank you for your time and dedication to make sure we had a good time, were well fed and you showed us people truly do still care. I did not realize how bad I needed this weekend. I am finally relaxed. Thank you so very much." Was signed Ralph.

Then another, "Leaving for this trip, I wasn't sure what to expect. I had the same feelings I do whenever I leave the house. Anxiety and apprehension usually keep me from going anywhere. Once I met Jon and Heather all that went away. This trip has truly touched me. I never thought I was capable of trusting people again, but you two have helped change that. From hanging out in the bunkhouse to the event, every aspect of this trip had helped heal me. I'm already thinking about coming back." Was signed Pete.

Overwhelmed. That was the impact upon Tricia. The power and truth. She read one more, "Wanting to say THANK YOU both for this awesome, amazing and memorable salmon fishing trip! I'm sharing my thoughts and feelings. First, you bring a warm welcome into my heart and mind of this amazing tranquility event. I feel overwhelmed with kindness, love, caring into the thought and process of what your soul heartily brought and showed each and every day, from start to finish, or what you so lovingly wanted this part of the WWIA to be for Wounded Warriors. My mind and body has remembered what slow and easy has been for me in the past. I feel I've excelled in who I am and who I once was. Which is a combination of happiness and a true blessing." It was signed Joshua.

It was the silence. A silence that had a voice. Tricia closed the journal, placed it on top of the closet. She sat back on the bed. She didn't cry. She wept, her insides twisted into a snarl. Not because of what she read. Rather, it was because of what she was missing… the peace, the blessings, the heart at….what was the voice saying? It was only murmurs but it was somehow important. She thought she knew. But for whatever reason…whatever reason in the world, she missed something. She knew the feelings. But what was she missing? Somewhere beyond the tip of her tongue, the pulse of her heart.

She sighed, a deep sigh. Closed her moistened eyes, offered a prayer, "Dear God, please help me."

She went to the bathroom, looked in the mirror, turned on the water, washed her face. Took a deep breath, wiped her face dry...and knew she needed to be on her way. Somewhere deep inside she was empty. But wasn't sure how to be as the wounded warriors were...at peace, experiencing a moment—packed into a couple of days, in which healing, blessing, love and peace came together.

Somewhere, somehow she would not remain empty. But she missed something...on how the emptiness could be gone.

In a flash the day had come into focus. The casting. The two-second wait for the jig to sink. The lift the rod, drop it, reel a bit and continue the ritual, again and again. It was when the ritual came to a stop... when the action began. When the fish was hooked and what she called *the ballet drama* with the fish began. The splashing and leaping.

Tricia was grateful for the time on the Skagit River. Even more, she was grateful for Jon and Heather, for their hospitality. She was grateful for their work with the wounded warriors. No, that was wrong. It wasn't a work; it was a ministry. A ministry of healing. She prayed as if she was wounded...which she was. It wasn't a bullet or an IED on the trail but it was sticky notes that hit her like a bullet.

Tricia looked back into the mirror. The eyes were red. But the face was dry, as were her eyes. It was time to leave. But, she hoped, maybe it was time to start...on a trail called healing. Possible?

Chapter 29

They stood by Hannah's car.

As Tricia approached them, Hannah raised her eyebrows and said, "See, Tricia? Wasn't that mind blowing and heart rendering?"

Tricia got closer, blinked her eyes, said quietly, looking at Jon and Heather, "That journal isn't a journal."

Jon looked puzzled, "That's not so, Tricia. It is a journal, what some of the wounded warriors wrote about their being with us. But, Heather and I believe, perhaps being better with themselves. There are some details I should have told you. But I thought against that so you could read and be impacted only by their words.

"I want to tell you about a couple of them…so you get an idea of their terrible experiences. Remember Joshua? He's amazing. A 4-time Purple Heart recipient. He was wounded twice by IED's, once by a RPG and was shot another time. And Craig. He has every reason to give up. Incredible, though, he doesn't…and we doubt he ever will. Craig was here only a month ago. He is a double amputee, lost both of his legs just below the hips because a roadside IED took out his vehicle and legs as well. He sat in the same chair you sat in today, Tricia. And, boy, could he cast. And it was great…he, excuse the phrase, had the hot rod. They all wrote from their heart and what they said, well," as Jon sighed and nodded, "Gives Heather and me great gratitude we can offer what they call Camp Stillwater. I like their choice of a name. Well, sorry to interrupt but I wanted you know something about their experiences and wounds. And you are sure? It is not a journal? I'm not clear on what that means."

Tricia clarified her statement, "What I want to say about it not being a journal. And, of course, this is overstated, but there are 66 books in the Bible. Your journal could be the 67th book. It came to me as biblical. What messages. What truths. And way off the charts above goodness, how much the two of you bring. Jon, you are more than a fishing guide and wrestling coach. Heather you are more than a gracious hostess and school bus driver. You…both of you…are ministers. And now to hear about the seriousness of the injuries, that gives me all the more appreciation. You both, because of your caring, bring healing and peace. That's better than wonderful. Maybe we should say it's wonderfullest!"

Heather bit the inside of her cheek, nodded, then said, "Wow, Tricia. That's the second loveliest statement I've ever heard."

Jon said, "What? What do you mean second loveliest? I think it's great Tricia is perceptive. But, the second loveliest?"

Heather gave Jon a kiss, 'Yep, the loveliest is when you tell me you love me. Nothing can be greater than that."

She kissed him again, "Got it, mister?"

Hannah tapped Tricia on the shoulder, "Well fisher lady and pastor… time we head back to Dodge."

Jon smiled, "Hey, don't leave us forever. Do check, Tricia, about your schedule next Thursday…got two seats for you and Hannah. And maybe we can track down that chum…bet the jig is still in its mouth."

They laughed.

Chapter 30

Hannah and Tricia drove out to the highway, on their way back to Mercer Island.

They were silent…for about 20 minutes…

As they drove west of Darrington, Hannah pulled the car off the road. Pointed to the right, "Tricia, what do you see?

All Tricia could see was nothing growing. A massive area…down the side of a mountain and stretching to the highway they were on.

"Actually, Hannah, all I see is mud."

Hannah agreed, "Yes, you are correct. But what you see is one of the most horrible times in the peoples' lives here…you see the result of a huge mud-slide. The rain and wind…as you can imagine, the torrential rain, broke the mountain's side, creating an avalanche of trees and roots and mud. Happened two years ago, March of 2014. I remember the facts, it engulfed almost 50 homes and other structures in an unincorporated neighborhood known as 'Steelhead Haven,' just east of Oso. It also dammed the river, causing extensive flooding upstream as well as blocking the road we're on, 530.

"It destroyed homes and animals and human lives. It brought national news here. But that's not most important. Yes, it brought devastation. But also brought people together. Jon, our guide, wouldn't tell us, because he's so humble. But he also is a volunteer fireman and he came to help. I cannot tell you. This used to be teeming with life, trees and a river and homes and a school and a church. Now, it's mud. They did find, finally, all who perished. But, you can imagine…this was horrific. The mud was everywhere. But the people who lost their homes and some of their family never gave up. Why? Because people like Jon never left them mired in mud. He and hundreds helped pull them out of the morass."

Tricia had read about this, hadn't realized it was on the road from Rockport to Arlington and then to I-5. She was stunned. To realize how terrible. To realize what a mud slide did. To see it was so much more impactful in its devastation than to read about it.

Tricia's cell phone rang, Beethoven's melody on cue. It was Sage's number.

Tricia answered as Hannah started the car and headed west.

"Hello, Sage."

Before Sage could say anything, "Oh, Sage. I've had a great day with my clergy buddy, Hannah Ball. We fished on the Skagit and caught our limit of cohos. I'm bringing most of them back…our guide filleted and vacuum packed them. Hannah has a large freezer in her church kitchen; she will keep them for me. Well, I mean, for us.

Which leads to an idea, want to share it with you. But I'll wait until I get back, maybe tomorrow. Think the idea could help our church's stewardship campaign."

Tricia stopped her stream of consciousness, "Oh, I'm sorry. I had shifted into the prattling gear. Let me start again, hello, Sage, how are you?"

Silence.

Sage then spoke, "Tricia, call me when you get home. Melita has resigned."

Chapter 31

Tricia thought she would faint. It was like *she* had stepped on an IED. Emptiness. Worse than that. She suddenly had trouble breathing, handed the cell phone to Hannah and barely got the words out, "Tell her I'll call when I will be home."

"Hello, this is Hannah Ball, I am with Tricia. We're coming back from fishing. Suddenly she's not doing well. She'll call back. Need to stop for a moment."

She clicked the phone off, Tricia pounded her knees, shook like the proverbial leaf and screamed, full throated, "I'm done. Totally done. Today, Hannah? It was Easter. And it was. Best day I could have ever wanted…even more, needed. But that!," as she held up the cell phone, "That is nothing but Good Friday. Horrible. Damn! Good Friday's not supposed to come after Easter. This is all screwed up. I'm done, like I just stepped on one of those ground devices those soldiers…"

She pounded her knee again, opened her window and started to heave the cell phone.

Hannah spoke quickly, "Tricia! Don't. Hold it," as she saw the rest area sign. "I'm getting off. We need to stop driving and start thinking. Obviously…"

She didn't finish her sentence because a couple of cars had slowed down on the exit ramp. Hannah was relieved Tricia put her window back up, simply laid her cell phone by her feet.

It was a large rest area, lots of parking. Hannah pulled in front of the bathroom, "Do you need to use it?"

Tricia shook her head, pointed to the last parking place, off to the side. No cars around. "No. But right now that's the only thing that's okay…I don't have to pee. But I do think I might have to throw up. Let me take a few breaths. How bad is this…when Good Friday…"

Tricia stopped, put her face into her hands, "Oh no! This is terrible!"

Hannah parked, let her window down a few inches, turned off the car. She rubbed her cheeks, pursed her lips, said, "Take your time, Tricia. Take those breaths. And then, if you wish, let's talk about *terrible* and identify it. And know this, our conversation will not be recorded for quality assurance. You can trust me."

A slight smile from Tricia. Hannah thought that was promising. Better than a scowl. She waited.

Hannah then spoke, "I assume that was the Sage you told me was your moderator?"

Tricia nodded, "Yes, it was. She only told me one thing. The IED."

Hannah didn't want to say anything because she felt Tricia would start explaining. She was not wrong.

Tricia started to cry, "Give me a few more moments, Hannah. A few more moments. I'm not cut out for ministry…I cried when I read the journal notes…and what the vets said about how Jon and Heather had ministered to them. Oh, they didn't use those words about hosting the veterans, but as was mentioned they do have a ministry. I couldn't help but think that my church members…now in Snoqualmie…wouldn't write that in their journal about me."

Hannah was quick to protest, "Wait a minute. Hold on. I bet. And it would be a safe wager. I bet if I handed them a page and asked them to write down what they thought of you and the first two worship services, they would have rung your praises. I bet you'd find words like inspirational, wise, helpful…"

Tricia disagreed, said forcefully, "But, Hannah, you and I both know that the value we have as a pastor is…or at least I believe it should be, much more than a sermon. It has to do with relationships, with trust, with what Creighton said to me far more than once, the key to an effective ministry is to be there with the people, to be a spiritual presence. And, speaking about presence, Creighton said when meeting with people, it's important to be a non-anxious presence. I cannot be that now. You know what? I feel now, deep in here," as she pointed to her heart, "like those people must have felt as the huge mud slide trapped and then covered them over."

Hannah said, "I do understand. But. Those are all negative images, Tricia…*mentioning IED's, mud slides, Good Friday.* There's got to be more. Please tell me, what did Sage say…it had to be one sentence."

The Lemon Drop Didn't Melt

Tricia actually smiled, "Yes, Hannah, a rather perceptive word, *sentence,*" as she finger-quoted the word. "Because I feel that I'm getting a sentence and the trial hasn't even been started…and the sentence is out-a-here, I'm finished. Ministry is now in the past tense."

Hannah nodded, "Yes, I'm sure that's how you feel…that there's only Good Friday and you're having a month of them. But," as she put her hand on Tricia's shoulder, "Maybe not. Maybe no harsh sentence."

Hannah then had an idea, "Hey, you're the detective, Tricia. Why don't you put on your detective hat…look at your situation as if you're a lady Columbo."

Tricia shook her head, looked at Hannah, sighed, "Sorry, right now I don't think any hat will fit. Not well at all."

Hannah had to say something, "Okay. Ms. Nothing. Let me," as she pointed to her chest, "Let me be Ms. Columbo."

Hannah snapped her fingers. "Yeah, let me be the detective, to see how Ms. Nothing can really be Ms. Something, emphatically Ms. Something very special. For a seminary professor once told me when there are shadows, that's only evidence the sun is shining somewhere. Yep, there are shadows for you. And now I'm wearing a new hat. I want to help you, if at all possible, find the light in the shadows."

Hannah put both hands out, facing upward, "So tell your favorite detective the facts…the whole facts, ma'am."

Tricia whispered, "What a helpful image….shadows as evidence."

Tricia took a deep breath, "Okay, here goes. Some of this Ms. Columbo, you already know, but from the beginning…"

Tricia had not forgotten anything. She wished she had. At least, she thought, how about partial amnesia? But not. Perfect memory.

Tricia started with the condom package. Because she figured none of the bad things was unrelated. Coincidence wasn't in her vocabulary. She mentioned the notes, the slashed tires, the visits she had had with Courtney, with Melita, with Jordon, even with Rider. She also mentioned the visit to the emergency room with Bradley and Sarah, the possible miscarriage, and the two delightful visits with her neighbors, Andrew and Abby and their two Kings and one Queen. She described the three gifts, the fishing pole and reel, the police badge and the fishing yarn.

Her eyes were now dry. For whatever reason speaking, putting words to all that had happened, that helped. She didn't have answers, but she did have facts. Maybe a start…and with that, maybe not a finish to her ministry. Because she didn't think in modest terms. To visit with Hannah lessened the worry. Even if for a small worry.

Tricia raised her eyebrows, "Now, the capper to my tale of woe. Sage said one sentence, that could be a double-entendre, 'Melita has resigned.' You saw my reaction…I went into shock. But, you bailed me out. Thanks for that. In summary, as I've heard others say, 'that's my story and I'm sticking to it.' Wish I could unstick to it."

As Tricia's shoulders sagged, Hannah spoke. "Okay, I think I have the events. And I am with you, I don't believe in coincidences either. But, do not rush to judgment about Melita. You don't know why she resigned. You are jumping to conclusions. That it has something

The Lemon Drop Didn't Melt

to do with her telling you last Sunday before worship about her medical situation. You don't know if she received a sticky-note. So, that would be a start. Maybe it isn't about her new pastor. Not for a breath. Maybe it has nothing to do with you. Maybe she feels with the impending lumpectomy she won't be in good health...or spirits, to get her job done as the church secretary. None of that is known, the cause for her resigning. So, the first step would be to learn the reason she resigned.

"Secondly, maybe she can be encouraged to change her mind. You speak well of your moderator. Maybe Sage can help. Actually, since Sage is aware of the sticky-notes and should the case be Melita has had the same given her, and especially since Melita knows about the note left in the pulpit that said you are next, maybe she can be part of the solution team."

That never occurred to Tricia, her eyes widened, "Ah, Ms. Columbo, that's good. Really good. I need to learn more and maybe, even though Melita has been described as the church's verbal newsletter, maybe she can see this does have something to do with you...but not an indictment to your untrustworthiness. Well yes, that can be the case."

Before she continued Hannah took Tricia's hand. "But let me say this, madam pastor, I trust you. I consider you my truth friend. And, after all, you cannot...you simply cannot let the bastards get you. And for sure, I'm not putting all those coho fillets in my church freezer, just to leave them there. You are my truth friend, and I hope you consider me no differently. Besides, not a note of this goes in our church newsletter."

Tricia smiled, "That's so helpful. And I don't consider for a moment there's more than one bastard, so it's not bastards."

"Oh, something I forgot. Jordon asked me the locations that prompted the sticky-notes. Creighton did the same thing. Not sure what that's about."

Hannah, raised a finger, "So? Maybe this has something to do with real estate."

"I don't understand. Real Estate?"

"Yep. What's the most important about a family when they buy a house? Sure, cost and resources to pay the mortgage are part of the decision. But, the most important part is location. In fact, when I purchased my home on Mercer Island, and contrary to rumor, not every house starts at a million dollars, location impacted. Who knows, maybe location impacts your situation…and maybe, just maybe, the nets won't remain empty and the mud flow will stop… plus, both practically and theologically, Good Friday never wins. Hence? Don't give in or give up, Madam Pastor. Don't give any more victories to Good Friday.

"Oh, I know," Hannah ended her statement, "I just slipped off my detective hat to do some preaching. Think maybe in all this you should do the reverse. Might ponder that."

She pointed to the cell phone, "if you feel okay about it," as she looked at her phone, "Give Sage a call back and tell her you can meet her at the church in two hours. We can do that."

Tricia dialed. Sage answered before the second ring. With a voice stronger than she felt, she said, "Hi, Sage. Sorry I was so shocked by the news about Melita that I couldn't speak. I can speak now. Hannah says I can be at our church in two hours. Okay to meet you then?"

Sage said, "Glad you called back. See you then. I'm calling Melita now…maybe we can make it a threesome. I'll do my best. Drive safely."

Nothing more was said, nor did it need to be. Tricia went deep inside and for reasons she didn't know she did feel a little better. She could see some light in the shadows…maybe that would be a sign that evidence, helpful evidence, was happening to and for her.

Tricia hung up her cell phone and then realized, "She'll meet us at the church and said she'd see if Melita could see us. But, Hannah, know how much you've helped. In case they ever bring Columbo back… and I'm surprised you even know who he is, but you do so that's a good thing…you should try out for being Columbo's partner. Yep, I'm perceptive—we'll get to the humility later.

"However," as Tricia pointed to the rest area bathroom, "First things first. I gotta pee."

Chapter 32

Tricia was sure, although it was somewhere in the middle of obvious, that the turn at I-90 and Exit 25 wasn't anywhere in the Bible. Yet, as she drove up the hill toward old Snoqualmie, not noticing all the shops and the school on the left, she did see the valley. Every time, every single time, even when the light was not bright, she saw the Snoqualmie River flowing west, she saw the mountains and could tell the larger mountain immediately. Especially Mount Si, the tallest mountain. Well, it wasn't the mountains she saw each morning in Breckenridge, Colorado. But now, Mount Si was more than high enough…and she saw it as a sentinel, maybe more, a guardian. That was better than mud to get sucked up by. And all the trees. The Douglas firs especially, tall, even regal.

She could think of Psalm 23 and the valley and the *even though I walk through the shadow…*

Yes, she knew it was of death. But she didn't think about that…about death. She thought about the shadow and Hannah's affirmation about shadows and evidence. There was something else Hannah said. It had the flash of importance but stayed elusive. Somewhere, hiding from Tricia, it was important. She came up blank...hoped she wouldn't be blanked forever.

She reached the time to turn. She needed to turn right and drive into Old Snoqualmie and her church. She could turn left, stop at Salich Lodge, walk out on the platform and look at Snoqualmie Falls, how powerful and picturesque. Or she could keep driving west along the Snoqualmie River and find the big drift the Issaquah guide shop had told her about. How a bobber and some jigs could get a winter steelhead. Ah, how temptation tempted her, almost pulled her arms, to turn left.

But she couldn't. She had called Sage to say she'd be there in ten minutes. She had to do this. Having no idea what she would face. Sage hadn't said she'd be alone. Also she didn't say Melita would be with her. In fact, other than a word of appreciation to Tricia for the time of arrival, nothing was said. Everything was to be known. *Even though....*

As Tricia drove up to the church parking lot she could see Sage standing against the front of her car, a blue Honda CRV. But there were no other cars. Looked to Tricia that Sage was alone. Not sure that was good...or bad.

As Tricia turned off her car, she thought of the next part of the shadow of the valley of death...she knew that...would she take it to heart and attitude. The affirmation from the psalmist after the valley of death, *for I will fear no evil...*

Ah, could it be?

"Hi, Tricia," said Sage as she turned and looked into her car. "I should have told you; we'll not be alone. I think it's important…"

Before she could finish her sentence the front passenger door opened and out got Melita. The way she looked at Tricia…the thought didn't miss Tricia, *looks like she's planning my funeral.* The looks that would kill…this was classic to Tricia. In fact, the last time she remembered that stony glare was from her ex-husband, only Tricia wasn't the one who died.

Tricia pushed that thought away and said, waving modestly, "Hello, Melita. Thank you for coming to meet me."

Melita spoke, seemed to Tricia she had lowered her voice…from soprano below alto, "Well, I'm not grateful to be here."

Melita pointed to Sage, "She said I should be here. Arguing was not to happen. So, I'm here. And it's likely for worse; forget the better part of any relationship."

Tricia could hear the tone…somewhere between angry and furious. She wasn't surprised, although she didn't know what to say next.

Sage took over, "We need to visit, in the very least. Tricia, why don't we go into your office?"

The temperature was unseasonably warm, about 65. She saw that both Sage and Melita were wearing jackets. Melita had a colorful scarf around her neck. She was pulling on it, but the impression was Tricia thought she probably wanted to take her scarf, walk over and choke Tricia with it.

Certainly going to her office made the most sense, although that might give a too crowded reality, so Tricia answered, "Yes, Sage, we can go to the church office, but it's so nice, why don't we go to our picnic table and visit there?"

It was a surprise that Melita agreed, but not without a slander toward Tricia, "I can do that. Because out here I can leave when I want. All I have to do is call Jacob and he'll get me. He wanted to come to be here with me, but I told him I didn't want that. I could take care of myself. I feel if we are in your office, Reverend Gleason, it will get too stuffy. Besides you might hide behind your desk."

Tricia saw more than handwriting on the wall and thought that maybe she'd end up with the shortest tenure of any ministry…three weeks… and forced to stop counting. It took no guessing the title of *Reverend Gleason*…Melita's way of distancing. Her way to destroy Tricia.

Even though Tricia didn't know a thing about what prompted the resignation…and maybe Hannah was right, the resignation had something to do with the upcoming lumpectomy…although Melita's attitude and tone indicated nothing about her upcoming surgery. It had everything to do with Tricia and that somehow how Tricia has caused the resignation.

They sat down at the picnic table. Tricia sat across from Sage and Melita.

Sage spoke the first word, "Tricia, I have told you that Melita resigned her position as our secretary. What I didn't tell you she also resigned her church membership. She said Jacob wants to have them find a new church, one where…"

Melita wouldn't let Sage finish, "...one where the minister doesn't betray her secretary."

She stood up, pointed, then wiped her mouth, pointed again, and spoke with almost a yell, "Somewhere the pastor won't go around and tell the world what she promised not to tell. You, Reverend Gleason, are an embarrassment, a damn embarrassment—and I won't be excused from my Latin—to our church and to your profession. Speaking of profession, what you need...more than anything... anything in the world...is confession. You need to tell me...and Sage...why you betrayed me. THAT is the reason I have resigned... both as secretary and as church member...and to think, this church has been my home...since I was a teenager. Jacob and I were even married in this church, our twin sons—you haven't met them yet and you NEVER will...were baptized and confirmed in this church. This church has been everything..."

She stopped, sat back down, began to cry. She shook her head, jumped up and started to walk away. All Tricia could think was how wrong this was. She now knew what was happening. A thousand questions came to her...but Hannah's words were clear, be a *non-anxious presence. Don't do anything. If she wants to leave, she must have the freedom to do so. And if Sage agrees with her, then I'll have to have a party of one...only I'll not be having a self-pity party. That's not to be.*

Sage got up, but she left her purse on the table and Tricia knew her car keys were in her purse. Sage stopped Melita about half-way to the car. They talked. Tricia couldn't hear, nor was she at all sure she should be listening. Sage reached out to hug Melita.

Tricia wondered, *Is this a farewell hug? Will Melita pull out her cell phone and call her husband, Jacob. Is this all there is? Indictment... but no proof, no other side of the story, no jury, no judge. Maybe that's what will happen, indictment and conviction. With a gavel pounding the picnic table and a judge asking for the next case to be brought to him.*

Melita and Sage hugged some more. But Melita didn't reach into her purse. Rather, Sage took her arm and brought Melita back to the picnic table.

Tricia tried not to look surprised or disappointed or jubilant. In fact, Tricia looked at her hands and thought in a flash about playing the chum salmon...how powerful it was. If only. If only in the next few minutes Tricia could show the same power, the same openness to... yes, she thought, to learn more.

Sage and Melita sat down. Melita looked at Tricia, "I'm not going to apologize to you."

At least she didn't say *Reverend Gleason*.

Tricia gave an understanding nod.

Melita looked at Sage, "You need to tell her what has happened to me. I cannot without spitting at her; I'm that mad."

Tricia could see the anger hadn't lessened. But whatever Sage told Melita, it had worked. They were back at the table.

Sage reached into her purse and pulled out a sticky-note and handed it to Tricia. Tricia read it, looked at Melita, "You aren't the first...it's the same calligraphy. What a horrible note, Melita, horrible. But I'm sure you can notice it's the same hand writing of the note you found on our pulpit, the one about saying I am next. It's the same calligraphy.

"But I can see, Melita," Tricia said, holding up the note, "If I had come to you about a surgery I was to have and have told you that I had only told you and I needed to trust you to confidentiality, and a couple days later I had received this note…let me read it…*your pastor has told church members you have cancer and will have a mastectomy*. Well, I would never forgive you…probably never. THAT would have violated our trust and our respect. It would all be out the window. Gone. Poof. No more. I would be furious."

Tricia paused, "Melita, I do understand…fully. All I can say is I have told no one about our conversation. I honored it. I am not lying. But I can understand your anger. Using an inelegant word, you are pissed at me. And, short of the truth, you have every right to be. Please don't indict and execute. That's all I can ask you."

Tricia thought of something else, which might get her back in the church secretary retention hope. "All I can share with you…is that I'd like to take this note—it's the same as others that have come to my attention. I can tell you the note on the pulpit is not the only one. And you aren't the only person who was outraged at me. I cannot share anything else…other than to say this is a serious matter, even more than that, it could destroy my career as a minister.

"To say that I cannot be trusted, to say that I violate confidences, to say that no one should ever confide in me? Yes, people can say that; I cannot keep people from rushing to judgment. And I certainly don't blame you for taking this into your own hands. It is understandable. But. And it's a huge but. I'm asking you to believe there are some very important people who have been impacted for the worse by Mr. Calligrapher. About this horrible person, we don't know, actually, if it's a man or woman. But…I trust those helping with this—and they are all official folk, are helping me to learn what in God's name is going on. No, I didn't say that right…they are helping me to learn what in evil's name is going on."

Melita looked at Sage, "Sage, what do you think?"

Sage didn't respond immediately, folded her hands, then said, "Melita? I cannot tell you what to do. You were willing to come here with me. And when you wanted to leave, you trusted me to come back to let Tricia explain some of the background. Not the rest of the situation, but at least you aren't the only one hit with this note-writing-business. And from what I can figure out it is ALL about getting Tricia. You were simply in the path of attack. Sorry, but that's how I see it. Thanks, Melita, for listening to Tricia. You ask me what should you do? I cannot tell you. I won't tell you. Because you are no one else's opinion…and don't be offended, certainly not mine. You have to decide what to do."

"I don't know what to do. My trust for you, Tricia, has lessened. I don't think it's disappeared, but it has lessened."

Tricia thought of something else, "Melita, before you decide, may I ask you another question?"

Melita nodded, kept looking down. But Tricia saw the scowl had left; Melita's hands were calm on the picnic table…and her cheeks were dry.

"Thanks. Who gave you this note?"

Melita answered, "It was on my back door. We never go into the front door. We park the car in the garage. Jacob and I came home and the note was sticking on our screen door. Jacob found it, read it. As I told you, Tricia, I hadn't given Jacob all the details. He has the greatest worry ability of anyone I know. So, first of all I had to update him about the initial diagnosis and the lumpectomy. Actually he thanked me for telling him. I was relieved about that. But he then told me this note upset him beyond upset—those were his words—and told me I had to resign my secretary position and we needed to get away from you—to go to another church. That made sense to me…at least when I was standing on the back porch. Never thought the back porch would serve that purpose."

Tricia began to get a fuller picture…she was relieved Melita dropped the Reverend Gleason moniker, "I have just one more question…do you know if any of your neighbors were told by the calligrapher that I had talked to them? Because I don't even know where you live. And I'm totally unaware if any of your neighbors are our church members."

Melita answered a calm voice…a good sign, "No, no one has talked to me. This just happened yesterday, but no neighbors have said anything."

"So, it may be, Melita, the note is made up…and is trying to drive a wedge between you and me…and even worse between you and our church. I understand you can and might continue to be mad at me… that would be heart-breaking to me personally…but honestly it would be far worse for this to separate you from your church membership with St. Andrew's. Look at it this way—you can put up with me for

The Lemon Drop Didn't Melt

a year…well, not even that long, for my licensed ministry contract ends next June. So, you can know that I will be gone."

Sage looked at her watch…only the spotlight over the picnic table kept the darkness away. "Ladies, our fifty minutes is up."

She smiled, "At least that's what a counselor would say. But, I'm no counselor, however. Yes, Melita, you asked me what I would recommend. I deferred. But now, I thought of something…so put it into the consideration bin. I can appreciate your wanting information about your lumpectomy not to be shared. However, there are SO MANY…in emotional terms a cast of thousands…of people in our church who love you more than you know…but I'm sure you know you'd win every vote about a favorite person. They will find out sooner or later about your lumpectomy…but I'd bet you they'll be better with you and for you—and all their prayers and casseroles—they'd prefer knowing it sooner. That way you can have a cast of thousands with you. Besides, I don't see Jacob cooking any time soon…and you may need to be in the hospital for a week or so, depending upon what the lumpectomy results are.

"So…oh my word, this is like submitting an argument to the court… but, no, not an argument, only a suggestion. You said the lumpectomy will be next Thursday…think I'm right on that."

Melita said, "Yes, at 9 in the morning at Swedish Hospital in Issaquah."

Sage said, "That's great. I'll be there with you; give Jacob a heads-up so he doesn't open up his lawyer joke book. But, here's the suggestion, Instead of resigning your secretarial position and your church membership, why don't you take a medical leave? We can offer that—we can get a temporary secretary—not a permanent secretary, only a temp. That way you can focus upon you…and the surgery…and the treatment.

"You may end up resigning. But I have confidence in Tricia, and honestly, Melita, I do trust her in this. Plus, remember she used to be a detective…so maybe she can put that hat on…but, of course, not until she's got her sermons ready. So this has every chance of being solved…give it some time. Then, later, when all this unfolds, you can decide about your secretary position. How's that sound?"

"Well," responded Melita, pointing to the table, "That isn't pulling my resignation off the table…but you make a good suggestion…I shouldn't keep the medical stuff a secret…maybe even, Sage, you could share the information this Sunday during the call to prayer?"

Sage looked at Tricia, "Well, how about our pastor doing that? Let her share in your support."

Melita squinted, rubbed her chin, "Guess that's okay…yes, that's okay. But, please keep it short."

Tricia nodded as they got up and walked to their cars. Tricia wanted to shout to the mountains, at least to Mount Si. And shouting would be inappropriate, but to herself she whispered, "Even though…but fear no evil."

In that moment fear wasn't around.

As Melita got in the car, Tricia said, "Melita, I do know where Swedish Issaquah Hospital is. I was there with some friends this past week. See you before your lumpectomy if that's okay. Because my mentor has written an eleventh commandment...always be with your church members or friends of church members before their surgery. And, honestly, Melita, I won't violate that commandment. Okay with you? I hope you nod yes."

Melita didn't laugh, but she said, "Thanks for that. I wouldn't want you to break any commandment."

Sage and Melita drove off. Tricia wanted to call Creighton and then Hannah. But decided against it. A prayer to God would be more than helpful...and all that was necessary. Plus a *thank you, Jesus* was in order.

She drove home...to think what a day. And in that moment she didn't think about mud slides or amputated veterans or a chum snapping her leader. She only thought that perhaps once she spoke with Jordon and handed him the note stuck on Melita's back door screen, good results would happen.

She didn't know how unlikely that would be.

Because she didn't know he was looking at her...across the street, parked in a dark lot. He could see them. Shook his head, "Shit. Double-shit. Why didn't the Pastor Bitch take them into her office? Damn. Sitting outside. Guess ramp-up time...still, shit for their staying out of her office."

He drove off, already knowing what was next.

Tick. Tick. Tick.

Chapter 33

Tricia had always liked the story. It wasn't her story, but it was from the senior minister of the church she had been a student minister with in Palo Alto. He had been a minister in Colorado Springs. He was also a volunteer chaplain with the Colorado Springs Police Department. There were 30 volunteer chaplains; they each took a night to ride with an officer. Their help came mainly at the most difficult cases, the homicides and suicides, the death notifications. Tricia smiled when he said his first death notification was at the wrong house. But even funnier, as Tricia remembered his telling her, was his first night riding with an officer.

He got in the squad car, introduced himself to the policewoman, Sue. Before they headed out for the evening—her buddy rode what he called the "O-dark-thirty" shift from eleven at night to about four in the morning—the dispatcher said to Sue, "Robbery in progress…."

Off they went, lights flashing, sirens blaring. Tricia's friend wondered what this was about? They never told him he would be sent to a robbery in progress. They pulled in to the back alley of a strip mall.

The Lemon Drop Didn't Melt

The alleged robbery was taking place in a drycleaners shop at the end of the alley. The back door was open. Sue got out, pulled her revolver. Tricia's friend sat there, as he said, "doing my best mannequin impersonation." Sue looked in and told him to get out; they were in this together."

Tricia loved the next part, and she told it well. "My friend said to Sue, 'That's no fair, you have on a bullet-proof vest.'" Sue didn't hesitate, "But, Reverend! Don't you have on a bullet-proof faith?"

Tricia loved that story; she had told it in a sermon in Colorado and the people were fascinated, very alert. It brought some good vibes to her yesterday in her sermon when she pushed on about having a bullet-proof faith. The people were double-riveted to her. Every eye was focused. Big-time. No one looked the other way.

After the service, Courtney didn't shake Tricia's hand, she grabbed it, tears in her eyes, "Tricia? That sermon? I think you were preaching to me…you hit the nail on the head. I need to know that faith is not for protection; faith is for endurance. Oh my goodness, did that ever speak to me. You also said that to be good won't keep the harm from happening. But to be good will bring us closer to God. And I imagine you know no one who needs to be closer to God than I."

Courtney sighed, looked over her shoulder and saw people were waiting to speak to Tricia, "Oops, I've taken too much time. I wish Rider were here…I'm gonna tell him about your sermon and what it means to me. Maybe he'll listen. He needed this sermon more than anyone I know. Thank you."

Yes, Tricia thought, her day was great…such a good thing. She needed the sermon more than Courtney, or the others. Wasn't a bad thing to preach to herself. She had chosen not to go outside again for the sermon, even though the day was a carbon of the previous Sunday. They stayed inside because they were serving communion and that was easier to do in their sanctuary.

She was grateful her comment about Melita's surgery went well. It was scheduled for next Thursday, so Tricia called Hannah to tell her fishing wouldn't work. Hannah understood, said she'd call Jon. Tricia also filled Hannah in on the visit with Sage and Melita.

Hannah said that often when church members are angry at God they don't want to say anything to God. They figure their pastor's the best conduit to God, so they should yell at their pastor. Hannah indicated something about classic transference.

Tricia told about the onslaught by Rider. She indicated that Courtney was in church, but not Rider. "That's assuring, Tricia. Thanks for sharing…it's good to have Sage in your corner. See? Not all lawyers are rotten to the core! It is rare to meet a lawyer who isn't always right, who never makes a mistake. Sounds like Sage breaks that mold."

Now it was Monday morning. Sage had contacted a temp agency to have a secretary. Since the newsletter had gone out with the individual or couple meetings with Tricia and she had posted the sign-up lists on the church bulletin board, the temp was there to mainly answer the phone.

Tricia would create the bulletin for next Sunday, but not today. She needed to look over the lectionary scripture lessons. She really didn't have a sermon in mind. She smiled about that because Creighton said one of the purposes of the lectionary was to keep the preacher from repeating, with some variances, one of the three sermons the preacher favored. He was so right about that, Tricia mused. Her basic supply of sermons did number three…and they each had been offered to her new congregation. Thought it was time for something new.

She reached for her calendar which listed the scriptures for each Sunday. The first was from Exodus chapter three, something about Moses being called by God and being asked to take off his shoes, because he was standing on holy ground. That got her attention.

But what got more of her attention was the knock on her office door. It was Jordon. He looked great. She saw immediately the slacks were creased sharply, his detective jacket didn't slouch..a great fit. She thought again how impressive were his looks.

They had only talked on the phone on Saturday. Jordon apologized but he had been sent to Seattle for a two-day seminar and couldn't see her. She updated him on the phone, indicating she had another note to give him. She told him about the meeting with Melita and Sage. He said he'd be able to come to her office Monday morning, if that would work.

And there he stood, good to his word. Tricia loved that; she would explain in detail what Melita had said and how Sage had helped. She looked at him again…but then saw something was wrong. It was in his face. He looked at her then looked away. Didn't ask anything but sat down in front of her desk. She offered to get up, but he put up his hand, almost like….well, it was something not good, he was almost wooden.

He asked, rather directly, "Thanks for this chance to go over everything. I want to make sure the details are clear."

He reached in his pocket, retrieved a small notepad and read what he had written. Up to her meeting with Melita and Sage. Closed the notepad, returned it to his pocket.

"All this is certainly not coincidental."

He reached his hand, "Could you show me the note to Melita?"

Almost like asking for her credit card to pay for the meal.

Tricia handed him the note, he looked at it and said to Tricia, "It does look like the same calligraphy. When did Melita share the information about her upcoming surgery?"

Tricia explained that it was a week before yesterday, in her office before worship.

Jordon then asked, "Was the entire conversation in your office…not outside?"

Something is really wrong, but I better not say anything.

She nodded, "Yes, all in my office. Although Thursday when we met, we stayed at the picnic table outside. Never went in to my office."

She pointed to the note, "The note is from the same person; he's out to get me. And honestly, Jordon, I have thought and thought about it. My new clergy friend, Hannah Ball, I trust her totally, asked questions on who would do me in…the same questions you'd asked…as had Creighton. But I cannot think of anyone whom I've offended who would want to stick so many needles in me.

The Lemon Drop Didn't Melt

"I know…that stick-pin image isn't the best, but it feels like I'm being set up and with each step it gets worse. Where will it go? Nothing happened yesterday and people were very polite after the service. Courtney was even there. She told me she couldn't have been more pleased with the sermon. Rider wasn't there…and honestly, I was relieved he wasn't there. Big-time relief. But, there wasn't another note from someone. That's a good thing."

"Well, Tricia, I wish you were right. But unfortunately there is another note."

He reached into his pocket, pulled out a note, unfolded it. It wasn't a sticky note, rather in a full sheet of paper. He handed it to her.

She read it and almost fainted. The blood rushed from her face. She looked at Jordon. His face was stone, his eyes piercing.

"Jordon! This is horrible! No, it's not horrible. It's malicious. It's wrong. It's evil. You know this isn't true! Where was this note?"

Jordon answered, almost like a monotone recording, "It was in an envelope, delivered to our main office desk. It was intended for my captain. He called me in this morning and showed it to me. It came Saturday morning. As you can see, it's in reference to when we first met in your home…actually in your home office."

"How wrong this is!" Tricia almost shouted. Anything but a whisper. "What did your captain say?"

"Well, he was disturbed. Actually he was miffed. He knows me and knows all about me. So, he knew I did nothing to trigger what the note accuses you of. But, still. We can never be too careful when investigating an incident. Often we go alone into a home. As I did when first meeting with you. So, my captain knew I was innocent. But, he wondered about you, Tricia. He wondered what kind of person you really are. He even said something about how clergy today...."

He didn't finish.

"Jordon? I'm devastated. Does anyone else know about this...other than you and your captain?"

He shook his head, "No, my captain and I have a great relationship. So. For the time being when I told him I had this appointment this morning with you, he said to share the note with you and see if you could shed light on it. I have to ask. Did you know this was being sent to my captain?"

"No!" Tricia almost shouted, her head shaking. "I knew nothing about this! This is horrible. I'm sure you told your captain about all the sticky-notes written in calligraphy. Did you explain all these other things that are happening to me? It has to be from the same person."

"Yes, I did. My captain is never leaning toward any person's innocence. That's his nature, so the only surprise is when he's wrong, when the facts unfold and let him know he's looking in the wrong direction. But, he did ask if I knew whether or not, Tricia, you know how to write in calligraphy?"

"Oh my God, Jordon. How could he ask that? That's an indictment."

She reached to the corner of her desk, grabbed a Bible, jumped to her feet, holding the Bible with one hand and placing the other on her heart, "Jordon Valentine, I promise before you and my God, I do not know calligraphy, I had nothing to do with this note and what it says, as you know and hopefully your captain believes, what the note accuses me of…never happened. I swear to God."

She sat back down, returned the Bible to her desk and then thought, "Your captain has the original note and the envelope, right? Hopefully there's some DNA on it…and to erase my culpability I'll go to your headquarters, give some blood, so they can register my DNA. Well, they could simply contact my captain in Salem because they have my DNA when I was a homicide detective. I'll even take the lie detector.

"Gotta ask…has there been any DNA evidence…or finger prints? Have you checked this note out…and the envelope?"

He shook his head, "Not yet. They'll be doing that today. And no. You don't have to provide blood…our captain's already contacted Salem."

Tricia started to shake, *oh no, his captain does think I'm involved in this…not as a victim.*

She read the note again…and wondered when this will ever stop. Headed for a disaster…a new mud slide, Good Friday all over again.

Jordon got up, his eyes not so piercing, "I'm sure you realize, Tricia, we need to focus on this. My captain believes me…and most of me believes you. I simply have to qualify that so I remain objective. You and I know what happened when we met in your home. The note is totally wrong; you didn't take your panties off for me."

Tricia didn't know how to respond, other than to whisper, tried to calm down, looked him in the eye, "Yes, it is wrong. You were professional. I would never do that. Never. We have to find this person, Jordon. Please keep me current. And if you have any more questions, call me…please? Plus I will let you know if anything more happens here or in my home."

He turned and left, walked away without saying good-bye.

Tricia got up…wanted to walk with him outside. That didn't happen. He closed the office door behind him. No good-bye.

She sat back down, the note screaming at her, "Captain, you need to know your detective Valentine and Pastor Gleason, when they met in her home…she tried to seduce him by taking off her panties…"

Sick. Perverted. Evil. No limits to inflicting damage. Tricia had many more words and phrases. Nothing that could be included in a sermon. She couldn't think a moment about looking at the Exodus passage selected for next Sunday. She felt that she was anything but standing, or sitting, on holy ground. She had no value; to take her shoes off would be presumptuous. And as she felt about herself right now, an insult to God. God wouldn't want her and would tell her to keep her shoes on. Or maybe. Something worse.

The note came to her again. She closed her lips, put her head in her hands. And wept. Silently. But not without the screech of pain and being wounded.

No holy ground under her feet. Maybe never.

Chapter 34

Tricia read and re-read the Exodus passage...they were only words at first...about the fact that, she figured, Moses thought he'd be tending sheep all his life. About hearing God speak to him, to get his attention. About how Moses pled incompetence [Tricia had remembered in seminary during her Old Testament class that Jeremiah had also protested. His out was he was a teenager. That made sense.] Asked to take off his shoes. And when Moses asked God, if he would get to Egypt to free the enslaved Israelites, he asked God who was sending him. God answered, nothing but a being-verb-sentence, "I AM WHO I AM sends you."

She read that and remembered her seminary professor delighted in that name for God. As explained in class there is no being verb in Hebrew, so what God was saying had to do with sending forth. Because God would always be with them. The translation was, "I will be who I need to be." Or something like that.

She more than pondered about the call to Moses passage, kept coming back to holy ground, which Tricia thought, at least for her, didn't exist.

She might not have thought that when in seminary, but the reality of angry church members and false accusations tore her apart. She had no thought, let alone action, to take off her shoes. None whatsoever.

Her muddling through the reference sources on the Exodus passage didn't really help. Muddling continued.

Until her temp secretary interrupted, "I'm sorry, Reverend Gleason, but I forgot to ask about how to transfer a call. A lady's on the phone, said you'd know who she is, gave her name as Sage Worth and said it was important."

Dread didn't ooze into Tricia's feelings, it was flooding. *What? Important?*

Tricia picked up the phone, "Hi, Sage. Our temp secretary said you wanted to talk with me."

Silence.

Never a good sign.

Tricia thought maybe she lost connection, "Hello? Sage, is that you? Are you there?"

Sage responded, "Yes, sorry, I didn't hear you at first. Got a minute?"

Tricia wanted to answer yes, I have a lifetime, but thought that was unhelpful, "Yes, I have a minute. What's up."

More silence. Never a good thing Tricia reasoned. Sage then said, "I want to share with you, just minutes ago I got a call from Micah

Dimmock, our executive minister. He wanted me to give you a heads up. He will be calling you later about this."

The *this* sounded onerous, as Sage confirmed, much to Tricia's dismay.

"Tricia? Micah called to say he had a visit in his office this morning, just as Micah arrived, from Rider Samson. Somehow Rider tracked down our Washington conference office. Rider filed a complaint against you and asked for the Committee On Ministry to have a misconduct review. Micah didn't go into detail but in summary it is not good. I hate to talk with you over the phone, but I'm due in court in five minutes, so wanted to give you a heads-up before Micah called you with what Rider contends."

"What? A complaint from Rider? Okay, I know he was outraged when he came to my house to accuse me of betraying his wife, Courtney. I tried my best to listen, to not enflame his fire any more. Sounds like I was a miserable failure. Actually, Sage, it sounds like I'm a horrible failure in many areas. Can you tell me what his complaint centers on? Bet it's something about betrayal. And you know about the other notes I've received and mounting anger toward me. Didn't you tell him about those last week?"

Sage said, "Yes, I did, Tricia. And Micah has appreciated being brought into the loop. Neither Micah nor I expected anything to come to either him or you or me. But. Rider's rage during his office visit this morning with Micah, plus a signed letter to be distributed to the Committee On Ministry, cannot be ignored or denied.

"As I said he and I are wrong. Look. But let's talk details later. My court appearance won't take more than 30 minutes. So, let me finish that and drive to your office. I can clear my calendar the rest of today. To visit personally is important."

"Oh," said Tricia. "Will we need the whole day?"

Sage didn't answer.

Tricia didn't push for her question to be answered, but she felt she should mention what happened to her already this morning, "Something else, though. The detective, Jordon Valentine, stopped in this morning with something—actually a note—that was given his captain in complaint of me. It was shocking. I don't want to detail over the phone, but will tell you when you get here. I'll stay put... and look to see you."

Tricia didn't want to say she'd look forward to seeing Sage. Who looks forward to someone pointing to the scaffold? That likelihood was in her mind. But what if it was correct? She thought again. Maybe Tricia was overreacting. Maybe it was much to do with nothing.

Still, the mention of a fitness review sent shudders through Tricia. Because she knew one of the purposes of the Committee On Ministry—it was actually an ethics committee—was to investigate charges against a minister. If the committee found the charges were true, they could take away the ordained clergy standing. In Tricia's case she wasn't ordained...that would come when she graduated from seminary, and that would be two more years of classes at Ocean Divinity School. Her status currently, and the Committee On Ministry had authorized it, was a one-year licensed ministry standing which meant she could officiate as a minister.

But, if all this crashed down on Tricia and the committee found the claims authentic, they could make sure Tricia never would be ordained. And they could vote their licensure for Tricia to be removed. Talk about Good Friday stalking.

Sage said, "Sorry, Tricia, for all this. But I do need to go…don't want to make the judge angry. I'll call when I'm on my way to your office."

"Thanks for the call, although it's very disturbing not to know the grounds for complaint. Another note about betrayal, I imagine. That note list is getting too high. We've got to get to the culprit. Betrayal? That's tough to handle."

Sage said, "It's not about betrayal, Tricia."

"It's not about betrayal…what else could there be? Please tell me. That will give me a chance to think back over the confrontation with Rider. Not betrayal? That was his complaint…that I had betrayed his wife."

Sage spoke quietly, "No, I'm sorry, Tricia. Not about betrayal. It's about seduction. Sorry I said that, should have kept it until I get to your office. Relax, I'm sure it's fallacious; I'm sure it is a strategy for Rider to rip your licensure papers out of your hands. Let me go over it with you when I get there."

Click.

Tricia never heard a word…the entire conversation with Sage was a blur…a nasty and toxic blur. The only word which wouldn't leave was the s word, *seduction?* Rider claimed that. *He's a sick fool. Ah, to paraphrase, hell hath no fury than a betrayed man.*

She wished she could smile. Let alone laugh. But the flood of complaints, the rush of woes…she had to leave the office.

Tricia looked at her temp secretary and tried to be natural and not frozen in fear, "Marie? I've got to run out for a while. Be back…if Sage calls—and by the way, she's our moderator, the head of our Church Council, the church's governing board. She will visit me in an hour or so. I'll be back before that, but if she calls before I return, please tell her I'm on my way back to the office. Then call me on my cell phone. Here's the number," handing over her new business card.

As she left the office she looked at the stack of business cards she had in her purse. For reasons she hadn't planned, she tossed them into the waste basket by the church entrance door. She thought perhaps such a toss would prelude another toss…the get-rid-of-you toss.

She didn't know where she would drive. It couldn't be far. So, it was back to Snoqualmie Falls. She got out, looked at the falls from the platform, looked down to see the water crashing on the rocks below. She looked downstream and saw how the water smoothed out. She didn't think about winter steelhead. She thought about herself and it caused her to tremble, "I need to find the smooth water. I don't see how to get there without crashing over the falls. I just don't."

She stopped uttering the self-demise option. Sat down on the bench, could still see the water pouring down on the rocks below. Then the look downstream, the river was not roiled.

Then. She looked down at her feet. And wondered. Where was holy ground? No way it was here. No way. When she looked up she wished for the clouds above to spell hope. But no. It was like a horrible message and she was sure she saw the word. *Seduction*.

She closed her eyes. "God? I need help. Please don't leave me. Please show me where the smooth water is."

Her cell phone rang, was the office phone.

She answered, "Hi, Marie. I'll be right there."

Marie responded, "Take your time. Your moderator just called. She said she had another meeting, would be here in two hours. Hoped you would be here. I told her that unless you called her back that would be fine."

"Ah, thanks, Marie," said Tricia. "I'm coming back in about fifteen minutes. See you then."

Tricia stayed seated and went over all the notes. She thought of the visit with Jordon and worried that maybe he had given up on her. But she did hope. She hoped that Jordon knew and told his captain she didn't know the first thing about calligraphy.

The key was to learn who did. She trusted, somehow, that her hope in figuring all this out wouldn't crash into pieces on the rocks below the falls, thus never making it to better water downstream.

Chapter 35

Tricia got out of her car in the church parking lot, in front of the "Clergy" sign. She then looked at the picnic table…that had brought her good luck. She'd actually prefer to visit with Sage there, but the clouds were changing from grey to black, which meant that rain would arrive. She hoped that was all the clouds turning black meant…rain and not anything worse.

As she walked to the church's entry door she heard a car drive up, turned and saw it was Sage. Great timing. Sage waved, turned her car off, got out and said, "Thanks for being here…your secretary, is her name Marie, said you were out. Doing some shopping? Maybe even at the North Bend Safeway?"

Sage put her hand to her mouth, "Oops, sorry to bring that up. Not thoughtful of me. Forget I asked it."

Tricia answered the easy part, "Yes, her name's Marie. She asked if she could start on the bulletin, but she needs to go to an afternoon job…she said it was okay for her to be late to that….but maybe tomorrow I can give her the information for next Sunday's scripture and sermon title."

As they walked to the entry door, Sage asked, "Got a sermon in mind?"

Tricia read that as a good sign…much better than being told someone else would preach next Sunday. Tricia wanted to slap her own mouth; she simply didn't know how to keep the negative forces that swirled her—couldn't keep them from popping up, the thoughts that pushed Tricia to the exit sign, at least mentally. "Yes, I am thinking of saying something about taking off our shoes because we're standing on holy ground. That story when God called Moses. It's the scripture lesson from Exodus, listed in the lectionary for next Sunday. Need to think about it more, though."

Tricia stopped and sighed. She opened the door for Sage, held it and said, "Oh, if only this church was on holy ground. There's something inside me that hints that maybe I'm causing the holy ground to quake."

Sage didn't say anything as Tricia introduced Marie to Sage. Marie had gotten up and was pleasant. She reached to her coat and said, "Nice to meet you. I will be back in tomorrow at 9 a.m., Tricia. Hope the two of you have a good meeting."

As Tricia opened her office door she noticed Sage held her purse in one hand and a large manila envelope in the other. She tried to be calm but wondered, with some nervousness, *what was in the envelope?* Figured it was probably about her. Also figured it might be a printed version of a mud slide. Oh, how the image of Oso keeps oozing in.

Sage sat down in front of Tricia's desk. Tricia sat in the chair next to her.

Sage commented, "Don't you want to sit behind your desk. You are the pastor here."

Tricia said, "I appreciate that. But honestly, I feel better not sitting behind all that wood. Less personal to be there. But, I know. We're not here to talk about authority and who's in charge. At least I think that's not the case. Please tell me what this is about, the charges I need to face."

"I will. I promise, Tricia. That's why I'm here. But before I talk about what Micah and I talked about, I have a question. Please remind me about when Rider Samson visited you. I know about the note. I know about his charges that you had betrayed his wife…and him. I know he was hostile. But, please go back over that again. What happened?"

Tricia had no trouble with that…the pushy and accusing Rider. His hostility, his being hateful, his accusations of her betrayal…easily remembered. She summed it up, "That, I think, is the essence, Sage."

"Yes," Sage said, "That's exactly how you explained the first time. Almost verbatim. That's a good thing, because the truth is always remembered. But not the lies. I believe that…."

She paused, but didn't open the envelope, and asked, "Tricia, a few questions. Was there any money exchanged? Did Rider hand you a $100 bill?"

Tricia was aghast, "What? No! No money was exchanged. We stayed on my porch. He was so hostile I didn't let him in. Hand me money?

Oh no! You wouldn't have asked that if he hadn't said something about money. Is that right?"

Sage didn't answer. Another question for Tricia, "Was there anything sexual about the visit? Anything intimate, or even suggesting intimacy?"

Tricia doubled her fists, pounded them together, "Sage. These questions. They are ridiculous. But, maybe not. Maybe they're questions that come from what's in your envelope. Please. Please share what I'm charged with…"

Tricia bit the inside of her cheek, shook her head, "Sexual intimacy? Not for a breath. No, a thousand times no. It was hostility, all from him. No sexuality in any way, manner or form. Sage? Would you please read me the charges?"

Tricia at first was glad she asked. But after Sage read the charges Tricia got sick to her stomach. Was afraid she'd throw up, "Sage, I'll respond but I'm literally sick to my stomach…not because any of that is true—it's blatant lies—but because it's so upsetting that he would write that about me. He's a monster. But, I need to…"

Tricia jumped up and went to the bathroom next to her office, closed the door and literally threw up, the agonizing gagging and then emptying her stomach. She felt empty—and that was because that was the condition of her stomach…but even stronger, the condition of her heart…empty and shattered…and all she could see emotionally was the water coming over Snoqualmie Falls. She imagined the rocks immediately beneath the falls. She locked on that image. She was unable to look downstream.

She washed her mouth out, dried her face and saw her eyes were swollen and teary. She tried to wipe the tears, but couldn't stay in the bathroom much longer. She needed to be with Sage.

"Are you all right?" asked Sage.

Tricia had no interest in diplomacy, "NO! I'm anything but all right. This is such garbage, all made up. But please. Read what Rider Samson wrote again."

Sage did, it wasn't very long, but it told a story that Tricia found horrifying. "I am filing a sexual misconduct charge against our new pastor, Reverend Tricia Gleason. She had betrayed my wife, Courtney, after Courtney has trusted Reverend Gleason with her heart. I was furious and needed to tell Reverend Gleason how she had embarrassed us and even more, was a phony to call herself a person of God. Suddenly Reverend Gleason…we sat in her home office… changed the subject. She wanted to know about sexual intimacy with my wife. So offensive. Then she put her hand on her left breast and massaged it. She didn't say a word, but her look was inviting me to massage the same breast.

"I didn't say a word. I was horrified. She reached in her desk and pulled out a tube of what she called a 'special intimate lubricant,' and said, holding it up, that when she used this, nothing would chafe. It would only bring me to the height of pleasure. She then got up, walked over to me and reached for my fly and said, 'I can make everything come. You will enjoy this. You will enjoy what I can do… and it will send away your anger.' As she started to pull down my fly I slapped her hand and stormed out. I need to share this with Reverend Dimmock. I hope the proper authorities will tear away any clergy recognition of Reverend Tricia Gleason. She's a disgrace, using sex to be a reconciling act. God-awful."

Sage put the sheet back into the envelope. Looked at Tricia, "That is what Micah received. He now wants to do some discovery, because this describes nothing even close to what he was told about you from your mentor, Creighton Yale…"

Tricia panicked, "No! Did the executive minister share this with Creighton? He cannot have. That's not fair! That's horrible. Who knows about all this, Sage…who knows?"

Sage put up her hand, "Tricia, listen to me. There, to my knowledge are only four who know now…you, me, Micah and your accuser. I don't know if he mentioned it to anyone…especially with his wife. I simply don't know. I cannot answer that."

Tricia said, "Sage, I cannot even imagine how sick his mind is. NONE of that happened. None. None. None. It's so untrue and so wrong! Obviously he's trying to rip my life apart. What happens to me through this would be a miscarriage…a terrible injustice. It's not true. He lies. He is a worthless human being. I must say this…I hate him for his doing this. He's such an evil man. To write all that…none of it happened. Well, he was right in saying he came to my home to rant. That is true. But nothing like that happened…it wouldn't happen. I have ethics. I know what responsible counseling is. This is horrible."

Sage said nothing. She nodded but didn't say she knew Tricia was telling the truth.

That bothered Tricia, but said nothing to Sage that would cause Sage to comment on the charges. Rather, Tricia thought a procedural question might temper her rage, "Sage, please tell me what happens next. Who gets this? Does it go to the Committee On Ministry?"

Sage answered, "Not right away. Micah will want to visit with you and ask you what happened. He will then make some reference calls on you…never mentioning this charge by Rider. Rather, he will be discreet and talk to your seminary advisor, the minister of the Congregational Church in Palo Alto where you were a student minister and with the Colorado executive minister. He will also visit with Creighton. It will be a general conversation. Micah will not mention these charges, but will say you have now started the licensed ministry in Snoqualmie and he is following up to see what they assess as your strengths and where you need to get stronger. He does this for every new minister in our conference. It will be generic."

"Well, I'm sure he has to do that, Sage. But honestly how can that reveal I am a person of integrity and respect others?"

"Oh, Micah can do that, Tricia," Sage responded. "He can pick up any nuances. But at no time will he mention the Rider Samson accusations."

Tricia shook her head, "I still don't understand. For Micah to do, as you say, discovery, how can he learn what really happened when Rider came to my house? It will end being unsolvable if it's 'he said she said.' I'll bet that's all that can be considered. Getting to the big question, who is telling the truth here? What about discovery on Rider? That's probably impossible. But, that's important too! This is about him as much as it is about me."

Sage nodded, "You have a good point. But I cannot promise anything in checking on Rider's background."

Tricia protested, "Sage, you're an attorney. I have been a detective. There are two sides in any conflict. At least two sides.

"I have to say more. Let me add, is this something Rider has done before when he's had trouble with his clients, has he been unfaithful to his wife and she's hammered him for it? In other words, Is this the first time he's made these charges? Maybe he asked one of his clients to zip his fly down and she refused. Or, let's be complete about this, maybe he's bi-sexual and a guy refused to grab his fly. I'm furious!"

Sage was quiet...she wasn't misnamed. She thought it was helpful for Tricia to, what she called, un-vent.

Tricia wasn't through. "Right now I've got my detective hat on, Sage. I will try to figure out how to make it clear that Rider Samson cannot ride me. He's such a bad excuse for a human being. He doesn't even deserve....well, I won't say that...but to have him around? Well, I didn't like him when he pounded on my front door. And now, I have no use for him. None. This could end my ministry...and to think of the cluster...no, that's the wrong word...the clutter of what's happening to me? Huh. Makes me wonder if Rider knows calligraphy. Maybe he's the culprit. I am grateful I didn't let him in my house. He probably would have grabbed me. I wish he were not in my life!"

Tricia sighed. "Well I guess I said too much...but honestly, Sage, what can I do?"

Sage didn't hesitate, "Well, honestly, Tricia, you cannot do anything. And I recommend you do nothing. I recommend, and cannot say this strongly enough, don't share this with anyone…not with your detective, not with your mentor, not with the pastor who took you fishing. Mum is the word. For now.

"And for sure, if Rider should be in church next Sunday, pay no attention to him. Even avoid eye contact. You cannot let him think he's got you. I'm pretty sure Micah will call you in the next day or so and will ask for reference phone numbers…the people I had mentioned. You really cannot do anything more. Micah and I agreed it was essential to share this with you. He can be trusted. He won't cause you a problem when he calls for additional references. And I know him well enough to know he won't send this to the Committee on Ministry, unless he's convinced the charges have some validity."

"Validity?" Tricia asked, "that should never be…because what I'm accused of…well I don't have to say anything more."

They stood up. No hugs. Not even shaking hands. Sage turned to Tricia, "Good luck on your sermon for next Sunday, Tricia. Maybe you can find some holy ground…I even knew a minister who took off his shoes before he preached. Some thought that was arrogant presumption, but most understood he considered the pulpit and the church holy ground…when they knew God was with them…and they affirmed they were with God. He said the holy ground had nothing to do with the earth…and everything to do with the relationship with God."

Sage got up to leave and said, "Well, that's one guy's version of the Exodus passage. Maybe that can help. In any account, Tricia, I'm sorry to be the messenger of this bad news. Take care of yourself. And call me if anything additional comes up…or you can think of how to verify that Rider Samson is not telling the truth. Okay? And know that I will be in church next Sunday. I will be here with you."

Tricia walked with Sage to her car. As Sage opened the car door, she said, "Sage? Well, at least now I know who hates me. And right now at least, I am incapable of standing above the same feeling toward him. What a…"

She didn't finish. She went back to her office, pounded her desk and shouted, "No! This cannot be happening. It cannot."

What she didn't know, because she couldn't see, but learning of the exchange between Tricia and Sage brought great joy. To know his strategy was working. He never figured Samson would be a helper. And then he thought to himself, maybe more than that. Maybe much more than that. The ultimate ramp up of charges against Pastor Bitch.

He sat back and started to game plan. A new option. A deadly one. And he'd remember where to get a tube of that intimate lubrication.

Tick. Tick. Tick.

Chapter 36

He stormed out, shouting all the way. How unsettling. That was the polite version for Tricia. Down deep she hated him and wasn't sure she could ever return to civility. But she tried.

Up to that point in the worship, it was almost too perfect. Some chairs set up, some new faces. She had found the sermon title helped, "Take Off Your Shoes." She even removed hers before she preached. She had been told once not to be too gimmicky, but have a purpose when something different was done. Well, it had been different to worship outside her first worship. So, taking off the shoes served a purpose. And to make sure the transition was smooth, that there wasn't a distraction, she wore new tights. No flaws to be seen on her feet.

When she decided to go with the theme that holy ground's not a piece of earth but the evidence of relationship—she loved that phrase, an example that phrasing skills had not left her—she knew the sermon almost preached itself, especially when she closed with putting her hands out, "My faith is this…you and I are on holy ground, because of the manner we care for each other."

The Lemon Drop Didn't Melt

Effective. And she had noted no one even peeped or uncrossed or recrossed legs or had the glazed look, that stare which said nothing was being heard.

She was nervous, but only inside, when Rider and Courtney showed up. They sat in the very back row. Rider never looked at her. She was grateful they came in during the opening hymn…so she didn't have to shake his hand. She was never into faking politeness. Fortunately, their tardiness kept that from happening.

Perfection was on a roll. Until the announcement when she invited people to give input, "Are there any concerns you'd like to share about our community? Because we don't want to be known for only tending to our own needs."

It was shattering, but not at first.

Everyone looked at Tricia. Scooter had raised his hand. He spoke softly, "Yes, next week on Saturday. A fishing time for us kids. Pond will be stocked with fish. Dad and I and my sister and brother will go. Does…I forgot."

Andrew stood up, held Scooter's hand, looked at him, "Hey, partner. Can I help?"

Scooter nodded and clutched his father's leg, nodding rapidly.

"Good. What we'd like to know is if you know of any children who might like to go fishing next Saturday; please see us after the service. We can provide the fishing gear and we'll have lots of worms. Scooter and I would love to have other kids join us."

Smiles everywhere.

Then the screech. Not a whisper, "That sounds nice…and I have a suggestion…and I insist."

All eyes looked to the back row. The tirade had just begun, "Don't look at me."

He pointed to the front, "Look at your pastor…not *my* pastor but *your* pastor. She needs to go fishing. She needs to leave. What you see is not what you get."

He spoke with a toxic tone, "Minister? You need to leave…go back to Tillamook or hell, whichever is closer!"

Stunned silence.

He then pointed to the exit sign, "See that, minister? And *minister* is so inaccurate. Don't just look at that exit sign. It's a message to you… for, to quote you, we cannot be on holy ground with you around. You'll never help that happen. Read the sign…and follow it!"

He grabbed his wife's hand…she was ghostly white…pulled her up and stormed out.

The silence was the worst silence imaginable. Tricia didn't know what to do.

Sage got up, "Folks? This outburst came as a shock to me…yes, to all of us. I'm sorry it happened. It shouldn't have happened. Uncalled for. Unnecessary. Very unsettling."

She then looked at Tricia, "Pastor? I apologize to you. You didn't deserve this. I'll make sure I talk with Rider to learn what's going on. You preached a good sermon," then looked at Scooter, "And you, Scooter, brought a great caring invitation. Thank you for that."

She stopped, looked at everyone, then at Tricia, "I am sorry for this. It has never happened before. Please don't think this is how we function in the church…I repeat, it's never happened before and I pray…never again. Not sure how we should end the service…"

Before she finished, Tricia, still stunned, her body shaking, said, "I'm sorry, too. This has never happened to me before either. I don't know how to handle it."

Abby stood up, "Tricia? We are all sorry. Why don't we sing the last hymn and you give the benediction and we can have our fellowship hour?"

Tricia wanted to rush up to Abby and hug her. She didn't; to hug in that moment was inappropriate. Instead she said to the members, thinking quickly, looked down at her feet, "Thanks, Abby. I'm looking down at my feet…you can see my shoes are still off. I'll keep them off now and I won't consider the exit sign a message. I do believe together we can create holy ground, knowing that life isn't perfect, we each make mistakes. A seminary buddy once said to me, 'I'm not okay; you're not okay. But. That's okay.' As a shock, this is a not-okay moment. Still, we'll do what we can to address this situation."

She looked to the pianist, "Let's sing a different hymn, don't even know the number. But let's sing what I hope we can realize…in each moment of our lives, 'It Is Well With My Soul.' That's my prayer. And another revision, instead of the Benediction we have printed, why don't we say together the Lord's Prayer again…offering it twice may help."

It was now three in the afternoon. She sat alone in her home office. Probably the best thing that happened to her was an hour ago her three neighboring royalty came. They had a gift…they each had a gift…cupcakes. They said they were sorry for her but that she needed to know each of their family was with her. That meant the world to Tricia, especially when they pointed to the chartreuse yarn and said as a trio, "Don't forget the yarn!" They knew Tricia needed to be cared for. Even though they didn't say it, they knew, and their parents talked with them about it. It was Tricia who needed the support of the church…almost like she was a community project for the church. And that was more important than a fishing pond. She felt better.

She knew even more, though. Probably nothing could be done with Rider…his anger, his wrath, his nothing-but-negative attitude…had to run its own course. She was tempted to pray that he would disappear from her life, but saw that as being selfish. The thoughts never reached words to God. But she knew God knew her every thought.

The neighbor Good Samaritans were exactly that. But, Tricia knew there was only one solid, reliable Good Samaritan in her life.

So she dialed.

His response, when learning of the morning sermon and member screech, was a quiet statement, "Tricia, there are times in our ministry when we have to focus on the smooth water downstream. But also, remember I told you once that every minister has at least three church members he or she liked to trade. Sounds like one has announced his trade worthiness."

Tricia smiled at that, then told him about sitting on the platform bench looking at Snoqualmie Falls. She honored Sage's request that nothing be said about the sexual misconduct charge against her. She knew Micah Dimmock would call him. But she also knew since she'd never had a negative review at her seminary or from her short ministries, Micah would learn, and her best buddy in the world would confirm, Tricia Gleason was a good person.

She then felt tired, her words drooped, "Creighton? Thanks for listening. You're the best at that."

"Hey, woman preacher, thanks for sharing. And remember, you CAN walk on holy ground. Pay no attention to the exit sign. And simply go about your ministry…Rider Samson…there are people you can do nothing about. Nothing. This is the truth. I believe you are the best. I can even create a new evaluation. You are the bestest.

"Oh, time's escaping for me. Sorry, Tricia, I gotta go meet some friends for a late afternoon brunch. Take care of you…and keep me linked…and if I can find a way for you to get to smooth water…and as you mentioned, stay ahead of the mud slide, I'll let you know. Tricia? I'm with you. Always."

Tricia hung up, the activity bouncing in her thoughts like a water bug. She reached up and put the yarn in her hand, held it to her heart. No words, but such a hope…

She put the yarn back on the desk, walked to the kitchen, ate one of the cupcakes. She never thought a cupcake would taste so good; even more, bring peace. But it did. She went upstairs and was asleep…fast asleep. Maybe the quiet provided a sleep for her. Maybe it was a silence that was helpful. She hoped her maybe would become a yes. Would it?

She'd find out. Much sooner than she'd ever realize…much sooner.

Chapter 37

It was *her* time, a private by herself time no one could take from her. It was the time when, and it was well beyond imagination, the insult of her marriage didn't reach her. When his tirade at church against Pastor Gleason could be washed away. She loved the by-herself-time. Loved it. Words could never reach the importance, the value. Precious and more than important.

Oh, she and he had it out all Sunday afternoon and most of Monday. Rider said his tirade "was needed, that bitch should never be a minister. She betrayed you, Courtney. I am a stopper. I am not one who puts up with breaking promises. I've sent in the report to her boss, although who knows how big his rug is…probably lumpy with all he no doubt sweeps under it.

"But he cannot do that with my complaint…no chance for that, because I will not be pushed away. I sent it overnight UPS a few days ago. If I need to, I will see this guy personally; his name is Micah Dimmock. Their office used to be on Beacon Hill, south of downtown, but now they're in a church north on 125th. I don't need an appointment. I'll wait another day, then he'll be seeing me. And, first thing, if I see a broom in the office, I'm taking it with me..."

His tirade was merciless, but that best described her husband. She thought of his intentions, but now, now and she hoped as long as this moment would last, he couldn't get to her. She reached to increase the heat of the water, water covering her entire body. The shower was her blessing. The one time...and honest to her heart, the only time she could not be embarrassed for the bruises. No one could see the inside of her arms where he grabbed her, his fingers almost breaking the skin. The purple ugliness of her thigh when he pounded her because she wouldn't do as he pleased with her.

Washed away, at least for a moment—his torturous management of her—the abuse, the demeaning he poured upon her...and it went deep. But she'd never admit it. Courtney didn't know what to do. She shampooed her hair, the water rinsing the foam away...it was her only pleasure...letting the water massage her hair and her stomach and her bruises. Maybe the water could, as she'd heard from a television preacher—she forgot his name but he had a great smile—wash her pain and her sin away. Not that she considered her sins equaled Rider's. But, she knew, he was never wrong.

It was therapy for Courtney...to stand in the shower...and let the water provide warmth...and dare she hope? Cleansing of the evil that came to her in the marriage. She even said out loud, "Thank you, God, for this moment of peace. Thank..."

She didn't finish. She hadn't seen him. She thought he had left for work. She was wrong.

He had *that look*, she could tell…what she called *the look of intrusion*. Well, it was more than that. The only word that worked he cleared out any ambiguity, as he opened the shower door and pointed to the bench along the far wall, "Time for us."

She knew it was never *for us*. It was only for him. He was naked, walked into the shower, felt the water, "Good temperature."

She knew he liked it almost hot. Courtney wanted to escape, but he stood in front of the closed shower door. She knew what he wanted. As he reached for her hand she knew he wouldn't be shaking it. Rather, he looked down, "My swollen friend would like your attention." He took his other hand and put it in his mouth, his body language of what pleased him.

She wanted to scream, but she knew if she did, he might hit her in the face. He was that cruel and would think nothing of damage he could cause. She didn't want to touch him, let alone what he wanted.

He let go of her hand, "Okay, guess you're not of an oral persuasion. That's okay."

He pointed to the shower bench… "Assume position. That is a position I know you like."

She was stuck. She knew what he meant. Never had he taken time… it was as he said once, probably well inebriated, "Time for the train to enter the tunnel."

She turned, put her hands on the bench. He had his way.

He thrust so hard her head rammed against the shower wall. He didn't care. His cry of relief shook her soul. To herself, "You bastard…I'm not a sex machine any longer."

What Courtney didn't know was how to make that come true. She was trapped, a prisoner in her own home.

He left, "Nice."

She wanted to say, "That's rape!"

But he went to his own bathroom—he had insisted they have "their own space."

Courtney stayed in the shower, letting the water drown her tears. What she didn't know was how she could not drown in this marriage. She thought to herself she needed to call Tricia again…and learn the new therapist's friend.

She was still in the shower when he returned. This time he was his lawyer-best, the camel coat, the beige shirt, the new tie that he bragged, "Look! I finally found a tie under $100." As if that mattered.

He arched his eyebrows, pointed to her, "How long you staying in there? Trying to become a prune? The wrinkles are showing. You are so lucky…maybe the luckiest woman in the world…that I have the highest water tank…so the hot water continues and our intimacy doesn't get cold water poured on it. But, please get out soon…so we make sure we have good hot water supply tonight---it would make a good night-cap for me."

He waved, "Thanks."

She looked down and saw blood on the shower floor. Damage. Would it never end?

Rider loved his domination…it came with his personality. And he knew Courtney wouldn't ever leave him…the dollars meant too much to her. And he was clever about the pre-nuptial, so that if he died before she did, her estate would hardly keep her going each month. She hadn't looked at the details when she signed the pre-nuptial.

He had left his car in the driveway. When he opened the door he didn't look in the back seat. He should have.

Suddenly a hand closed his mouth. The sharp point of the gun was against his right ear. He looked up to the rear-view mirror, but the man was masked, a scraggly beard at the edges.

The voice was deliberate, even, almost casual. "Mr. Samson, I believe. You need to know you define *bastard* better than anyone I know…."

Rider tried to turn his head, tried to reach his front door. He couldn't. The gun pushed harder against his head, the hand on his mouth so strong he couldn't open his mouth. Suddenly he became sick,

The voice continued steady, "I could put this in your mouth and then have your hand hold it. Suicide. But not for my purposes. For, Mr. Rider Samson, you are not the end. You are the means to an end. This situation is a two-part scene. The first will be for your beloved pastor, Reverend Tricia Gleason. The second, which unfortunately you won't witness, will be against Reverend Tricia Gleason. Won't do any good to tell you anything more, or how you figure in the great plan I have…besides you won't remember it anyway.

The voice stopped.

Rider couldn't hold down his jumbled stomach. He thought he'd throw up. But he never made it.

Craaaaaaack. Craaaaaaaack.

The masked man slipped out the back side door, put the revolver in his pocket and walked out the driveway.

He wasn't seen. He knew that he wouldn't be seen…for the Samson home was in the new toney section of Snoqualmie, each home nestled on five acres, with trees fencing for privacy. And, as the masked man thought, for anonymity. That would change…but not right away. The game plan would be kept.

For. There were a few more things to do.

Tick. Tick. Tick.

Chapter 38

Courtney had called Tricia and was grateful Tricia could see her right away.

As she left, she looked in the mirror by the back door, was relieved the make-up helped smooth her face. She couldn't smile. And she ached inside. The damage, physical as it was, was not as serious as her emotional fracturing. Something needed to be done.

Courtney stood on the porch, turned to lock the back door. Walked down the stairs and started toward the garage.

She looked and saw Rider's car in the driveway, the motor on. She could see he was slumped on the steering wheel. It looked like he had fainted.

She walked up to the car. She saw he wasn't asleep. She saw the holes in the back of his head. Then saw on his lap the mess…it looked like blood and vomit.

"RIDER!!!! RIDER!!!"

Chapter 39

She always….never an exception…smiled when her cell phone played "When The Saints Go Marching In." Only one came with that call… her cherished friend, Creighton Yale.

Tricia answered, "Well, hello Reverend Saint. What can I do for you?"

He didn't hesitate, "Hey there, Reverend Gleason. This is a check up on Tricia call…any of the bad taste left from yesterday? Just checking on your pulse rate this veritable day after."

She laughed, "Ah, Creighton. You are the bestest. Not me. But you. Yes, I'm feeling much better this morning…cannot explain why, but this is a new day. And with it, hope arrived. Actually it's been a better than good morning. I didn't count them, but I'll ask Marie…think there've been at least five calls from church members who expressed how horrified they were by Rider Samson's tirade last Sunday. They said they supported me and I should not give his screaming frenzy the time of day. That felt good. Really good."

"Great to hear, Tricia," said Creighton, "great to hear. I hope the routine will return…no fuss, no flap and no sticky notes. Really my hope; more to the point, my prayer. Got any visits set up with members?"

"Yes, I'm pleased. Have three this afternoon in my office and then two tonight. At that rate, I should be able to have visits with almost everyone right after Thanksgiving. I'm not taking notes during the visits, but write down the basic information when they leave. That seems to be a good way to manage the recall."

Creighton said, "I am curious. Anything more about your tirade attorney? Or anything from your executive minister? Just needed to ask because I realize the problem that is."

"No," Tricia replied, "but I cannot say I haven't thought about how to get out of his charges. But, honestly, I'm good and he hasn't bothered me. And maybe it's self-delusion, but I'm not worried about it. I sense it's not going to be a problem. Not for a minute."

Creighton signed off, "So glad to hear that, Tricia. Keep casting those nets to the right side of the boat. Hope the news continues to be good and you, at least down deep, will be all right. Later…"

Click.

Tricia thought she'd be just fine. She thought life would take a normal pace. She had no clue—none in the world—how that would change. How wrong that could be. And how down deep she wouldn't be all right. And, worse. How that might not ever change.

Her cell phone rang; it wasn't the "Saints" melody.

Chapter 40

She didn't recognize the number but it was a Seattle area code, "Hello, this is Tricia Gleason."

A new voice, "Hello, Tricia. This is Micah Dimmock. I would like to visit with you today, if at all possible. I'm headed to Issaquah for a meeting with one of our ministers. Might I come by your office, say about 2 p.m.?"

Tricia knew what this was about, but remained calm, not indicating worry, "Thanks for calling. It would be great to see you," she lied.

"Two o-clock would be fine. I'll be in my church office. See you then."

She started to hang up, but Micah said, "I need to tell you, and I believe Sage your moderator has given you a heads-up. I need to visit with you about some allegations filed against you by one of your church members, Rider Samson. It will be good for us to visit, Tricia, so I can appreciate your take on all this. See you at 2."

Tricia remained positive, "Yes, it's both good and important we visit. Sage did tell me about the allegations…and believe me, I want you to hear me on this."

Click.

In one way Tricia was pleased, so she could fill her executive minister in, with hopes she could avoid anything more.

Her cell phone rang. It was Jordon, "Tricia, I need to see you right away. You in your office?"

His tone was sharp, not harsh but very clipped.

She said, "Yes, I'm here."

Jordon said, "I can be there in five minutes."

Tricia was hoping he had good news about the calligrapher. That was her primary hope. The calligrapher needed to be identified. Then she could figure out why all this was happening to her.

Marie buzzed Tricia, "Your detective is here, Tricia."

He knocked and then opened her office door.

His look? Something bothersome about his face. Not a glower, but seriousness…and no doubt, very official.

Tricia pointed to the other chair in front of her desk.

Jordon sat. "Tricia, I have bad news. Very bad news. Rider Samson was murdered this morning. His wife, Courtney found him slumped in his car's front seat. My captain was called and sent me over here to their place. The scene has been secured. Mrs. Samson's devastated. She is with a neighbor right now. She's being interviewed as you and I speak."

Tricia turned to stone. All she could do was shake her head in disbelief. She looked up, "Murdered? How in the world? That's horrible. Murdered?"

"Yes," Jordon answered. "He was murdered in his car it looks like. He was on his way to work. The scene's very messy."

"Can you tell me how?" Tricia asked.

Jordon, because that information would only be known by the killer, had to cover all his bases, "We don't know the how yet. My detective partner, Arlene Tiffany, is getting that information. It's still all in a preliminary stage. Mr. Samson's wife said she had called you for an appointment and that they were members of your church. So, I thought you should be given this information."

"You say she's at a neighbor's house? I need to see her. Can I head over there? I am her pastor…was his pastor, too. He was murdered? That's unbelievable."

Tricia's mind raced faster than ever before. She couldn't imagine such a scenario. Not even in her worst imagination could this happen. And then it hit her…what she had said to Sage about her dislike of Rider Samson, how he had erupted their worship against Tricia in last Sunday's worship and how he had charged her with sexual misconduct, how Micah Dimmock would be visiting her in the afternoon, a visit to explain Samson's charges of sexual misconduct… and how it had shifted from he said/she said to she said/he's dead.

"Tricia?", Jordon waved his hand, "You asked if you could visit Mrs. Samson. I'm sure you'll want to do that, but unfortunately not now. Perhaps you could see her later…to work out how the church can conduct Mr. Samson's funeral service."

Tricia looked dazed. Well, truth front and center she was shocked. And it showed. Her eyes were glazed. To think Jordon had said she couldn't visit…but she was unclear what followed that. Something about a funeral service?

She didn't want to keep the conversation going, so she nodded as if she understood, got up.

Jordon remained seated, "Yes, I can understand this is a shock. But, before I do, do you have any other questions?"

Tricia shook her head.

As he got up, Jordon looked at Tricia and tried to be casual, but Tricia, her detective pulse taking charge, knew that the question needed to be asked, "Oh, Tricia, one more thing. Did you have meetings here at the church or in your home this morning?"

All she could think of was INDICTMENT!!!

She responded quickly, "No, I didn't have any meetings. I was at home until about an hour ago."

He nodded, but it wasn't a nod of understanding. She sensed he had more questions. He walked to her office door. "I'm very sorry I had to bring you this news. But I wanted you to know since they are members of your church and you are their pastor."

Tricia knew that was polite and literal. They are church members. She also knew her contempt for Rider Samson, but her anger, well short of homicide, was real. And publicly? Such a downer. She could see him standing on her porch, she could see the sexual misconduct claim he filed with Micah Dimmock, she could see him ranting at worship and tromping out of the sanctuary and she could see herself making the negative claims about him to Sage. It was true, she had no use for Rider Samson. But, will all that about him that is useless, come back to haunt her?

And. Maybe worse?

Tricia walked unsteadily to her desk. Her hand shook as she hit the coded number. He answered right away.

"Creighton? I need you."

She then decided, without thought and not really caring whether or not she should do this, she needed to dial another number, "Hannah? This is Tricia. Got a minute?"

Chapter 41

Melanie beamed, "Well, look at this? My two most favorite ministers? Hey, who said women cannot be ministers? I'd fight against that!"

She had shown Hannah and Tricia to a corner table, one they requested, well off the path for new customers at the Issaquah Café. They had told Melanie they only wanted iced tea and some English muffins…this time there'd be no meatloaf or Swedish pancakes. Melanie had brought the order quickly and said, "Well, reverends, I'll not bother you…will give you all the time you need to work on your sermons…just wave when you want something."

Tricia hadn't mentioned to Hannah about the situation, but Hannah could tell something was wrong. As they sat at the table, Hannah said, "Something's wrong, I can tell," as she reached for Tricia's hands, held them gently.

"I'm here and have no meetings. The time is yours, Tricia, the time is yours."

Hannah then pulled her i-phone out of her purse, clicked it off, "No one can bother us…why don't you do the same? So this is only a Tricia and Hannah conversation…no quality assurance compromised."

The silence wasn't awkward for Tricia. Because Hannah was with her…and Tricia knew she could trust Hannah…what she would call a truth friend.

Tricia pulled her hands back. Then said, "Thanks, Hannah, for being here. I really need a friend."

Hannah smiled gently, squeezed Tricia's hands, let them go. "Tell me what you'd like."

When Tricia finished with the details, summarizing as well as she could, Hannah said, "I think I have the various incidents in order. What will happen now is your executive minister will be at your office at 2 p.m. today. Do you know if he knows about the murder?"

Tricia replied, "I doubt it. Or he would have called about that. He only said he had charges to inform me of, charges filed by Rider Samson. I just thought of something, isn't that weird, charges from a dead man…might say charges from a dead man walking. How can I defend myself when the accuser's unable to respond? And for sure, Hannah, no one could hear his charges, and I only visited with my moderator and my best friend about it."

She thought of the other shadowy thought…more accurately to Tricia, the other full darkness thought, and said to Hannah, "And this, Hannah. Such a terrible possibility, but I thought of it. Before he left my office this morning, Jordon Valentine asked where I had been this morning? All I could think of was I might be a suspect. Are you kidding me? I could be a suspect. Ah, what headlines, 'Local Church Minister Murders Church Member.'"

The irony dripped but Hannah would have nothing to do with that, "Whoa there, soldier. Stop that thought. Right now."

Tricia agreed, "Yeah, you're right. Innocent until charged and proven guilty, right?"

Hannah protested, "No, not innocent until proven guilty. It's clear to me," as she hand-quoted, "Innocent because she is innocent."

"Tricia, your time and energy and focus should be in answer to a couple of questions. First. What is your pastoral responsibility to and for Courtney Samson? Two, what do you need to do to make sure you are not caught up in the homicide charges? And three, think of fishing tomorrow with Jon…catching coho will be great release, moments of being set free. I know you said you couldn't go fishing with us… but I think, given the seriousness of all this, you need some casting fun-time."

"I hear you, Hannah. Most of all thanks for being here. I do need to be a pastor to Courtney. And I do need to think of next steps—Creighton can help me with that. He's been through some legal snares with some of his clergy when he was an executive minister…in fact, when one of his ministers and his wife were bludgeoned to death, one of the church members was a suspect, so Creighton got involved with the police and the member's attorneys. I'm sure he can be counsel for me.

"But, for tomorrow? I still cannot include fishing, which is like taking my breath away. Tomorrow, though, Melita has her lumpectomy and I need to be there. For me, no doubt, more than for her. Still, I need to be a pastor…for her and for her husband Jacob. Oh, by the way, he still won't talk to me; he believes the note about my telling others about her lumpectomy is valid. I also need to be a pastor to Courtney. Melita did say her lumpectomy might be postponed. Don't know that now."

Hannah said, "That all makes sense. We will have to put fishing on another day…the coho are still trembling when they hear your name."

Tricia said, "Hey, that's a good one. I saw a t-shirt that said that… about fish and trembling. Oh don't I wish it would only be the fish who tremble when they hear me. Don't I wish."

"Stop that, Tricia. It's so unbecoming to plan a self-pity party. I know I'm being sharp with you…but please don't mire yourself. I will be with you…got it?"

They got up, Hannah had paid for their less than sumptuous meal, although Tricia only managed one sip of her iced tea and the muffins weren't tasted.

They stood outside the restaurant, Hannah said, "Oh, we didn't go into it. But I'm assuming Sage will be involved in all this…I hope she's a supporter of you?"

It was a question Tricia didn't know how to answer, "Hannah, I do hope so. I want to talk with her and believe she'll want to be with me. In what manner she will be with me, I don't know.

Hannah hugged Tricia…a firm hug, leaned back, "Be good to you, Tricia. Be great to you. Because that'll reflect who you are."

As Hannah walked for her car, she turned, "And one more thing, Pastor Gleason, and it's from you, find the light in the shadows."

Chapter 42

Too nasty for the picnic table. Tricia would have preferred meeting there—in thought of when she and Sage and Melita met to work through Melita's anger. The rain and blustery wind kept them in her office.

She had met Micah before—he asked her to call him by his first name—but not in these circumstances.

She asked, "Micah, did you get the horrible news about Rider Samson?"

He hadn't, and looked puzzled.

"It's the worst news possible…he was murdered this morning. I've called Sage to tell her this terrible news and that you and I were meeting now. She said she was on her way home, had no afternoon appointments and wanted to meet with us, especially given this dire situation."

A tap on Tricia's office door, Tricia looked up, "Come in."

The Lemon Drop Didn't Melt

Sage walked in.

Tricia couldn't tell what Sage was thinking…but that was revealed quickly, "Hi, Tricia and Micah. Looks like we have a much more serious agenda than we had anticipated. Rider Samson's murder is and will be page 1 for us. Which doesn't discount his charges against you, Tricia…."

Micah pulled a third chair and looked at it, "Hello, Sage…why don't we all sit down."

Tricia didn't think she should say anything…because she didn't know what they were wanting.

Micah started, "Well, first off," as he held up an envelope, "Here is the claim from Rider Samson. I need to check with our conference attorney on how I should proceed, since the man who pressed the charges is dead."

He paused, looked at both of them, "Do you have any suggestions?"

Sage replied, "I think, Micah, we don't toss the envelope. But I also think to pursue it right now would not be either prudent or timely."

Tricia sensed where this might head, thinking of her conversation with Jordon and the possibility of charges filed against her. She wanted to keep a positive attitude, so said, "I hear you, Sage. But, honestly, if Micah thinks this should be reviewed by the conference Church and Ministry Ethics Committee, I will be more than pleased to meet with them. Of course, Rider Samson cannot respond, but I want to tell what happened. I want the committee to hear from me."

Micah said, "I hear you, Tricia, and will duly note that when I meet with the attorney. I just think the murder overwhelms everything else. And I can only say, if I were in this situation with a church member who was hostile toward me, and I do know he walked out of worship with lots of contempt toward you, Tricia—if that happened to me, I'd want to make my case. However…"

He stopped his sentence, tapped his chin, "I think we need to press the pause button…at least for the next few days. Nothing about this situation, that is, Tricia, his charges against you, will be changed. The charges are filed. There's no need to jump into that right now. Let me visit with our legal counsel, to make sure we're not irresponsible. And go from there."

Micah lifted a finger for emphasis, "Do know, Tricia. The committee doesn't know about this. I won't share the charges against you with them right now. Too much swirling around his death. I want to add, though, I hope the detectives and the district attorney's office check everything out."

When he said that Micah looked at Sage, who nodded, "Yes, Micah, good point. I know the county district attorney, who will be involved… is probably at the death scene now. He's good people and I'm sure will want to visit with you, Tricia, since it's pretty well known that Rider spoke against you last Sunday at the end of worship. So, to wait is prudent; thanks, Micah, for your call on this."

Tricia thought of letting it go, but she couldn't. She said, "I'm asking for just a couple of minutes, if I may."

She thought she saw Sage rolling her eyes, and Micah had no response. Tricia didn't hear a decline of her offer to share, so she said, "I simply

The Lemon Drop Didn't Melt

want you both to know…and I will tell this to anyone who asks, what Rider Samson…and I'm not pleased or indifferent about his death—that is horrible and I lament it. In all that, though, I want you to know that what he charged me with, the sexual misconduct, never happened. We stayed on my front porch. Yes, the front door was open, but I didn't invite him in. Nor did I ask him to come visit me, nor did he call to ask if he could come. A thousand no's to his claims.

"Okay, I realize he cannot speak for himself, but it's more than important that I tell both of you, I'm not guilty of Rider Samson's charges. And, as you know, Sage, I've been hassled—big-time—by all kinds of onerous notes, that are false accusations. The situation needs to be examined. But now. With Rider Samson's murder, my issues aren't that important. I do understand that…but sometime I want to find out who's really trying to do me in."

She was quiet. Micah and Sage nodded agreement.

Micah said, "I think you know, Tricia, that I'm making some calls for background on you. I have a list of names—can you send me their cell numbers? I can also appreciate this is a daunting time for you. We will do what we can to support you. Please keep me current on any developments. I do understand from Sage that various notes have been sent to you or to church members. That's totally wrong. And I'm sorry for that. All I can is I'm sorry for the troubling situations. And I'll not share any of this with the Committee On Ministry…at least for the time being. And if that changes, I will call you before I touch base with them."

Sage looked at Micah, "Thanks for being here…Tricia has had lots of difficulties…not by her hand. Now I need to notify the congregation of Rider's death. Plus, I will need to work with Tricia about our church providing funeral services. Such a tough time. Knowing you are aware, Micah, that's helpful."

She then looked at Tricia, "Tricia, got a couple more minutes…we should go over some details."

Micah left, "Keep me in touch with everything, Tricia. Take care of yourself."

He closed the door.

Sage said, "Why don't we sit down. I have a couple of questions."

Tricia didn't think it was a question; rather it came across as a non-negotiable demand.

"Tricia? I am aghast at this, the murder of Rider. I trust the county DA so all the investigation will happen in good order. What I don't know…and you I doubt can answer this…I don't know what your relationship can be to the funeral. Because most of the congregation was in church last Sunday…and they heard Rider tell you to leave."

"Can I interrupt, Sage? Why do you reference that? Are you looking for something else? Did you talk with my detective contact, Jordon Valentine? About Rider's murder?"

Sage shook her head, "No, I only know about this from your call. Haven't talked with him.

Tricia made a decision. No time to think it through, "Sage, let me share something. When Jordon told me this morning about Rider's murder—and he made it clear it wasn't suicide—he asked me what I had been doing this morning, where I was, was I with anybody.

"It hit me, and I know what good detective work is, it occurred to me that I might be a suspect. I couldn't believe that because I know I had nothing to do with Rider's murder. But I also know that I wasn't home this morning…I had been down along the Snoqualmie River and then came back to the hill by my house to meditate, to think about all that's happening. Mount Si give me inspiration, so I sat there for over an hour. I will add I talked to no one. I didn't see anyone. Just sat. Alone."

Sage looked understanding, "I need to say this, Tricia. I don't know how you feel. I can only imagine how your mind is racing out of control. That's not a surprise. But I want you to know that I care about you. I can appreciate being caught off guard by Jordon's questions…"

She paused, then said, "I realize this is a mess, from everyone's perspective. I'm also aware you have a great mentor and friend, Creighton Yale. He thinks the world of you…hopefully you've called him…or if not, please do call him, so he's aware of all that's happening."

Tricia felt better, "Yes, Sage. Thanks for mentioning Creighton. I have called him and he asked if he could drive up here, sensing how critical my situation is. He should be up here in a few hours…so, that will be good. He's the best friend in the world."

"That's very helpful to know, Tricia. One thing's pretty clear for me… and you and our church right now…boredom will not happen."

Tricia smiled, "Yes, that's true. I've never prayed for boredom. Maybe that might be my prayer this afternoon."

Sage got into her car, rolled down the window, "Hold on, Tricia. Don't let go."

She drove off as Tricia returned to her office.

What she didn't see, had no earthly clue to. He was watching her, clucking to himself, *This could not be developing better...in fact, it's perfect. Shouldn't take too long...will make it clear...anyone who thinks the Pastor Bitch is innocent of homicide? How wrong they'll be.*

Tick. Tick. Tick.

Chapter 43

Tricia asked, "Do you think this is the calm before the storm, Creighton?"

He tapped the kitchen table, "Don't consider it prelude…or postlude…consider it as it is. This is a nice, quiet time. And as you've found since arriving in Snoqualmie…"

He stopped, nodded as if a new idea popped in his head, "…arriving in Snoqualmie. Tell me, Tricia, what's been the best part of being here…let's look at the positive."

Tricia always appreciated Creighton. More than anyone she had met, he could keep the perspective, never too hyper, never too comatose. Those were his words to describe the extremes people often reached when life was overwhelming, especially when they only hoped to be whelming. She thought about his question and answered, "Okay, the best. Not chronologically, but as it now can be listed. First is the family who's befriended me, especially the children. Such a good and fun family. I'm hoping to go fishing with them next Saturday. Of course I expect you to be with us, to fish in the neighborhood pond next to the police station. I'll provide the gear and the worms. We'll join the neighbor kids and their parents.

"Second, meeting Hannah the Episcopal rector from Mercer Island. She is a truth friend. And with that, the time we fished on the Skagit River. Lots of catching with the fishing. And third, the worship service, even with the tirade explosion by Rider Samson."

"Okay, Tricia, you know the next question…"

She did.

"Yep, what is the most negative. Definitely the murder."

"Before you go on from that, Tricia," Creighton asked, "any updated information?"

"No, Jordon Valentine, the detective, called me just before you arrived, to say what he thought would be happening. He's not a detective for Snoqualmie; they don't have one. He's with the Major Crime Task Force in Snoqualmie and North Bend. It's a detective team that covers this part of King County. He's now on the murder case, especially since he is familiar with all my love notes."

Creighton laughed, pointed at Tricia, "Love it. Did you catch the verb? Tricia, don't ever lose your cynicism. That will keep you more balanced, so you don't tip over and not get back on even keel….okay, go ahead, what will happen in the murder investigation?"

"I don't know all the details," Tricia said, "But Sage is familiar with some of those dynamics. The body has been taken to the King County Medical Examiner's office. They will figure out the bullets. Sage somehow found out, I don't know how but she told me, that

Rider was shot in the back of the head. Two bullets that remained in his head. So, they will know the kind of gun used. Sage didn't know if the gun was found. But, since he was shot twice in the back of the head, that means it was no suicide.

"So anyway, the murder is number one in the bottom list. Second would be all the love notes. I still cannot figure out how that happened. And third…my list only has this third and maybe it's at the top of the bottom…"

Tricia coughed, cleared her throat, sipped some water, looked down. She felt horrible, didn't want to share with Creighton. And yet he was the best friend in the world, how could she not share?

Creighton wasn't a psychic, but he knew Tricia better than well, said, "Tricia, take some breaths. Obviously this is all serious stuff. Share what you'd like."

She did. She told him her *inside wrestling about ministry.* How the joy she felt when fishing. How the troubles mounted for her and seemed to increase exponentially. She said that there was something—actually two somethings lurking, "Creighton I am in a struggle about whether to continue in ministry. I'm not shutting that door; truth is I'm not shutting any door to my future. But. And it's the biggest conjunctive but in the world, there are lurking two unknowns…one the worst and one the best."

Creighton smile, "Wow, a best and a worst. Take them in the reverse order. Please?"

She so appreciated Creighton…what an incredible friend…and Tricia knew he would never give up on her.

"Okay, reverse order. The worst? That somehow I will be thrown out of this licensed ministry because I will be somehow be implicated, perhaps as an accessory, to the murder."

"Whoa, woman. Where in the world did you pick that up? You said you didn't do it. Actually, even though you know how to use a revolver and even though you were a great detective, there's no way you would have murdered Samson. No way. Besides, you indicated when he was murdered and you were here," as he pointed to the kitchen.

Tricia shook her head, "Yeah, I was here and I spent an hour up on the hill looking at the Snoqualmie Valley, the Snoqualmie River and especially at Mount Si. I was meditating, not murdering. But. Ah, another conjunctive but. No one saw me. I didn't use my cell phone. I didn't see anyone walking their dog along the path. No one. Nothing. And I do know the murder happened about 9 a.m. I was up on the hill then…without an alibi. At least something that can be corroborated. Valentine, the detective, asked me where I was. Creighton, that's a question that tracks down, as it is put, *persons of interest*."

Creighton raised his hand, "Okay, of course you are a person of interest. A point on that…did you ever say anything to anybody about your contempt for Rider Samson?"

Tricia sighed, "Yes, unfortunately I did. I told Sage our moderator that I had no use for Rider Samson, after I learned what his note said about me. That's pretty judgmental. In fact, very judgmental. Plus, Creighton, more than 80 people saw him piss all over me in worship, telling me to go to hell or Tillamook, whichever is closer."

Creighton smiled, "Did you tell him which was closer?"

Tricia appreciated the moment; Creighton wouldn't let the exchange push her deeper. It hadn't.

"No, I was speechless. The best part of that was that very afternoon the neighbor kids, who were in worship when the rampage by Rider Samson happened…all those kids are angels impersonating human beings…they brought me cupcakes…they each made one to give me. Is that special…or what?"

"See, Tricia? You are loved…okay, back on track…you think you may be accused of having some part in the murder. I cannot emphasize this enough," pointing to her, "That can be dealt with. If you need an attorney, I have a contact here in Seattle. If you need help in figuring out who might have murdered Samson, well, I hope Valentine and his team will figure that out. But, in any case, I think that you and I…and maybe your buddy, the Episcopal Rector, can visit to make some sense out of it. In any case, it's not just jargon, Tricia, you have never stayed down when knocked down. And you know, getting up is what life's all about. Okay, that's preachy…but it's crucial to never forget that….now time to switch…what's the best?"

She smiled and Creighton caught it, "See, young lady? I see it? Clear. Very clear. You are smiling! When you think of the best. Bring it!"

She loved his spirit…he always had the ability to never be in a position to give up. Never.

Tricia said, "The best? The best is catching the killer. And you know, what? I believe…and hope to prove…the killer knows calligraphy. I believe down deep…down very, very deep…that all the *love notes* that have pinned me down…THAT person is the guy who whacked Samson. Now, the best is still to happen."

"Do you mean to catch the killer?" asked Creighton.

"No, the best is still to be remembered. Let me explain. Early in this I had an idea…but it fled. It went somewhere into the shadows and for the life of me…and that may not be just an expression, for the life of me I cannot retrieve it. It was an aha moment that escaped. I keep thinking and thinking and thinking. But it's gone. And for reasons I cannot label…when it returns, yes! Yes! For me. And, who knows?"

Tricia didn't continue, she was spent emotionally.

Creighton looked at his watch, "Wow, how time flies, whether or not you're having fun. Guess it's time to get some sleep…thanks for fixing up the guest room…that should be fine. Do we have a game plan for tomorrow? I can stay through next Sunday…and I hope to do more than clap and cheer for you, Tricia. I want to help in whatever way I can.

"And, who knows? Maybe the aha moment will happen…it just may be. Keep searching. Although it might be like fishing…how often does the fish strike when you think the fish will strike? I know that answer: never! So, I guess it's best to not think about aha coming back."

"Oh, wise man, a guy named Creighton Yale. Thanks for helping me out…I'm not sinking…not swimming, but like Peter, I won't sink."

"Hey, that's pretty biblical…might even think about it for next Sunday's sermon…Peter and Jesus walking on the water. Well, for Peter, he sank."

He looked at the clock again, got up, hugged Tricia, "See you in the morning. Sleep well."

Tricia planned to do that. She didn't hope nothing bad would happen through the night. In truth, because of Creighton helping her spirits not fall apart, she didn't even think about it.

When she got to her bed—the master bedroom was on the first floor, the guest bedroom upstairs—she noticed a package on her nightstand. She picked it up. *Ah, Creighton, how special is this?*

It was a package of lemon drops and next to it, a CD. She knew what was on the CD, and the purpose of the lemon drops. Yet, she wasn't ready to take a lemon drop…not yet. But, hopefully some day. Some day.

She offered her prayers and reached to turn off the night by her night stand. The darkness had never bothered her. Her prayer voiced hope. Tricia didn't consider it selfish to pray for herself. She needed all the help she could get. And she knew. She knew no matter what, Creighton would be with her. His presence always brought her goodness. She trusted that wouldn't change.

The morning would arrive. Would it ever.

Chapter 44

"They make better Swedish pancakes than I…at least I was told they serve the best Swedish pancakes in the Seattle area."

"Okay, Tricia. If I have Swedish pancakes this morning, make a promise. A binding promise…you WON'T tell my doctor."

"It's a deal," Tricia said as she pointed to the Issaquah Café, "There it is…a wonderful restaurant and a great lady to serve us…I hope she's there."

Tricia parked, looked up at the car parking next to her. The driver got out and looked at Tricia and Creighton, "Ah, perfect timing…one of the gifts of ministry."

Tricia and Creighton laughed at Hannah's humor.

Hannah came over to Tricia, gave her a strong hug, then turned to to Creighton, "Ah, you must be the more-than-famous Creighton Yale… is your last name real or was it Community College?"

The Lemon Drop Didn't Melt

Hannah reached to shake Creighton's hand, he opened his arms, "Let's move beyong the politeness…you bring Tricia comfort and hope…so I want to hug a thank-you. Because you see, I'm more into gratitude than presumption. And yes, I'm her mentor," as he pulled on his hair, "the white hair gives me away."

He then pointed to the restaurant's front door, "Ladies…shall we?"

Tricia was pleased that Melanie was working.

They were seated by the hostess as Melanie waited her turn, "What a treat for me," she said, "bringing God to our restaurant. How special is this…two ministers…"

Creighton interrupted, "Yes, ma'am," as he pointed to her nametag, "It says Melanie. Tricia bragged on you, said you were a 12 on a 1-10… unless, of course, you changed nametags with another waitress."

Creighton shook Melanie's hand, "Guess you'll just have to put up with a third minister…hope you can handle it!"

Melanie beamed, "Wow, early in the morning. What a start for me. Like the Seahawks scoring three touchdowns in the first quarter."

Melanie pumped her fist, "Yes, go Seahawks!"

She handed Creighton a menu.

He put up his hand, "Thanks, Melanie. But, if you won't tell my doctor, I'd like to try your Swedish pancakes. I hear they also are a 12."

Melanie held up her notepad, "Ladies? Oh, I mean, pastors? What can I serve you?"

Tricia looked at Hannah, nodded, "Let's make it an order of three Swedish pancakes, Melanie…that's easy to remember. And three coffees…that work, Creighton?"

She knew it would, she even knew he preferred Hazelnut coffee.

Creighton looked at Tricia and Hannah, "But what will you be having to drink?"

Melanie got it, "Wow, this table has been changed. It used to be a table for patrons to eat their breakfast. Now? You've changed it into the stage for Comedy Hour. Be right back with three coffees, and sir, I assume you know that to share is to be golden. Or something like that."

Relaxed, enjoyable. Tricia could feel it. But. She knew the agenda was not humor. She knew it wasn't Swedish pancakes to die for. No. A thousand times no. She had called Hannah late last night, to ask if she could meet them for breakfast, that Melita's surgery had been postponed and with a trembling voice that her antagonist church member, Rider Samson, had been murdered. Would she have breakfast with her and Creighton? Hannah said she had cancelled her fishing trip, somehow sensing she would be needed. So there they were…and for sure, anything about Comedy Hour was an illusion. The comedy left the table as Hannah looked at them both, then focused upon Tricia, "Tricia, I see new worry lines…and from what you have told me…they have cause. Yes?"

Chapter 45

"Oh my, oh my, Tricia. What a mess. Hard to keep everything straight. The murder? What to make of it."

Creighton and Tricia nodded, "Yes, Hannah, I think I've told you everything. I told Creighton. Creighton? Did I miss anything?"

He shook his head, 'Nope, that was an excellent summary...too bad there's no good ending."

Hannah sipped her coffee, "I have a question. Have either you seen Joe Kenda?"

"I am both sleepless and clueless, Hannah. What's this about?"

Creighton said, "I agree with Tricia, although, at least not yet, I'm not sleepless. But certainly. Clueless fits."

Hannah smiled, "As you updated me on all the events, the what has happened, I thought of Joe Kenda. Because centered right now is the murder of your church member, Tricia. Joe Kenda is a homicide detective in Colorado Springs. Thought maybe you would have heard about him, Tricia, when you were in Dillon, Colorado last summer.

"Anyway, there's a television program detailing his homicide cases. He's solved more than 300 homicides. And yes, even though we're looking at only one, maybe some of his strategies can apply."

Tricia said, "No, I've not heard of him…but, please, Hannah, continue."

"Okay, what hits me on your situation, Tricia, is probably basic for you when you were a detective. It goes like this. When someone's murdered, who's the first person of interest? It wouldn't be you, Tricia, his pastor. Although I did see a program when the pastor was the guilty one. But. A huge but. That's not the case here. The first person of interest would be his wife. Did she—you said her name is Courtney—did she ever share about their marriage, that it wasn't good? You had relayed what Rider Samson had charged you with and how he disrupted worship."

"Yes," Tricia nodded. "She was very unhappy in her marriage. In fact I promised her I would give her a new therapist."

"Okay, Tricia, that's one person of interest. And yes, you can be another, given his public act during worship. We need to acknowledge that…he despised you…and you told your moderator you have no use for him. That's certainly in play.

"….but, there might be others. The detective involved, and I imagine he'll have help, but check on Rider Samson to see if any of his clients might have killed him. Or, maybe there's animosity in his law firm. Or," as Hannah tapped the table, "just maybe, he had an affair and told his girlfriend he was not continuing his relationship with her, so she shot him."

Creighton smiled, "Ah, Hannah, you must be a Joe Kenda cousin."

Tricia agreed, "Well, maybe not. But, honestly Hannah, you help with your inquiries."

"Thanks, Tricia, there is one more thing, no make that two, I'm thinking of. First of all, you are innocent. I believe that. I know that. I am sure of that. Yes, you have no alibis for when the murder happened. Meditating on a hill looking at a valley and a river and a mountain is nice. But, no one can verify, not even God. Oops, sorry, don't want to take God out of this. But, the point is you are innocent. Act like it. No matter what happens, never lose focus that you are innocent and be resolved to center upon that. No matter what. It should be out of innocence and not defensiveness and fear that you function. Preach next Sunday. Continue your interviews with church members. Be you.

"And, a second thing, actually in the form of a question…I have asked it, I'm sure more have asked it. Let's assume someone's out to get you. You can cover the bases of who that might be."

Creighton raised both hands, "Good point on that, Hannah. I know you're not finished, but I'm sorry I need to jump in. Tricia and I have gone over the culprit list and the biggest culprit of all is her ex-husband. He was not a good person. But, he's buried in an urn in a pauper's grave in Tillamook. He was shot dead, which solved a horrible crime spree. And yes, he would be suspect number one. But, in spite of a movie theme, dead people not only don't walk, they don't kill a church parishioner from St. Andrew's Church in Snoqualmie. So…the who is key, but no one comes to mind. Am I right, Tricia?"

Tricia spoke in a whisper, "Yes, that's true."

"Thanks for that, Creighton, but there's more than the who. In Joe Kenda he has some basics when solving a murder…the who, the how, the why. We don't know the who, but we do know the how. It may be, though, the key is the why. What would the motivation be? Because, Tricia? You weren't selected out of the phone directory and you ended up winning the frame-for-murder-lottery. This is not random selection.

"Those are my two things…oh, a third. Gosh, this is rapid-fire," as she looked at her i-phone, "but I'm sorry, I need to get going. Here's the third, has there been something consistent about all this?"

"Yes," Tricia said, "All the love notes. Well, Hannah, I called them love notes. The mysterious calligrapher. Valentine even asked me if I knew calligraphy. How indicting is that? As if I wrote all those notes to make me the poor victim, acting on my own behalf to destroy my ministry?"

"I'm sorry for that, Tricia…his question. But, I can see that he needs to cover every base…cannot get to home plate without circling the bases."

Creighton then asked, "I have an idea, Hannah, and it comes from a question I asked Tricia and Tricia said Sage and Valentine also asked it, what led to the notes? That is, the location of the notes."

"I think that needs to be looked at, I agree, Creighton," offered Hannah. "It sure needs to be looked at."

Hannah got up, "Sorry, I need to get back to my office. Let me pay," as she reached for the note.

Creighton grabbed it first, "Nope, you are both my guests. This will be a theological seminar, taking reality and doing our best to not sink."

Hannah smiled, "Thanks, Creighton. I get the next tab. Got it?"

Creighton didn't hesitate, "Good. If you let me pick out the restaurant. I know there's a great sea-food restaurant on Lake Union."

Hannah started to leave, stopped and came back, "Oh, no one's said this, but I imagine we all agree this conversation is not recorded for quality assurance."

She left.

Tricia turned to stone, didn't even blink.

Creighton saw that, thought something horrible happened.

Tricia could barely be heard as she whispered, "Quality assurance."

She blinked, beat her fist on her heart, "Creighton, it came to me… what has been hiding. Yes!"

Chapter 46

"Tricia? Make that double-Tricia. Only one word in response, in the largest letters possible: WOW. With three exclamation points. You make sense, you make the best sense in the world. I believe you have it nailed. What we might end up calling the *cause and result* case. You can figure out every single love note—I like that irony—all of them focused upon you and trying to bring you down…with a crash and burn. But, you got it. You absolutely got it. Call Detective Valentine, I'll bet he will agree, and will immediately bring his team to check out your theory. What a focus…and all from Hannah saying *quality assurance.*

"Ah, that's my favorite minister, a lady named Tricia Gleason. I'll bet you, although I've never heard of him…I'll bet you that Joe Kenda would be proud of you. Great!"

Tricia drove with new resolve. It didn't break the case of who murdered Rider Samson, but she knew that everything was connected. She knew it a thousand times over, once she thought of what she couldn't remember.

She beamed, "Creighton, I'm feeling good, pushing great. Can you tell?"

The Lemon Drop Didn't Melt

"Ah, your body language makes that clear…no wrinkles, no fisted hands, no darting glances as if you expect someone to jump out of a shadowed corner. Nope, that's my Tricia. Yes!"

He pointed to her, "Go ahead, call the detective. I assume you have his number…ah, so to speak."

"Creighton, stop that. He's a detective who will help me. Period. Don't get into the double entendre swirl, although you are a master of that."

She looked ahead as she turned off on exit #25 to Snoqualmie, saw the parking area by the police station. *Ah, what an irony. Not to turn myself in. Nope. To set myself free.*

"Detective Jordon Valentine."

"Hi, Jordon, this is Tricia. Got a minute? Would love to visit with you. I think I've unlocked a mystery and wanted to share it. But, not on the phone. Can we meet at my house? It's such a lovely day, we can meet on my back porch. My wonderful friend," as she winked at Creighton and he pump-fisted in affirmation and acceptance, "Creighton Yale is with me. I would like him to join us. Can you spare a few minutes? Won't take long. I can put everything together."

No response. None. *Did we get cut off?*

"Uh, thanks, Tricia, thanks for calling. I'm caught up now in the Samson murder investigation. We just received the medical examiner report. I need to go over it with my captain. Plus some new information he was advised, has been received. Let me get back to you."

Click.

The gleam and glitter left. Something deep inside, because she had an intuitive barometer, wasn't right. Not just what he said, but the tone of his voice. Tricia paid attention to tone, to inflection. It wasn't good. How could that be? She knew…for a certainty…no ambiguity…she knew how she had been impacted. She could trace every note, even the condom package. She needed the very detective Jordon Valentine to help her. She couldn't do what needed to be done. *Quality Assurance*. THAT was the key.

She turned to Creighton, "He cannot come to see us now. Said something about the M.E. report and some new information that his captain received. Said he'd get back to me later."

"Relax, Tricia. Relax. You are making too much of nothing. He needs to focus on the homicide investigation. I'm glad you didn't tip him off about your theory. There's time for that. You just need to be careful to consider your home and church offices off limits. Got it?"

"Yep. That's why when he gets to us we need to be in the back porch…or in his car."

Tricia headed up and then down—the path to her house. And she thought about being up but now was going down. She hoped that was only the contour of Snoqualmie Parkway…and had nothing to do with her situation. Nothing at all.

She was wrong.

Tick. Tick. Tick.

Chapter 47

Tricia felt good. Creighton knew that. Because he knew her like a daughter, like one for whom he would help in whatever way it mattered. And, for Creighton, helping always mattered.

He felt so good it was time, "Tricia? Your liquor cabinet?"

She pointed to the cabinet over her microwave.

He reached up to see what he wanted, "Ah, see you have my beverage. Time for sipping."

He reached for the Glenmorangie single malt, held the bottle up, "Tricia, it's like this…if no single malt in heaven…"

She smiled, "Yeah, you're not interested. Plus, I'm not looking to heaven, but I'm good for two fingers. Yes, time for sipping."

She looked at her cell phone and was getting anxious it was silent.

Creighton felt a two-fingered amount was good for each of them, added a splash, raised both glasses, "To you, Reverend, Fishing Guide, Detective…to you!"

He handed Tricia her glass, they clicked the glasses.

Tricia walked to the back porch. The weather, unseasonably calm and warm for October, made it nice. She brought her cell phone, laid it on the glass table.

Creighton knew she wanted to talk with the detective, but thought a healthy diversion would benefit, "Tricia, how's next Sunday's sermon look? Got something in mind?"

She said, "Yes. I even have the sermon title. I've always thought the sermon title should lay the groundwork, more than a title. Next Sunday it will be "Walked On Water Lately?"

He raised his glass, took a sip, beamed at Tricia, "I'm drinking to that!"

Glasses clicked again, "Will get to my idea in a minute…but I never asked you this. What was your favorite sermon title? You must have more than one."

He appreciated her question, "Nice. Sure, worked on the titles myself. Some come to mind, but the very best…when I was an executive minister and preached in every church my first year, I preached only one sermon…could fill in some details about the particular church's situation, but the title became my theme. I think it's worth a drum roll."

He nodded to Tricia, "Please?"

She tapped the glass table.

The sermon title I loved the best and preached the most goes like this, "The Poverty of Wealth."

"Whoa, preacher," Tricia exclaimed. "That's beyond good…in the best direction."

"Yes. It gave me a chance to talk about what's really important to God…and to them…has to do with what the members did with all their gifts…."

He didn't finish, but looked to Tricia, "But hey. This isn't about me. This is about you for next Sunday…so…tell me about walking on water."

Tricia spoke about how the scripture about Jesus being in the boat, lots of stormy weather. He looked up and saw Peter walking toward him, walking on the water. Peter looked at Jesus. But then he looked away at the water and how the wind frothed the water into large waves. Peter then sank. Tricia laughed when she told Creighton that she could make a case, when Peter sank, that was when Jesus called him the rock. Jesus then reached for Peter and brought him into the boat. Tricia then said she would end her sermon by saying that Peter sank but he didn't drown.

She then said to Creighton, "In many ways my dearest friend. I am not Peter…but at the deepest level I cannot deny that I am. No, I'm not walking on water. But I do feel that I'm sinking…sinking…sinking. I can only hope that I won't drown…or in the images coming to me and with me, especially in my heart, I hope I'm not heading over Snoqualmie Falls nor is a mud slide about to engulf me."

She reached for Creighton's hand, "Please know, Creighton, you are keeping me from drowning and you don't look like a mud slide advancing."

Her cell phone rang.

"Hello, Tricia? This is Detective Valentine. I'm sorry, but something has come up. I am not able to see you tonight. Maybe tomorrow."

Tricia made a decision, went and closed the back door, walked to the corner of the back porch, and said, "I can appreciate this. But, I need a couple of minutes…please record this conversation for quality assurance…I simply HAVE to tell you what I believe is going on. My wonderful friend, Creighton Yale, knows what I'm about to say…but, please let me tell you. It's crucial to me…."

She closed the call, "Thanks for listening, thanks for listening. I hope you'll follow up for me. Good night."

She walked back to the table, sat, took a deep breath, "Creighton? I hope he believes me; we need him to verify my theory. Yes, it won't make an identification, but it will be a huge step in the right direction. I absolutely believe you and I know what's going on."

Creighton asked, "You looked disturbed when you first answered the phone…something cause that?"

'Yes. He's always said he was Jordon. This time, though, it was formal, he said he was Detective Valentine. Like he'd never met me before. Like something was going on and he needed to create distance from me. Not a good introduction, but I'm sure I'm overreacting. I do believe he will follow-up and help me, because his department can…and should do that. Which hopefully means they will find the calligrapher. So. Yes, he came on formally. But I don't believe that is a problem."

Tricia had no idea, but would learn soon enough…she was wrong. It would be a problem…more than she ever imagined.

Tick. Tick. Tick.

Chapter 48

"Let me make the call, Tricia," Creighton said. "I know, nothing to really worry about, but honestly you cannot be too prepared. No one has to know, other than you and I and my friend. I hink it's prudent to cover that base."

Tricia didn't know how to answer. So she asked a question, "Creighton, to get an attorney? Isn't that being too defensive, almost an apology for something I may have done wrong. And I know. You know. Hannah knows. I did not kill Rider Samson, although through the night my mind raced that all this is connected, including the Rider homicide. Isn't getting an attorney a concession that I've done something wrong? I think it's too defensive."

"You may be right, Tricia; you may be right. But, let me say, my attorney buddy works for a major Seattle law firm. He does criminal defense work. One of the best. I don't think it's defensive. Nope, my take is to let me at least call him? That's being wise."

Tricia started to answer but was interrupted by a knock on her front door.

No one had called, although she hoped she would have heard from Jordon Valentine. She opened the door and almost fainted.

There were four uniforms on her front porch.

Jordon didn't smile. He looked all business. He handed an envelope to Tricia, "Reverend Gleason? I'm handing you a search warrant. Please let us in."

Life crumbled for Tricia as the four uniforms came in to her house. Creighton held her arm. Jordon pointed to the open door, "Please excuse yourself during our search."

Creighton felt Tricia would protest, so he said, "We'll leave immediately, officers."

They went out to the driveway and saw three police cars blocking Creighton's car. Some neighbors stood down the street. Tricia was aghast. Numb. Frozen in fright.

Creighton dialed his cell phone, waiting, "Yes, this is Creighton Yale, please connect me with Randy Linquist, he's expecting my call."

Tricia's eyes glazed and her mind pin-balled. Thoughts out of control. *A search warrant? Am I a suspect. Am I a person of interest. This HAS to do with Rider Samson's murder. It just has to. But I'm innocent. How can they do this? Why didn't Jordon give me a heads-up. What are they searching for?*

"Tricia? Are you all right?"

She looked up. It was Abby. Abby opened her arms. Tricia almost collapsed.

Creighton looked at her, "Hello. My name is Creighton Yale; I'm Tricia's pastor. I don't know what this is about either. Tricia is in shock. This a horrible situation. We don't know the why for this. I'm sorry we cannot say anything."

Abby stepped back, "Oh my goodness. Tricia, I'm sure there's a terrible mistake. Please let me know how Andrew and I can be of help. I'll head back home. I'm going to call Andrew right now and ask him to come back from his office. We want to be helpful. In whatever way that can happen. I'm so sorry for this," as she waved to the police cars, I'm so sorry. You can count on us for whatever's going on. Do let me know. I'll be at home and I'll see if Andrew can get back.

Tricia hadn't picked up on Creighton's call. He wasn't holding his cell phone.

He spoke, "Tricia, that was a call to your new attorney, Randy Linquist. He's in a meeting right now but will call back shortly…"

Creighton looked up as the four uniforms walked out of Tricia's house. One of them was holding two large bags. She couldn't make out the contents.

Jordon walked right by her, not even a glance. One of the other uniforms said, "We're finished and we'll be in touch with you. Have a nice day."

Creighton cringed and wanted to ask him what part of *up yours* needs to be explained. But, somehow he tampered down his rage and said with nothing but feigned toning, "Thanks, officers; we'll wait for your call."

He even waved, although he thought a middle finger salute would be more honest.

His phone rang, "Creighton Yale. Oh, hello, Randy, thanks for calling back…"

Creighton explained the situation and then said "We'll be right there."

He said to Tricia, "We're headed to Randy's office, please get in the car…I'll close up the house. Randy will be waiting for us."

Tricia never heard the clucking, but it was there. For the calligrapher heard the police…just as he had hoped. He had planted the revolver where she would never find it but knew the police would…and his cleverness was better than impressive in planting the lubricating jelly tube in her upper-right office dresser drawer. Ah, the seeds couldn't have been better planted in his note to the police captain. Such genius. And he knew. Revenge was his. He looked in the mirror and saw the most beautiful face in the world…his. He winked and then smiled and affirmed himself, "YES". He turned his neck and saw the scratch had almost healed. No problem. Only success. He should buy himself a trophy. Sweet!

Tick. Tick. Tick.

Chapter 49

"Tricia, I cannot tell you to relax. So I won't. But, we don't know what the search warrant was about. But we do know you absolutely need to have legal counsel. Randy is better than the best. He really is, has been a criminal defense attorney for twenty years."

"Creighton, I now realize you are right…to get me legal counsel. But honestly, there's no way I can afford someone like that…in a huge law firm? Way above my pay grade."

"Don't worry about it, Tricia. This will work out. Randy's one of those attorneys who knows how to spell pro bono. But he and I have a very reciprocating relationship. I don't know how else to describe it. Almost thirty years ago Randy and his brother Reggie were in my church youth group. They went swimming and Reggie drowned. It was worse than horrible. I was able to help Randy and his family. We bonded. Somehow that happens in the worst tragedy. Since then Randy has sent some of his clients to me…the ones who believe God is really pissed at them and that's why trouble haunts them…and now, Randy understands. There's nothing he won't do to help you…

and in turn, help me. So, don't relax because you won't. But, do trust me. This is the best next-step. He will be the best for you. I know it.

Tricia heard most of what Creighton said, but it all sounded positive. She needed the positive. She reached into her pocket. The yarn was always there. She clutched it and whispered to herself, "God, please don't leave me."

"Pardon me, Tricia? Did you say something?"

"Yes, I did," as she held up the piece of yarn…don't want to let this go…and I hoped that God wouldn't consider me a stranger."

"Ah, don't ever go there. To unfriend you? Never. I won't give permission for that…because as you've learned about me long ago…I am not a scribe; I am one with authority."

He parked in the law firm's lot. He and Tricia took the elevator to the lobby floor.

The elevator door opened.

"Ah, Randy. So good of you to meet with us!"

They hugged.

Creighton turned to Tricia, "Tricia this is your new friend. Randy Linquist. Treat him well."

Tricia liked Randy Linquist already. His handshake was warm and firm. His eyes connected. They said to Tricia, "I am grateful to meet you. Let's go up to my office and visit. I'll do whatever I can to help. But first. I need to listen."

Tricia felt better, much better. Randy was calm, certainly non-anxious. A great first step.

His office, what a view of Lake Union and the space needle and looking west, for Randy had a corner office, the range of mountains, some snow already in place.

He asked them if they wanted any refreshments. They declined. They then sat at a round table. Tricia liked him even more because he didn't sit behind a large oak desk. It impressed her he was not into power and control; rather he wanted to learn and then to support.

Randy said to Creighton, "The hour's yours, you two. And Creighton, I have never forgotten your primary key to relating. For I understand your mantra when communicating, that I should keep the ratio of two ears and one mouth."

A good start. A very good start.

Tricia reached into her pocket, touched the yarn and whispered, from her heart, "Thanks."

Chapter 50

Tricia explained. Randy took notes but had advised that this session wouldn't be recorded, "Let's just go where you lead us, Tricia. You are our starting point…and I'll be Velcro and not Teflon to make sure you're in the best you can be."

After filling Randy in Tricia looked at her watch, "Oops, most of my sermons never reach fifteen minutes…cannot believe it…I gave you three sermons worth."

Randy laid his pencil down and smiled, "I never fell asleep, so I had insomnia—which I don't—you wouldn't have cured it."

Creighton said, "Okay, Randy, what do you recommend?"

Randy answered, "Nothing," and smiled. "Let me explain. Especially for you, Tricia, you really don't have to do a thing, at least in one area. That is, do not talk with anyone about our meeting or about any of the content you mentioned. For sure don't talk to the detective. If you are asked to come in for questioning, do not agree to that. Call me and demand that I be present. That's crucial. Silence will be virtuous and only to your benefit."

Randy looked at his notepad, "While you were speaking I wrote down some next steps that I think we should consider. Let me list them. I will then Xerox a copy for each of you…kind of a to-do-list…some for me and some for you. Plus, don't let me forget," as he reached to his desk and grabbed a business card, "here's my card with both my office and cell numbers…no hour is a bad hour to call…just consider me your 25/7 counselor…the extra hour is my bonus contribution."

He held the list. Tricia noticed the sheet was still, not shaking. A firm grip. She felt the vibes of confidence and competence, a great combination.

Randy listed his agenda: Not necessarily in order, "Make sure your moderator knows only the skeletal reality of your home being searched. Unless we hear something from Detective Valentine or someone in their office, we don't know what they went for in your house. You mentioned they carried out two bags but couldn't tell the contents. So, to say you don't know is all you have to say. They certainly have not said you, Tricia, are a person of interest. So, until that might be…it isn't the case. I more than hope you're okay to preach next Sunday…carry on as if nothing has happened."

He raised his hand for caution, "Okay, I know…that's perhaps not likely, because some things have happened. But, preach as a preacher and give them hell. Well, not right. Give them heaven. Oh, why should I even comment. Simply preach, Reverend."

Tricia said, "I remember a clergy buddy," as she glanced to Creighton, "who once said the preacher's job is to preach as if you have nothing better to do. I'm pretty sure I can do that. In fact, Randy, I promise both you and Creighton I will…next Sunday. I agree on our visiting with Sage…and I say our and not I…because I think it's only good and helpful for Creighton to be with me for that. In fact, we'll try to see her yet today."

She nodded to Randy, "Thanks, Tricia, glad to hear your spirit. Because what I sense is you can preach very well…and I also believe you are innocent of any culpability in this situation.

"Okay, back to my list. Let me tell you, assuming you are a person of interest, and given the full narrative I cannot imagine you wouldn't be, here's what I want to do. First, I will call Detective Valentine and tell him I am your counsel. I've never met him but I do know the captain. He's a good guy and will be fair. That's helpful. I will also ask Detective Valentine for all the, as you describe them, the "love notes." We have a great handwriting expert who can analyze the notes. Amazing what they can tell. With me so far?"

They nodded. Actually Tricia sighed, clasped her hands together, "Yes, please continue."

"Next. I think you're right on target with the how of this, namely how the notes were sparked. Well, maybe not the condom package, although I do think that was part of the entire mess you've had dumped on you. I will check with the North Bend Safeway. I want to make sure I have the date and time, Tricia, you were there—and see if they have security video. Maybe that will show us who put the condom package in your shopping cart. Won't hurt to try.

"It is clear, though, almost everything else happened when something critical was revealed to you either in your home office or your church office. That was keen of you to say when you and Sage and Melita reconciled it was at the outdoor picnic table at the church. What I will do, and this can be done without anyone knowing, is I will check out both offices to see if your hunch is spot on. But, I won't advise anything be done about that. I will tell you why if necessary."

Tricia knew exactly what Randy was suggesting, for as a homicide detective for the Oregon State Police she had a similar situation…and not doing anything ended up being everything. She knew for sure she and Randy were on the same page.

"A couple other things. I know the medical examiner, thinking because it was a homicide, the head woman will have done the autopsy. I have a couple of questions for her. She's almost always very thorough, although we did have one case where we asked about a particular part of the body and she indicated they had not checked there. So, let me see what I can learn. Often the autopsy brings new information and bam, the right killer."

He stopped to go over his list, looked up, "For starters, that's what I have. Any questions?"

Tricia said, "Randy, I have no questions. But I want you to know that I can spell the word…let me show you….g….r…a…t….i…t…u…d…e"

Randy looked at Creighton, "Hey, she's good. We'll be in great shape. You got anything, Creighton?"

"No, Randy. But I share Tricia's appreciation. As you can tell she's very perceptive. Guess we be on our way."

Randy stood, took Tricia's hands and held them. "Preach well, Tricia. Glad you mentioned what your sermon will be…and as it applies for you…yes, I can appreciate you feel like you're sinking…and I appreciate the image of Snoqualmie Falls and the mud slide. But know, you can be like Peter…he sank…and you feel you are, too—but he didn't drown. And I'll do everything in my power to make sure you don't either. Keep me updated…and I'll do the same."

He turned to look at his desk and saw the light flashing on his phone, "Oops, gotta get that. Take care."

They walked into the elevator and went down the twenty floors. Tricia dabbled her eyes.

Creighton picked up on that, "Hey, there. Why so sad?"

"Come on, Creighton…tears happen because of sadness or grief. But they can also happen because of joy. I'm feeling the latter and the former is staying away…at least for now."

Chapter 51

"You know? It's crazy, absolutely crazy. Here I live in Issaquah and I've never been here. A neighbor once told me they make killer Swedish pancakes…oops, bad wording…sorry. They make great pancakes, so I'm going to check that out."

Tricia could believe Sage, as she and Creighton sat across the Issaquah Café table from Sage. Tricia confirmed, "Well, Sage, I've been here twice and I will give them a 5-star."

Creighton chipped in, 'That sounds great. But. What's your scale? Someone once told me I was a ten, I felt good…until he told me his scale was one to one hundred. Ah, that minister, he was into self-elevation. In fact, once some clergy buddies got together for a picnic. No one thought to bring some, what I would call hearty beverages. This better than good minister—just ask him and he'd agree—stood up, held up a glass of water and asked, 'red or white?' But, enough of the banter," as the waitress inquired of their order.

Tricia was disappointed Melanie wasn't working. The waiter, though, looked at Tricia, "Pardon me, ma'am, but aren't you the minister?"

The Lemon Drop Didn't Melt

Tricia was puzzled, "Well, yes. I'm not wearing a clergy collar. Does it show somehow? That I'm a minister?"

The waiter smiled, "No, I don't think so. But, and I probably should mute this but I won't. You are Melanie's favorite customer. She has bragged on you both times you were here. She doesn't brag very often, but she said you're well above a ten…and her scale's a one to five. Don't want to put any pressure on you. Oh. Forgot to tell you, as he pointed to his nametag, my name's Pistol, I haven't changed nametags with anyone."

Creighton laughed, "Pistol? A baptized name…or the manner of living?"

Pistol smiled, "Ah, given to me by an older brother…he thought I was small but effective. I think that's what he said. Okay, let me do what I'm supposed to do…please let me know which of our Swedish pancakes I can get for you…with or without blueberries?"

Tricia liked him, although the name didn't help. Not because of what they needed to discuss. She was pleased Sage could meet them. It was not only Randy's suggestion, but she felt she needed to bring Sage up to speed.

Sage said, "Well, I wish he had another name, but he seems nice enough, right?"

She was smiling, which was helpful, for Creighton needed to know where and how Sage was.

Tricia and Creighton brought Sage into the situation. They had agreed that Sage would find out the details sooner or later, and for them to remove any uncertainty, that was a way of bringing Sage into their trust.

When they completed their summary, Tricia asked, "I'm sure you have questions, Sage. Please let us know. But before you ask that, for me, and I don't want to leave this out, it's more than important, if you will, what do you think should be said this Sunday during worship?"

Before Sage could answer, Pistol showed up with their order.

Sage reached for the syrup, "Tricia, of course, that's the key question. I will answer, because I have an idea. But it's important we are not on different pages."

Tricia looked at Creighton for his response, a habit she never regretted, for his response, given his experience and wisdom. To Tricia, Creighton was more dependable than anything, "Sounds okay to me. Why don't we enjoy the pancakes, then deal with my question?"

Creighton gave no expression, but took a bite of his pancakes. Tricia considered that his response…eat and then visit.

As she ate, Tricia's mind went to and fro. Something she hadn't talked about with Randy popped up. They hadn't discussed what triggered the search warrant. It had to be the calligrapher, it just had to be. For nothing that was bad happened that he didn't orchestrate. She's had to explore that later…hopefully Randy could help on that.

Sage laid her fork down, rubbed her stomach, "My stomach and I thank you, Tricia. This is the first time for me here, but it won't be the last."

She paused, "Now, to your question. First, I want to thank you both for bringing me into the loop. I sense your style of leadership is helpful."

"Style of leadership?" Creighton asked.

"Yes, one of our previous ministers, who will be left as Reverend Anonymous, because we hardly knew him, once said to me he considered there were two kinds of ministers...those who were democratic and those who were effective. He was the latter, hardly ever clued us in with his ideas before he presented them formally to our council. We had no idea where he was in his vision for our church. And you know the saying, without a vision the people perish. Well, he didn't last.

"Let me put it this way. As a congregation when it comes to numbers were aren't big at all. But, when it comes to loyalty and energy and love for one another, we are huge. All of which is to say, and I more than want you both to speak to this, I think we should somehow be democratic...without, of course, divulging too much. Because we don't want to hurt your case, Tricia. And, for one, oh, more than one, let me say I trust you. I do believe the search on your house didn't just happen. Certainly you are a person of interest. But, look. So is Courtney, and who's to say Rider didn't tick off one of his former clients. So, let's not keep this cloaked in secrecy. The problem is, I honestly don't know how Sunday morning should be handled. For that will be key."

Creighton smiled, "I appreciate that we should cast Tricia as the direct shadow to Reverend Anonymous. But, on the other hand, and let's face it, Tricia is not out of trouble yet. We don't know what was taken from her house. I go with the search had a prompter. I go with none of the *love notes* were coincidental. But, let's face it. All this could explode on us. It could."

Tricia said, "Sage. I'm not for shrouding everything in secret. And now, I'm not into full disclosure. Yet, at this point I'm not arrested. Yes, there was a search of my house. And yes, I believe, no matter how trustworthy each of us is…most of this will already be part of our members' vocabulary. And what is worse? Rumors? Or rumors?"

"I have an idea," Sage offered. "Tricia, you impress me as being well organized. Which means I cannot imagine you don't have your sermon in mind, maybe even the main points. Mind sharing a preview of your sermon? Reason I ask is my idea…let me share it now. I think we experience worship as if nothing's wrong. For sure, and I cannot imagine, Creighton, you haven't counseled Tricia on this. Tricia? You are innocent. Don't act otherwise.

"Anyway, here's my thought…regular worship, an inspiration sermon, because although I missed one, the word with members is you are an excellent preacher. Finish the worship, except for the benediction and closing hymn. Then turn the service to me and let me speak to the congregation…not to deny we don't have a difficult situation, but to let them know I believe in you and ask the congregation if they have any questions."

Creighton looked at Tricia, "Tricia? What do you think? I think it makes sense. Certainly at the end of worship, because first of all in any situation we should focus upon God and not turn the worship into a business meeting. On the other hand, to say nothing about the difficulties, well, we'd become anonymous ostriches."

Tricia wasn't sure what should be done. However, deep inside? She trusted Sage. She knew Sage was in her corner. She had Creighton with her, no matter what. And she didn't want to be silent about her situation, especially with the congregation.

She had an idea, "Sage, I believe your game plan is better than anything I could come up with. However, will you do me a favor? Would you call our attorney—I will give you his number—and see what he thinks. He might even give you the topics that can be included and those that shouldn't be. Would you do that?

"Oh, one more thing. Our attorney said, and consider this in the what if category. If the revolver is found...and Randy doubts it will be...but if the revolver is found, a ballistics test seeing if the bullets that killed Rider Samson came from the discovered revolver...that takes at least four weeks. So, worst case scenario? If I'm somehow brought into that, it's not that I would be charged immediately, particularly not by next Sunday. So, all things considered, nothing should happen soon."

Creighton wasn't happy, "Tricia, I'm sorry. But why even mention the revolver? Do you know something we don't? That doesn't sound like the voice of innocence."

"Creighton?" she said. "No I am not guilty. But once you told me... and I know it is said by many when difficulties lurk, hope for the best and prepare for the worst. Just trying to think of the worst that can happen. That worst is unfortunately not something we can forget about. It may be I will be more than a person of interest."

Sage said, "Yes, Tricia. You can shift from a person of interest. But how about this? Instead of shifting as a person of interest to a person charged with Rider Samson's homicide? How about the shift be to a person of exoneration?"

Creighton raised his glass of water, "Ladies? What will it be? Red…or…white?"

Creighton picked up the tab as they got up, "My treat. That is non-negotiable."

Sage said, "Creighton? Thanks for the super Swedish pancakes. Even more, thanks for being here. Best medicine in the world for Tricia."

Tricia agreed, "Yes, Sage, that's right. But you are part of that now. Please let me know if there are other recommendations for Sunday during or after worship. I hope you can reach my attorney…"

"I will. He's got a great reputation. I'm positive he'll help us outline what I should say."

Sage waved and headed to her car.

As she and Creighton walked to his car she had an empty spot in her stomach. It was an emotional emptiness. Because she remembered a previous time when going to her car after a meal at the Issaquah Café. She saw Creighton's car…and it was not leaning to one side. She breathed more easily that no tires were slashed.

She was also breathing easier because of the visit with Sage. That was good. Sage could be trusted. With that the positive vibe they were in a restaurant and not in her office. She'd look forward to hearing from Randy if her theory of cause and effect was correct.

Chapter 52

"Hey, Tricia. It's Saturday night. Since you've indicated you're in good shape with your sermon for tomorrow, I thought you could tell me about your fishing trip. Sounds like it was more catching than fishing…and the way in which your new guide, Jon and his wife, work with…no, make that care for the Wounded Warriors. How impressive."

Tricia was only too pleased to talk about something positive, with no snags. In fact, losing the chum salmon was a plus; that monster fish needed to be released anyway.

"Yes, Creighton, it was a positive time, all around. Even when seeing the mud slide…I had no earthly idea the scope of the slide but some did survive. Still, a tragic event and I think about it…because for now, some of what I'm facing…it's as if the slide is oozing its way to me. But, to fishing…"

Her cell phone rang, saw it was Sage, "Hi, Sage."

"Hi, Tricia, hope it's not too late..don't want to interrupt your sermon thought."

"No, not a problem. Creighton and I were about to discuss fishing."

"Obviously," Sage, said, "that's a great topic. I wanted to update you. I just had an executive committee meeting. I had forgotten to tell you that I didn't want to have tomorrow happen and have none of our committee be uninformed…"

Tricia's heart sank, fearing the worst. She said nothing.

"You can relax, Tricia. Our committee, the five of us, are in full agreement. Well, consider that four-fifths in agreement. But, then never believe that unanimity happens, especially in our situation. The only person who is hesitant…he's not a surprise. In fact, he will be in church tomorrow for the first time. Don't think you've met him because he couldn't attend when our executive committee met with you for the first interview."

Tricia remembered his name, "Is that Connor Wright? I can remember that name, for I knew a Connor a long time ago."

"Yes," Sage answered. Connor is the one who had some questions if…well, to put it directly…you should continue serving us with the cloud of Rider Samson's murder hovering. You probably don't know that he and Rider were best friends and would go hunting together. So, the tragedy of Rider's death is tough for Connor. I want to tell you that he is fully aware of your background and he knows of your work with the Oregon State Police, as a fishing guide, the whole deal. He pointed out with appreciation that you did help solve the murders when you were guiding on Tillamook Bay, and the murder

The Lemon Drop Didn't Melt

in the Congregational Church in Palo Alto, and most recently, the two murders in Colorado. He wondered if that reality is what came with you…murders. He then said that if you hadn't come to Snoqualmie, he believed his buddy wouldn't have been murdered."

Tricia asked, "Oh my, what did you say to him?"

"Well, you'll be pleased to know I didn't need to say a word. In fact, you might not know this, but Rachel Fish is probably your best supporter. As you know, she's currently a principal at our high school. She took the same information, completely rejected Connor's theory that you being here caused Rider's murder and said, these are her words, 'Connor? You need to get to the half-full side of this. We don't know who murdered Rider. Of course it's the most horrible tragedy. But the half-full approach is Tricia has the abilities to help solve this homicide. I don't believe she has the ability to commit such a heinous crime.'"

"Wow, Sage. How could you remember all that?"

"Tricia, that's not verbatim but it's close enough. It ended our conversation. We didn't have a vote, but the consensus is I should speak before worship ends tomorrow. They'll all be there and will be, as Rachel described a *quintet to support our pastor.* Simply wanted you to know. So, Tricia, you be about preaching and I'll be about supporting."

"Oh my, Sage," Tricia replied, "A great way to end my evening. See you tomorrow."

Tricia looked at Creighton, raised her glass of water, "That was Sage, let me tell you the good news. But, before I do that," tipping her glass in his direction, "I prefer chardonnay, so that's what this has now become."

They clicked glasses, "Well, Reverend, I like your attitude. Good for you. No, more, good for all of us."

Tricia sipped the water, no chardonnay flavor whatsoever.

Her phoned clicked again, she didn't recognize the number, decided to answer it, "Hello, Tricia Gleason."

"Okay, Tricia, I realize it's late. This is your favorite attorney…at least most recently."

"Oh hi, Randy, something wrong?"

"No, I don't think so. But I want you to know one of my staff, she does all the heavy-lifting for research and discovery in our law firm. She was able to meet with the manager of the North Bend Safeway. He said they did have a security tape for the day you were in and he'd give it to us. I'm getting it tomorrow, so maybe Monday morning we can review it. May show nothing…but at least we have the tape. That's a good thing. Don't know if the leading actor will make an appearance. But, we'll have to see.

"I also want you to know I had a fine conversation with your moderator. She has a fine reputation in Seattle in our Bar Association. She and I agreed that tomorrow she will head the informal church meeting and will only deal with generalities. Thanks for having her call me."

"Oh, thanks to you, Randy, for this update. Creighton's staying next week, and I know he'll be pleased to be my chauffeur to your office Monday morning…would 9 a.m. be okay?"

"Sorry, but how about 10:30 a.m."

"It's a date, Randy…have a good day tomorrow."

She told Creighton and he said, "Sounds good. Only one problem. I left my chauffeur hat in Beaverton. That all right?"

They laughed.

Tricia felt better…the day had been good. She would hope tomorrow would be better. She hoped speaking in generalities would be acceptable to the congregation, even to Connor. The breathing came easily to Tricia. It had been a while. She prayed in gratitude for feeling better and that the new day would be good.

She loved the easy breathing.

What she didn't know. Her breathing would almost stop, sooner than she'd ever anticipate. It would not be a surprise she welcomed. It could turn everything.

She slept well and got up to live the new day.

For the time being.

Tick. Tick. Tick.

Chapter 53

Conner Wright jumped to his feet and pointed at Tricia, "Sage? I've listened to you," as his arm swept the room, "we all have. I even listened to the sermon."

He wiped his mouth, pointed to Tricia, "But, Reverend Gleason I don't believe you are from Kansas and I know your name's not Dorothy. This is a serious situation. I know the police went into your house yesterday. And I know...."

He clutched his chest and then doubled his fist, "I know my best friend, Rider Samson, was shot down in the front seat of his car. I wasn't here in worship when he stomped out letting you know how unwelcomed you are."

Sage walked toward Wright, he pushed her back, "Now, it's my turn. You have given us generalities. We are talking about murder here and that shouldn't be as if nothing has happened. We have a minister who is at least a person of interest. Why would the police get a search warrant? I'm more than sure," irony dripping, "they weren't looking

The Lemon Drop Didn't Melt

for sermons. No, they wouldn't have gone into your house, Reverend Gleason, if they didn't think you had something related to the murder.

"Rider had talked to me about his visit with you in his home. Such a disgrace of you, to choose seduction as a persuasive tool…"

The congregation gasped. Tricia was trapped, at least emotionally. She didn't want to say a thing, because that would be gasoline to his fire, no matter how correct she was. No, she thought, his name is Wright and that could be spelled without the w. At least as he saw it. It was Wright and not Wrong.

Tricia could see the congregation was shocked at the word *seduction*.

He wasn't through, "I will not simply smile and clap. You know what I think? I think we're not Peter. I think we are sinking and I do not believe as a church we won't drown. We won't! This is a mess, Sage. No matter what you try to say…hey, I am on the executive council. And yes, we did meet last night and yes I did go along with your plan. But, I'm festering inside…a horrible sense that to move on, to simply say something will work out…is in denial…naïve denial. I change my vote. I do not believe we can simply maintain that all is well and we should simply move along as if nothing has happened. There is no yellow brick road in sight…and there won't be. This is a mess. Yes, I repeat myself, but I can say it a thousand more times. Rider Samson is dead. No one's been arrested, but face reality folks, the police didn't get a search warrant for our pastor's house without the possibility she's more than a person of interest. I've had it and I think you, you, you, "as he pointed to many gathered, "should walk with me. I'm not gonna think we can function with a possible murderer for a pastor. No!"

He stomped out.

Sage took a deep breath, was relieved no one jumped up to speak or follow Connor. She had been in fiery court battles when shouting for control happened. She knew. She knew that to be above calm would be imprudent. She waited for the murmuring to stop. It did.

"Friends? Connor has obviously revealed his feelings. I regret what he said. I also regret we have a very difficult situation. I cannot go into details of what is being done now to clarify the situation. What I can tell you, I think it is important now. I am in constant contact with Tricia and her mentor, Creighton Yale, is here. We also have some legal counsel, because it is only sensible that Tricia be supported.

"I hold with what I said," as she picked up the hymn book, opened to the closing hymn page, and ask, because we are a Christian community and we are covenanted to be together, if you will stand and we'll ask you, Tricia, to deliver the benediction and sing together the closing hymn, it is a hymn about faith and how loving mercy comes from God."

Tricia stood, could hardly put three words together. Before she spoke she saw a handful of people leave. Dreadful. Still, she simply said, "May God be with us. Amen."

The congregation barely repeated their *Amen* and Tricia, so everything didn't fall completely apart, said, "Let's sing the first and last stanzas."

The piano was louder than the singing. That had never happened before. But it was also true, Tricia never thought the church would explode. Which pushed her to the possibility she should resign. Maybe that would be better for the congregation…and for her.

Her only hope was they'd not be in the same position next Sunday. And she hoped there wouldn't be a congregational meeting to fire her. She had some time on that, for a specially called congregational meeting required one month's notice, so nothing rash would happen.

The people left, all except Sage and Creighton and the Gladstone family. Abby said to Tricia, "Tricia, we are so sorry. So very sorry. We do not support Connor. We are saddened about this horrible murder. We cannot even imagine how difficult this is for you. Please, Tricia, don't give up. We don't believe for a minute our church…or you…will drown. Let us know how we can help."

They each hugged her, Cynthy turned as they left, "I hope the yarn helps."

It did. More than ever.

But she didn't know if the yarn could be a life preserver.

Chapter 54

A tap at the door, barely audible. Creighton saw children on the front porch, had a hunch who they were…the ones Tricia anointed her royalty, two kings and a queen.

"Oh, how special for you to be here! I'm sorry, but your favorite minister left for a little bit."

Creighton saw the cupcakes, each held high by the baker…make that bakers. He saw their parents walking up to the porch, "Wow, your cupcakes. I bet you each made them, right?"

They beamed and said in chorus, "Yes, for our pastor!"

Abby and Andrew joined in, "We wanted to tell Tricia that our gifts are a small measure of lots and lots of love for her. She's wonderful!"

"Wow, how gracious, how wonderful. I'll tell her. She's taking some time to be on her favorite hill, wanting to reflect. She speaks so fondly of you…and of the ways you care for her. She also loves the valley and the river and the mountain, I forget its name."

Scooter said, "I know! It's Mount Si…the highest we see here. Although my parents said there are higher mountains in Washington."

Creighton replied, "Thank you, young man. I wish Tricia were here. She will be delighted to return to some great cupcakes. That will make her day."

Scooter had another thought, "Oh, I know where she is. I've seen her there before."

Abby was curious, "Scooter, you know where she is? Where and when did you see her before?"

He pointed around the corner, "It's up that path to the top of the hill. There's a nice bench there. I saw Pastor Tricia sitting on it. I didn't want to bother her. I was on my way to the swings."

"You were?" Andrew asked. "Do you remember when that was?"

"Yeah, we didn't have school…forget the day…we didn't have school that's all I remember. And, don't want to forget, saw Pastor Tricia sitting there. She was there when I went to the playground…and when I walked back home, I remember she was still there. Like I said I didn't want to bother her, so I didn't go up the path."

Abby said, "Thanks for sharing, Scooter. Hey, guys, let's get going. We've brought love. That is important."

Creighton agreed, "Absolutely important. The most important to Pastor Tricia. I will be sure to tell her and she will love the cupcakes. Oh, can I ask a little question?"

The chorus was in good voice, "Sure!"

"Do you think it's okay if I have one of the cupcakes?"

"Yes!" the chorus answered.

Creighton closed the door and would be sure to give the cupcakes to Tricia. She would be pleased, a very helpful shift from the haranguing of the morning…a very helpful shift.

Chapter 55

Football was a nice diversion. Both Creighton and Tricia loved the Denver Broncos. However, Snoqualmie was Seattle Seahawks fiefdom. Tricia smiled, as they listened to the Seattle ESPN station, as the sportscaster went on and on about the Beast Mode guy. That would be the Seahawks Marshawn Lynch, who had been injured. They said that was the reason Carolina beat the Seahawks yesterday… and of all things it was in Seattle. Was the first home league loss for Seattle in a long time.

The ESPN diversion didn't last long, as Creighton and Tricia found themselves muddled in traffic heading west on I-90. Tricia insisted on driving and wanted to talk about her situation. She turned the radio off, "Creighton I'm nervous to look at the Safeway security tape."

He nodded, "I think I know why, but go ahead, I don't want to interrupt."

"Well, all of this happening…and you know the list that goes from a box of condoms to the murder of Rider Samson, is not only related. It has to be someone who knows me. It has to be. So. What if the tape shows the person who put the condoms in my shopping cart? What if I know him?"

"Come on, Tricia. That's a good thing…because we then know the foe…and to know the foe can only bring good news."

She wondered, "Good news? I think it could bring bad news because this guy's really clever. And if we identify him and he knows it, it could end up, excuse the phrase, being murderous."

"Tricia! I don't know if there's medicine for you…but I would give almost anything if there was an anti-paranoia pill. Anything."

Tricia tapped the steering wheel, "Okay, point measured and made. So, let's not jump to anything until we get to Randy's office. Instead, although you explained last night, tell me again about the cupcake visitors."

He smiled, "Ah, one of your gifts…to give people a new name. *Cupcake visitors.* That's good. This is what happened."

Tricia knew the importance of the visit from the great neighbors, "Creighton," she padded her chest with her right hand, "Creighton Yale? Did you say that Scooter saw me? Because I was sitting on my now favorite hill…and it was the morning that Rider was murdered. I didn't think I had an excuse…but Scooter's my get-out-of-prison card."

"How so?" Creighton asked.

Tricia smiled, "Because I didn't think I had an alibi for when the murder happened. Of course. I didn't do it. But if I couldn't account for where I was…I'm dead…and that's not so to speak."

"Tricia Gleason...great of you to make the connection. But, I wonder, if a seven-year-old boy could be reliable?"

Tricia spoke forcefully, "Of course he's reliable. After all, he did make me a fishing rod, reel and line. And he wouldn't make it up. In fact, remember the conversation yesterday you had with them...and I bet his parents...their names are Andrew and Abby? I bet they can recall, subject and verb of every sentence. In fact, without divulging any particulars, make sure to call them after we visit with Randy... and let's tell Randy...simply covering our bases."

Creighton looked up and pointed, "There's the garage, let's park and go to the cinema."

Chapter 56

They sat down in Randy's office.

He began, "I have what I think is good news. I want to start with that…although you might consider it much less than good. In any account, my gratitude. For letting my investigators be in your home yesterday morning—please forgive them for not being in church—and then yesterday afternoon in your church office. You get a perfect score, Tricia. You are right."

Tricia smiled, "I am really happy to hear this. It only made sense when I linked the notes with what preceded them…the calligrapher had to have awareness of what was said. No other way that could happen. I don't believe I'm dealing with a conspiracy of many; it's a conspiracy of one.…so, both my offices are bugged. Did you remove them?"

Before Randy could answer, Creighton raised his hand, "Oh, Randy! I hope you left them. You didn't take them out, did you?"

Randy pointed to Creighton, "How perceptive. Ever been to a police academy? I had mentioned something about that in our first meeting…that if there were secret bugs we should not remove them."

"I understand, Randy," Tricia said. "We don't want this guy—and I'm assuming it's a guy—to know we are on to him. Good, they are not removed. We can now be careful what we say…and I won't have anyone share intimate confidences in either office."

Randy raised his eyebrows, "Well, Tricia, we need to discuss that. You are right—don't you have serious, confidential conversations with anyone. But, on the other hand, we might be screenplay writers. We'll hold that card for now."

Tricia thought something she hadn't raised before, "Randy, can you—oh I know you can so why ask—I think there's a GPS on my car, that the murderer knows not only what I say in my offices but also knows where I'm headed. Why else would my tires be slashed when I met Hannah at the Issaquah Café? Would you check that?"

"Well, I didn't ask your permission, Tricia. I guess this is simply assuming you won't mind…checking out your car is happening right now. And. If we find a GPS we'll do nothing with it. I call it the pattern of neglect…all with a purpose."

Creighton said, "Tricia, this makes all the sense in the world…heinous sense…but still, sense. That can explain the plumbing truck in front of your house…because, hey, very clear, it doesn't take thirty minutes to put a note on your home office desk. And the bugging of your church office? That happened the time when the U R NXT note was put on your pulpit. Happened before Melita showed up that morning. Making sense. But now…."

Randy nodded, "Yes, it's time to look at the security tape...I've looked at it...some of my colleagues have looked at it. And there is someone we have seen who's dropping something in your shopping cart, Tricia. So," as he pointed to his video equipment, "show time!"

Tricia wanted to see the tape. But she didn't. The tossing and turning had to do with some fear what she would see. And yet, Creighton had told her this could break the case wide open. Why wouldn't she want that? She wasn't sure either, but inside she was empty...a sense of worry and anxiety that mounted.

The tape began, "There," said Randy, as he stopped the tape.

They could see. A bearded man putting what obviously to Tricia was a box of condoms. She remembered leaving the cart. *Was I away from the cart that long?*

But she couldn't see his face, only the scraggly beard. She could only see him from the side and his image wasn't clear enough to identify.

Randy said, "We cannot make a bigger image. This guy's clever, he probably knows where the cameras are...and we've looked at the previous thirty minutes and the same amount of time after you left, Tricia. He doesn't appear again. Only this moment...we can call it *the drop*. No one else has this guy—let's call him the Calligrapher—put something in their cart. So, that's all we have. I guess it isn't much."

She didn't recognize the guy, didn't know anyone with that kind of beard. Sure, she felt, he could have grown the beard...or it could be fake. She couldn't tell. Had never seen him before. Never.

The Lemon Drop Didn't Melt

Still, she asked, "Can we go through the sequence again…when he approaches to when he leaves my cart?"

They did. Tricia couldn't figure out anything.

The third time she watched it. And focused not on his beard or his long hair. Then it hit her. Like a smash in the face. As if she couldn't breathe. Choked with what she saw. Worse than that…a grip on her throat. *This cannot be.* Her thoughts were overwhelming her. *Impossible.*

She about fainted and barely whispered, "Is there water I could have?"

She reached for the glass of water Randy handed her. As she grabbed the glass, looked back to the video screen, she dropped the glass. It shattered on the floor.

Tricia fainted, a collapsed heap in her chair. She then crumbled to the floor before either Randy or Creighton could reach her.

She fainted. From shock. From an awareness that she thought impossible. Yet. It wasn't the beard or the hair. It was…

Tick. Tick. Tick.

Chapter 57

"Tricia, you okay?" Randy asked, as he used a wash cloth on her brow.

She looked around…at first it was like being in a deep sleep, suddenly awake and having no idea where she was or what was happening. She looked at Randy and Creighton, then it all came back to her…*the most horrific* was all she could think of.

"Yeah, I think I'm okay. Guess I checked out…not the best of manners, right?"

Creighton put his hand on her shoulder, "Tricia, you did faint. Weren't out for very long. But both Randy and I were worried. Everything seemed to crash down on you…something you saw. You were looking at the guy who put the condom box in your cart. You looked and looked and said, you had never seen him before. Then you closed your mouth, your eyes got bigger than saucers, you pointed and your eyes rolled up. That was it. We didn't catch you before you fell from your chair. Do you remember all that?"

She nodded quietly, "It was his, Creighton. It was his."

Creighton had no idea, "I'm sorry. You say it was his? Help us with that."

She spoke slowly, each word like its own sentence.

When she told them, Randy said, "Well, you may be right, Tricia. But, hey, that wasn't a custom made jacket. I've seen lots of them at Cabela's. Just happens to be one like you remember."

She shook her head, "No, Randy. It isn't any old Cabela's jacket. It's the only one with that slash on the right shoulder."

Randy had turned off the video, went to turn it on again.

Tricia struggled to stand up, pointed crossed fingers, "Don't! Please don't! It's too much for me."

Chapter 58

Randy's desk phone buzzed him.

He answered, "Yes?"

He nodded and plugged in the call, listened and pulled out a notepad, "Just a minute, let me write that down."

Randy listened and wrote a few sentences, "Thanks for this information. We'll expect your results. Please get back to us as soon as you can. More than appreciate your giving me this."

He smiled, "Well, Tricia, I am obviously unaware of what the Cabela's jacket means. But, that call is potentially very good news on your behalf."

Tricia looked at him; it was almost a blank stare. She knew Randy had said something to her, something about a call from the medical examiner about the autopsy."

Creighton could tell Tricia was in a non-register state, looked at Randy, "Thanks for this. We sure hope the results are what we are thinking."

He turned to Tricia, "I'll explain on our way home, Tricia. The shorthand is, the call said the autopsy of Rider Samson revealed skin tissue under two of his finger nails. They're checking the DNA. They will get to us soon."

Randy and Creighton nodded to each other, the body language that Creighton should take Tricia back to her home.

As they left, Tricia looked at Creighton, looked down, looked up again and broke into tears. "Creighton…oh Creighton. It was his jacket."

Chapter 59

On the way to Tricia's home, Creighton called the Snoqualmie police captain and was able to reach him. He gave him an update of what they learned and asked if the captain could arrange for Detective Valentine to meet with them…at Snoqualmie Police Headquarters… and for the captain to sit in. The captain could do that, but it would have to be at 4 p.m.

"Yes," Creighton said, "That's great. We'll be there. Maybe you'll have the DNA results; please check for us. And thanks for understanding this is a very surprising situation. Thanks so much for understanding my protecting my favorite pastor. And for our bringing Randy Linquist on board. I'm glad you and he know each other. That helps. That helps a great deal. See you at 4 p.m."

He looked at Tricia. She looked straight ahead as they reached Mercer Island Exit #7. He thought of driving to Hannah Ball's church—Creighton knew how much Tricia appreciated Hannah. It was more than fishing. But he didn't exit. Now they needed to get home. Tricia, if she could, needed to get some rest.

He looked at her again. She wasn't looking ahead. She was staring. Her cheeks were now dried but her eyes were glazed. As if the worst thing in the world happened. All from a frozen moment on the video. Something about a jacket.

Tricia said nothing more, shook her head when Creighton asked her to explain. She said she'd tell him later, "Not now…not now."

"Hey, maybe I should drive," as he pointed to an exit. "Why don't you get off here and let me drive."

Tricia blinked, slapped her forehead, looked at him, "I got it. Driving will be okay."

But she didn't know if anything else would.

Chapter 60

The sleep happened. She awoke by shouting, "NO!"

Creighton opened her bedroom door. Tricia was sitting up in bed, clutching her chest. She shook her head, opened her eyes, "Creighton, did I just yell something?"

"No, Tricia," he lied, "It's time to wash up. We have an appointment with Detective Valentine and the police captain in the captain's office."

Tricia was shocked, "What? Am I to turn myself in? Creighton! I didn't kill Rider Samson. I didn't," as she reached for Creighton.

He hugged her, "I know you didn't, Tricia. And I believe the police don't believe you did either. We need to visit with them. I asked for the visit. It will be good to make sure we're not standing on separate pages. It will be okay. Trust me, it will be okay."

Tricia slapped her hands, "Oh, now I remember. I fainted in the lawyer's office. Did I tell you why I fainted? Why I am so upset?

I mean, if I cannot tell you I cannot tell anybody. Anybody in the world."

He only nodded, *if she's ready to share, so be it.*

"It hit me, Creighton, when I saw the video. When it froze on that one moment I froze. I think I mentioned the jacket. It wasn't any ordinary jacket. I recognized the slash on the right shoulder...."

Tricia gulped, looked to Creighton, locked on his eyes, "Creighton. It was Travis' jacket. I'd know it anywhere. It was Travis' jacket. He was standing there, putting the box of condoms in my shopping cart. I don't believe it. But it was Travis."

Creighton realized Tricia saw what she saw. But he also knew it couldn't be Travis. For the very simple reason that Creighton was with Tricia when Travis was shot dead by the FBI agent. In fact, it was like yesterday for Creighton. It was a terrible way for justice to be realized. And Creighton then said, "Rustin Townsend."

Tricia looked puzzled, "What? Rustin Townsend?"

"Yes, Tricia, he was the FBI agent who helped us. We left and Rustin took care of Travis' body. Tricia? Travis is dead. That may have been his jacket. I think all Travis' clothes were sent to the Tillamook Goodwill. Someone must have picked it up for a dollar. And you know how that goes…coats like that go from one soup kitchen to another."

"I know," Tricia said, "but Creighton? Can we be sure? I'm overwhelmed with fright now. What if he didn't die?"

Creighton looked at his watch, "Hey, we gotta go…let's meet with Valentine. I'm the one who called the captain and asked for this meeting. Oh, do you remember the call Randy got before we left his office?"

"Call from Randy? What?"

"No, Tricia, a call to Randy when we were there. You were just coming out of your fainting spell. He was called about the autopsy of Rider Samson. They discovered skin tissue under two of his finger nails. The DNA testing is happening. And," in his attempt to bring some hope and a good spirit, "I bet you your DNA is not under his finger nails. That's not to say you weren't under Samson's skin…. oops, strike that comment."

Tricia couldn't smile, but she loved Creighton so much she wasn't bothered by his skin comment. He was her strength and that wouldn't change…unless it got stronger.

She stood up, "Okay, driver, let's get to some justice."

"Now, Reverend Gleason," Creighton said, "That's better…you're headed in a good direction."

Creighton smiled because they had visited in the master bedroom and the door to her home office was closed. A good thing.

As they drove, Tricia said, "I forgot, Creighton. I forgot to thank you for the lemon drops. Great of you to gift them. And to think that troubles melt like lemon drops. Not yet for me. But, when Connor Wright screamed at me and talked about Dorothy and her red shoes and the yellow brick road I thought immediately of the lemon drops. Some day. I have to believe this, the lemon drop…"

He finished for her, "Will melt."

He then started to sing, even though his musical toning was somewhere between *forget it and absent,* "Somewhere over the rainbow..."

Tricia smiled, "Creighton? Mind if I turn on the radio?"

He laughed and gave her a high-five.

Chapter 61

"Hello, Tricia," as he shook her hand, "I'm Benton Harbour, police captain and friend of your attorney, Randy Linquist. Thanks for being here."

Harbour turned to Valentine and nodded. Valentine was no longer wooden, he shook hands with Creighton and Tricia, "Glad we can meet here."

Harbour was pleasant and relaxed, not rigid, "Good, let's sit at my table. There's plenty of room. And Tricia, I hope you don't mind but I will record this visit…how do they say it when you order a plane ticket on the phone," as he quoted his fingers, "for quality assurance."

Creighton picked up on it immediately, "Captain? That's the magic phrase, *quality assurance*."

"Oh," Valentine asked, "How so?"

The feel of the visit was positive and encouraging to Tricia. A good start.

Captain Harbour said, "Creighton you said you had some updated information from your attorney, Randy Linquist. By the way Randy and I have worked together before. He's good people. So, Tricia, might you—and Creighton, please partner up with her—share what you've learned? We can then go from there."

Tricia indicated chapter and verse. Explained that she learned her car was bugged as were her home and church offices. Even mentioned the note sent to Harbour about the charge she had taken off her panties in front of Valentine.

It was shocking to Creighton, "What? That was the charge?"

Harbour laughed, "Yes, the only constant with the note…it was written in calligraphy. But, I have worked with Detective Valentine for five years and even though his name might indicate otherwise, Tricia wouldn't have done that…and in hearing some of her church members talk about her, she'd never do that. For, after all, she used to be a detective, right?"

Creighton laughed, "Yeah, yeah. Detectives are pure. Well, in some cases they are pure as the driven slush."

He raised his hand for correction, "But. Of course that's in no reference to anyone in this room."

Tricia was feeling better as she looked at Creighton, "Sorry Dr. Yale, but I need to continue…"

He clapped.

Tricia continued.

When she finished Creighton said, "One more thing. Yesterday in the afternoon Tricia went to the small hill up the path from her house on Kendall Peak Street…"

"Yes, I know it," said Valentine. "A great view of the valley, the Snoqualmie River and Mount Si. I've been there and find it a helpful place."

Creighton nodded, "Yes, well Tricia went up there because yesterday at worship no one sang the Hallelujah Chorus. One of Rider Samson's buddies screamed at Tricia and told her to leave! Anyway, while she was up there the neighbor family stopped by. They are members of the church and had been there yesterday during worship when the church member exploded with his venomous comments. The neighbor family knocked on Tricia's door. The kids…beautiful and so thoughtful…each held a cupcake they had made for Tricia…their way of helping her feel better after the morning attack.

"I said she was up the path to the top of the hill and then the older son, I think his name is Scooter, said he knew where that was. He said he had seen her and he put it this way, 'I saw Pastor Tricia up there the morning we didn't have school. I was headed to our playground and didn't want to bother her. But, I know it was her…and thought she was praying as she sat on that bench. It was in the morning.'

Valentine said, "Dr. Yale, are you sure that's what he said and when that happened?"

"Yes," Creighton said, "I'm sure. Abby, that's their mother, confirmed there was no school that day. It was a teacher's workday. And I know, that is the morning Rider Samson was murdered. How wonderful is that…saved by a seven-year-old-angel?"

Tricia didn't see a scowl. Jordon raised his brow, "Well that can certainly help."

He looked at Tricia, not saying her name, "What a summary…and for you both to learn from your attorney that there are listening devices in both your home and church offices, that certainly explains how the notes were on track. It certainly could be they were recorded."

Tricia smiled to herself at Valentine's detective cleverness, *got it… don't want to agree with too much…more miles to travel on this case.*

"Yes, that makes sense…also makes sense why the plumbing truck was 30 minutes at my house," Tricia said, "And no one was in the church when that note was left on my pulpit. So. That could have been when the bug was hidden in my church office. That's how I look at it. Because the notes notwithstanding, I never revealed any of the confidences. Never," as she knuckled her hands together.

Tricia sighed, "Well, that's about it. Thanks, Creighton, for filling in what Scooter said."

She didn't say anything about seeing Travis' jacket in the Safeway security tape. She and Creighton had discussed with themselves. But for now t's good to keep that discovery with Randy and the two of them. It could always be offered later to Valentine and Harbour. They'd want to get more information from the detectives.

Harbour's phone rang, "I need to get that. You don't have to leave… my secretary is blocking my calls, except one. Hold on."

He went behind his desk, took out a note pad…wrote. Tricia noticed his eyes looked surprised. Ended the call, "Thanks for this. Great to know how competent and timely you are. Take care."

He hung up.

Came back to the table.

Looked at Tricia, "Do you know a Travis Gleason?"

Chapter 62

Tricia reached for a glass of water. Creighton put his hand on her shoulder.

Harbour wasn't sure of her reaction, "I'm sorry, Tricia. I only asked if you know a Travis Gleason. That call was from our DNA forensics staff…I asked them to rush their testing on the tissue under Rider Samson's finger nails. The DNA said it wasn't from Samson. It is the DNA of Travis Gleason."

"He's dead," Tricia said softly.

Valentine looked baffled, "You know him, Tricia?"

Tricia looked at Creighton, he nodded, "Go ahead, Tricia, start with the security tape."

She did, "This is knocking me out. What you learned, Captain. Let me explain. We did keep one discovery from you. Please don't be offended; I didn't know how to deal with it."

She explained the security tape, the jacket with the torn sleeve.

"That was my ex-husband's jacket. He's dead. Both Creighton and I were there when he was shot. The FBI agent shot him."

She looked to Creighton, "What's was his name?"

Creighton replied, "Rustin 'Townsend. I was there when Gleason was shot. Tricia and I left, but we just anticipated Townsend would have taken the body. We didn't verify; saw no reason for that."

Harbour asked Tricia, "So, we have the DNA of a man you say is dead."

He turned to Valentine, "Jordon, go check for us, you know how to reach Townsend. Ask him to verify."

Valentine responded, "On it," as he jumped up and walked to another office.

Harbour shook his head, "If we link all this together…and as I've reviewed the case, the links from one of these situations to the other…could be unrelated, but I find that unlikely. Does that mean, Tricia, your ex-husband didn't die? Maybe he wasn't killed? Or. At least that his jacket was on the security tape…and as the autopsy shows, his skin tissue…."

Valentine returned, "I was able to reach Townsend. He said the timing of my call is more than curious. One of his friends owns the Tillamook Mortuary. Just last week the mortician said to Townsend that an urn had been dug up at their pauper's cemetery. It was the urn…and Townsend swears he was dead…of Travis Gleason."

Creighton raised a question, "I hate to ask this, detective, but, might it be possible that Gleason wasn't killed? That all this has veracity to it…and…for his urn to be stolen. Weird. Something that Rod Serling would come up with…or Stephen King…"

Tricia started, "There's something inside me that…", but she couldn't finish.

Harbour looked at his pencil, tapped on the table, "Geeze. Something just came to me. We had mentioned it earlier. Here's the situation. The four of us—don't worry about the autopsy results, forensics won't convey that information right now—the four of us are the only ones who know some things…that at least in this moment, seem worth counting.

"First, we have enough evidence to not indict you, Tricia. You are no longer even a person of interest. Two, we believe Rider Samson was murdered by someone whose identity is unknown. I don't want to say Samson was killed by a dead man. We simply know what the DNA shows."

Creighton's eyes got big, "Captain. I have an idea. Based upon your two points…Tricia is innocent and someone else murdered Samson. Our goal, our purpose, nothing less, is to identify the murderer, who somehow is making Tricia's life a horrific situation."

Tricia agreed, "Yep, Dr. Yale, you are on to something. I can feel it…. oops, I interrupted," as she pointed to him, "Preach it Reverend!"

Creighton smiled and winked at Tricia, "I'm about to. I'm about to. Knowing what we know and knowing what we need to find out…the killer has no idea what we know. The congregation has no idea what we know. We," as he pointed to Harbour and Valentine and Tricia, "we are a quartet of identifying and catching the killer. Here…here is what I am thinking of…."

When he finished, Harbour slapped the table, "Hot damn, minister, looking at Creighton, "In a previous life..were you a detective?"

Creighton shook his head, "No, but maybe my idea will work out… then you can give me one of those plaques that I done good…and I done it well."

Tricia saw how the game plan had a possibility, "I want to try it. But, it's important that no one else knows…and important we leave my offices bugged and no GPS be removed from my car."

She then looked at Creighton, "Well, sir. Since this is your idea, I think we should be co-conspirators. You on?"

He nodded and saluted her, "Yes, ma'am. At your service."

Tricia looked at Harbour, "If you don't mind, Captain. Might this be unrecorded now…just in case everything doesn't work?"

Harbour got up, reached under his desk, pushed a button. "Ready?" Three heads nodded.

Creighton said to Valentine, "Detective? Ever been in a play before… or on a stage?"

He shook his head, "Nope. I did try out for our senior play in high school, but didn't get the part."

Tricia smiled, "Well, I am a believer."

Valentine asked, "A believer? In what?"

Tricia didn't hesitate, "I believe now you'll get the part."

Tricia reached into her pocket. The yarn never felt better.

Chapter 63

He pounded on her door, yelled her name, "REVEREND GLEASON!"

Tricia waited.

More pounding.

She stood by her office door, "I'm coming! Have some patience!"

She looked at him, "Well, Detective Valentine. You sure don't look like Cupid. To the point, what do you want? You've already made my life a mess with your home invasion…don't think I'll ever gain back respect with the neighbors. No chance.

"Okay. Well, it's not okay. But why are you here?"

"Reverend Gleason, I'll try not to be cynical, but that's difficult. Official business."

"Official business? I don't see a search warrant."

She slammed the door in his face.

More pounding, as Valentine shouted, "I can get all the neighbors up with this yelling. Why don't you take a smart pill and open up. I won't even say please."

Tricia smiled. Couldn't imagine how Valentine didn't make the school play part.

She opened the door. It was hard to hold a firm, outraged attitude, "I'll not be nice, but come in. Tell me why you're here."

He walked in, Tricia pointed to her home office, "Since you are official…there, in the corner is a chair. Got it? Sitting in the corner?"

"Reverend Gleason, why don't you take a civility pill. I'm actually here to give you a warning. How's that for matching up to my name?"

"Warning? What's this about."

"My captain knows I'm here…I want you to know we're about to change you from a person of interest to an arrest."

"What! What in God's name are you talking about?"

Valentine answered, "Not in God's name. In your name. We now have corroborated evidence that you murdered your church member, one Rider Samson."

"No! That's absurd. You did the search warrant drill, but you never told me what you, quote, ripped me off for."

"That's easy. We found what we thought was the murder weapon. And. The petroleum jelly?"

That took Tricia by surprise, "What, a revolver and petroleum jelly?"

"Yep, on the lubricating matter, we know what you tried to do to convince Rider Samson, when he met here with you, with, how might we say it, the s word?"

Tricia was taken aback, so faking it wasn't at issue, "You've got to be kidding?"

"Nope, look at this picture, good ol' KY."

He handed her the picture, she gulped. It was a picture of KY lubricating jelly, sitting in her top desk drawer. She could only shake her head.

"But, you didn't use the jelly tube to kill Samson. Nope, you used the revolver."

"It must have been planted!" Tricia screamed.

She thought she heard the window shake. Good.

"Yeah, you may be right, but more than likely not. We've rushed the forensic testing and the revolver found in your lingerie drawer is the gun used to kill Rider Samson. The bullets came from that gun... no mistake."

Tricia put out her hands, "Okay, I am innocent. But, evidence is evidence. Where are your handcuffs."

"Well, the only reason I'm here is to be alerting you. A warrant for your arrest is coming...probably later tonight. You better call your church. The pulpit will be closed to you."

"You cannot do this!"

Valentine turned, walked to the door, opened it and stepped to the porch. He leaned back, "Be seeing you later this evening. Next time I'll use the doorbell."

He closed the door.

Tricia yelled, "Creighton? Get in here; you still in the kitchen?"

He was closer, just down the hall from her office, "Tricia! You look terrible. What happened?"

She waved him into her office, "This is not good. I am arrested for murder. God-awful. Everything looks worse than…I cannot even think of the word…well, I don't care…it looks shitty. They're coming for me later tonight. Dreadful. That's the minor version."

Creighton said, "Well, let's not wait. I have an idea. He cannot serve you if he cannot find you. Right?"

Tricia smiled, "Well, no. What are you, the master of logic?"

"Here's my idea, call the Rockport guy…he's into helping wounded veterans, right? Call him and see if we can stay in their bunkhouse tonight. And. What will help you, don't tell him why, but use your pleading and begging voice and ask him if we can fish with him tomorrow. We'll go up there tonight and fish tomorrow. That way you'll be out of sight if not out of a warrant arrest."

Tricia picked up her phone, nodded to Creighton, "Creighton, you are a genius," as she dialed.

"Jon? Don't know if you remember me, but this is Tricia Nelson. I need a favor…don't know if it's possible, but know if you can help, you will be the hero of the decade. Can my mentor, Creighton Yale, and I stay tonight in your bunkhouse and just possibly, very just possibly, fish with you tomorrow morning?"

She waited, then said, "Yes! We're on our way. What time will we launch from Roger Miller Steelhead Park out of Rockport tomorrow? That's great...see you tonight. And I bet I get the first coho after our 8 a.m. launch. Great! What? No, Creighton Yale's not my boyfriend. He's my favorite friend, though, older than time. He's my mentor, my minister. And. We know how to be discreet. No problem."

She closed her cell phone, "Well, Creighton, your idea is a winner. I only wish I was. And to think, the detective picked through my underwear. How embarrassing. Ridiculous."

They packed and walked to Tricia's car, which they had left in the driveway, so they could be followed. They almost burst out laughing, but Creighton gestured to Tricia, rubbing a finger over his lips.

When they got in the car, "Wow, Tricia," Creighton remarked. "How good of us to call your fishing guide an hour ago. My. What a great job of a convincing conversation. Well, impressive, even if it was one-voiced. And I bet Jordon Valentine lied. I bet he did get the high school lead in their senior play."

Off they went. Hoping the mission would be better than successful.

He reached to click off the recording. He thought, *everything's in order. And for sure, I know the boat launch. Wonder if they have room for a 4th? Time is now. Why wait for a trial when I can be judge, jury and injector...a new version of the death penalty.*

Tick. Tick. Tick.

Chapter 64

Never. Never before had Tricia sat in a boat about to be launched… and been filled with anything less than full joy that the day would be spent fishing. It was her pulse, the pulse that never failed to ignite her joy and fuel her energy.

But not today. To say her feelings were mixed? Probably accurate. She and Creighton made it to Jon and Heather's log cabin paradise. Arriving there at night, to see the lights illuminating Jon's ten-year project, it took her breath. Probably always will.

What she didn't want was for her breath taken away to be nothing more than a metaphor. They didn't talk about much. Heather went to bed. She had to get up pretty early for her school bus route. She had made them dinner, always, as Jon described her, "the consummate hostess." He called that spot on. She excused herself, "Hope you have a great day…lots of catching. I'm sure Jon told you he has to be off the river at 1 p.m. He needs to be at the high school, a meeting with the principal then the assistant wrestling coaches."

The Lemon Drop Didn't Melt

Tricia knew this. Jon had told her that. What she hoped was the fishing trip, probably a very dramatic boat ride if she played her cards right, wouldn't take until 1 p.m. She didn't tell Creighton, but she put her own revolver in the back of her long john underwear, fastened to the lower back. She knew you could never be too prepared.

They really didn't talk about anything…Creighton excused himself right after Heather had. He said he'd be ready for lots of catching in the morning and went to the bunkhouse.

The mixed emotions were real. It was great news to be fishing. But. It could be the most terrible day in her life. She sat there. Jon had everything ready. Creighton had taken the adjoining boat chair in Jon's sled boat. Creighton tapped the arms of the chair, "Well, this makes each of us a captain, right?"

Tricia's smile was forced. Not Jon's, "Yes, Creighton, only the best for preachers."

Jon turned off the trolling motor and cranked up the jet motor, "Here we go!" As he shifted into the reverse gear.

The shout froze them…and to Tricia, froze time.

A man running at them from the parking lot, "Wait! Wait! I want to join you!"

Jon paid no attention, started to back up.

The shot shattered the window of his boat.

Jon's eyes looked in shock as the man jumped on the bow of the boat, held his revolver at them, "Time to go fishing, boys and girl. I think you have an extra seat," as he pointed to the third seat by the fish box, "so I won't have to stand."

He waved his gun at Jon, "You are Jon, right? The wounded warrior hero? Well, I ain't no wounded warrior, but this one will be and being wounded won't be even close to the final…"

He said to Jon, "Go ahead. We've have lots of time…I want to enjoy the trip."

Tricia looked at him. No longer the scraggly beard. She saw her ex-husband…perfectly clear. She looked again and realized it wasn't her husband. He had been killed. This guy, quite a physical resemblance didn't have the scar. So, it wasn't Travis Gleason.

He said nothing, "Okay, you two," pointing to Creighton and Tricia, sit down. Captain, head out…to your favorite fishing hole. I'd hate for all this to end when you're not casting at, what go guides call it? Their 95% hole? Head to that. And then we'll anchor."

He took off his pack, set it down, looked at Tricia, "Hey, Pastor Bitch, do I look familiar? Yep."

He then reached for his pack, pulled out a box of condoms, "Hey, you remember this, don't you?"

Then pulled out a tube of the KY jelly, "And this? Bet you can remember where each of them was."

The motor roared down the Skagit. Almost an irony it was a day to never forget. At first that had nothing to do with the dire circumstance. It had to do with the glorious sunrise…the quiet river, the mountains, some already dusted with snow and the glorious orange glimmering red sunrise. The circumstance took over.

"Do you recognize him, Tricia? I bet I'm right. It isn't Travis. It's his identical twin brother."

A shot was fired over Creighton's head, "Shut up, you bastard. No more from you. Next time I won't aim so high. Shut the hell up."

Tricia nodded, "What is your name? I know now you aren't Travis… no scar on the bridge of your nose. You probably don't know this but when he was seven he and a neighbor buddy took terms throwing sawdust on each other. The buddy lost his grasp of the shovel and it hit Travis…he was furious because the doctor, a neighborhood doctor, stitched the wound without using Novocaine…and laid Travis on his dining room table. After the stitching, Travis got up, the doctor's wife offered Travis a box of chocolates and he threw the box to the floor."

She paused, "But I bet you didn't know that, did you?"

Jon slowed the motor down, "Here we are, the 95% hole. But today I bet it's the 100?% hole. Sir, whoever you are, I'm now going to the bow to release the anchor."

He waved the gun again and stepped aside, reached into his pocket and pulled a second revolver, pointed at Jon, then turned and pointed at Creighton and Tricia, "I've got each of you. Nothing. That's what I expect from you. Nothing."

Jon lowered the anchor. It held. He walked back to the back of the boat, turned his jet motor off. Looked at Tricia, "Sorry, Tricia, but you were saying?"

"Yes, thanks, Jon, I was saying to Mr. Revolver...make that Mr. Twin Revolvers, that I bet he didn't know that about his brother."

She then said with a soft voice, the tone in total contrast to her inner turmoil, "But, I bet you didn't know that. In fact, I get it. You are a twin brother. But I don't know your name? I would bet it's not Gleason."

He scowled, "I shouldn't even respond," as he put a pistol back into his pocket. "But, I do want to do what I've waited to do. I want to bring you a special greeting from my brother."

He reached back into his pack, it was lying on top of the fish box, lifted out a rectangular container. It was brushed gold.

Tricia got it, "Ah, Travis' urn. We heard it was stolen."

The smile appeared crooked, "Yep, digging an urn...did you know they're not six feet under?"

He laid the urn down on the front seat, opened it and reached in.

He picked up a handful of ashes and tossed them at Tricia, "This, you Pastor Bitch. This is a special greeting from my brother. You!"

He tossed more ashes, "You! Killed him. I learned all about it. You are horrible. A minister? No way. But you've fooled everyone."

Creighton didn't protest, "I know Travis' name. In fact I was there when he met his Maker. But I don't know who you are. You look like Travis. But, do you know why Travis had to be killed?"

"Sir! I don't give a rat's ass. He was my brother. You," pointing at Tricia, "killed him. So now, in your honey bucket hole, you need to die on his behalf."

"My, oh my," Creighton said, "You have it all wrong. You don't know what happened. But, that's not the point."

Before he could answer Jon said, "Hey, you are obviously on a mission. But I am too. And if this is my final hurrah, I want to do some fishing."

Jon then looked at his boat, "But, damn. Can you believe this? A 20-year Skagit River fishing guide who forgot his net? Look, my screw-up. Hey, we have to present a good front to those neighbors in their modest home in the Cedars. Let me call my wife, Heather. Sir, you'd like her. Ask her to bring my landing net."

Tricia echoed the option, "Mr. No-Name…"

He interrupted, "My name is Quentin Bridges. But don't call me that. It's too Aussie."

Jon picked up his cell phone, "I'll text her."

"Don't you dare do that. Call her, I want to hear what you say. Go ahead," as he pointed to Jon's phone, "Call her. I bet you know her number."

Jon saw it was 8:30 a.m., Heather should be at home. She answered, "Honey, guess what? I really screwed up. I forgot the landing net. We're right in front of Hannah's favorite hole, in front of the yellow ladder….no, Hannah's not here, I'm just pointing out where we are. It's right by Eileen's house. I see smoke coming from her chimney so

I know she's home. Anyway, please bring the landing net. I'll look for you....am I all right? Never been better, you know how that goes, our favorite jingle, 'Hey, guess what? I think I just saw a honey badger down here at the Cedars,' in front of Eileen's house. Will look for you....yes, I love you, too."

He clicked his phone closed, "No problem. Will be about 30 minutes..."

Tricia asked, "Now that we are ashes to ashes and dust to dust," as she brushed off her dead husband's ashes, "why don't you fill us in. You obviously didn't know him. But I hear an accent. And you said something about an Aussie name. That mean Australia?"

Tricia knew that *diversion* wasn't an option; it was a necessity.

He bit.

"I didn't know about Travis. But, I'm a travel agent in Australia. A couple from Oregon called me to arrange for some travel here. When I met them, turns out they are from Tillamook, Oregon. When I met them at the airport they were in shock. They said I could be the twin brother of their favorite fishing guide named Travis Gleason. They showed me his picture. So, I did research, and sure enough, to my amazement, I had not a twin brother, but an identical twin brother..."

He raised his revolver, "But that's shit. I need to do what I need to do," as he pointed the revolver at Tricia.

Creighton stepped forward, "Go ahead and be a hero. I have the short straw; start with me."

That was more than surprise to Tricia, "No, Creighton! He's not after you; he's after me."

The identical twin lowered his gun, "I need you to know...I did some research and learned that Travis and I...I was named Trenton Gothridge at birth...had the misfortune of having a very sick mother. We were born in 1980 and then there was no ultra sound. Our mother didn't know she'd have twins. She wasn't married, had hidden her pregnancy. When my brother and I were born it was a shock to her. I learned our mother had a severe depression and with immediate emotional and coping problems and no money resources, she was advised to adopt me and my brother out. With that I learned my brother, Travis, was ailing...maybe our mother had lots of cocaine use...so he was hospitalized. He was adopted by the Gleason family in Garibaldi, Oregon. They changed his name from Gothridge to Gleason.

"Turns out at the time a family visiting a church in Portland wanted to adopt a child. They felt sorry for me and adopted me. The problem was they got transferred to Australia which became my home. I had no idea I had an identical twin brother. Then the visit with some people in Tillamook.

"I made arrangements to get to Tillamook. I didn't want to tip off Travis ahead of time and thought it would be the surprise of the century. And. On the very day I arrived in Portland," as he pointed the gun at Tricia, his arm didn't waver, "You, Pastor Bitch, had my brother killed. You must pay for that. Revenge is more than getting even. YOU! Will. Pay. For. His. Death. Carrying his ashes with you."

He clicked his revolver.

CRAAAAACKKK.

Chapter 65

No one moved. Except Quentin. His head exploded, blood and shattered skull spewed. He staggered, then fell into the river.

Jon pointed, as Tricia reached for him, "Tricia, leave him. He will be good food for Mr. Chum."

She sat back in the chair that was much more comfortable than she was. She put her hands to her face and wept.

"I don't believe it," as Creighton pointed.

Out of the modest cabin stood Heather, holding the rifle. Following was Jordon Valentine, holding another rifle. He pointed to her, "She said she could shoot a bear at 100 yards. Who am I to argue?"

Tricia looked downstream. The body floated. Then sank.

She reached for her yarn, held it and continued to cry.

Creighton held her, "Tricia, it's over. I bet the lemon drop will melt."

Epilogue

The moment could have shattered Tricia. It didn't. Both Jon and Heather had saved her from dying in the sled boat, covered by her ex-husband's ashes. Jon understood when he explained that he and Heather had a "secret code" that only said "danger in every way." He also said that Heather could "shoot a bear at 200 yards."

That drama was now in her rear-view mirror. Advent and Christmas happened. Candles were lighted on Christmas Eve. Somehow the singing of "Silent Night, Holy Night," candles raised high, made it clear to Tricia. She would not leave ministry. At least not now.

Her mentor, Creighton Yale, said he understood her inner struggle. He said that every one of us was pure, but in his manner to bring humor and truth, "Yep, Tricia, we're pure as the driven slush." He also included the Bible when he pointed to her neighbor children, "Remember, Tricia, they need you. They trust you. They would be devastated if you walked away. At least now. Be good on your commitment to serve this year in Snoqualmie as a licensed minister. You have no reason to leave. The kids are telling you that you matter. A decision on returning to seminary can wait. No egg-timer pushed at you to decide, at least not now."

Tricia nodded as the months got checked off her personal calendar. She believed the "danger people" were not around. She had enjoyed fishing the Skagit with Jon. That was her "fishing fix." She also found her getaway place for a couple of days was Forks on the Olympic Peninsula. Floating the rapids of the Calawah River with a new guide, Bob Bell, gave her the joy of playing a steelhead. And watching the eagles soar and seeing the tree that was supposedly dead, but had another tree growing out of its dead center. A very good sermon metaphor. But more. It brought her personal hope, that growth was never in a cul-de-sac. Growth could be.

The next "big season" in church life happened. She appreciated Lent, for it gave time for self-examination. Tricia wanted the congregation to engage her...they did...and no exception of appreciation came her way. For her especially, the inner struggle of "next step" continued. But, somehow, maybe it was the smooth gait of ministry with the Snoqualmie church people, the struggle was real but not beleaguering.

She found that Creighton's question was answered. He inquired, "Tricia, how will you make sure your congregation doesn't amputate the Gospel?" That meant, of course, ministry was to help the church members be involved beyond self-examination. Linking the church with Hannah Ball in serving food monthly at the Methodist Church in downtown Seattle gave them an awareness that people in need should never be neglected. They also provided their recreation hall a place for after-school care giving. And, no less, they discussed creating a mission team that would travel to Port au Prince, Haiti to work with a new program called The What If? Foundation. To feed and teach. Okay, Tricia thought, it would be only for a week. But maybe a week in being with those who had great struggle would give them perspective on how their own lives should never be self-indulged.

The Lemon Drop Didn't Melt

And nothing else. Tricia could say, "No amputated Gospel for us; we'll give arms and legs and hearts to helping others. That's the least we can do."

That didn't mean resolution. But for these months, washed clean from her ex-husband's ashes and helping the congregation live with more wisdom and courage and love. That wasn't academic. It was real and evident. It tugged inside her…"ministry or fishing or…" She kept that to herself. But her inner self was never in full mute.

She was delighted Mary Tricia Murdough was born to Bradley and Sarah, her neighbors. They wanted Tricia to know their gratitude and hoped their daughter would have the wisdom and courage Tricia had shown them. As Sarah said, "Tricia your visit to us in the hospital when Mary Tricia may not have made it…that will be with us forever. You ARE a caring presence. And all three of us are the better for it. Thank you."

And of no less value, Sarah's negative and controlling boss left Amazon. A good step. So aware of Tricia's love for them they joined the church. They asked Tricia if she would baptize Mary Tricia. That meant birth and new life was more than a resurrection truth…it was real and alive and connected. Made for the best Easter Tricia ever experienced.

Still, Tricia knew the days would not be uneventful. And she knew the piece of chartreuse yarn would always be in her pocket. Even if gnarled and knotty. Still, she wouldn't give that up. Never would give that up.

And then. A surprise happened. She was more than surprised. It was as if her ex-husband was one of triplets. She knew that wasn't the case. But she wondered again about ministry. Was it a place that was never distant to harm's way? She sighed…and was grateful… the yarn hadn't left.

About the Author

Dr. Mark Henry Miller is a retired United Church of Christ local church pastor and Conference Minister. He and his wife, Diane, and their faithful buddies, Faith [English Cocker] and Caleb [Lord Cavalier Spaniel] live in Leander, Texas. Born in Portland, Oregon, he graduated from Stanford University, Yale University Divinity School and Eden Theological Seminary. "The Lemon Drop Didn't Melt," not unlike his four previous novels, includes lots of life, ministry, fishing and murder, but seldom in that order. This novel's venue is Snoqualmie, Washington, 25 miles east of Seattle but not distant from daunting stress moments for Tricia Gleason. For those interested, Mark's four previous murder/mystery novels are available on www.authorhouse.com, Amazon/Kindle, Barnes & Noble. For any questions or if interested in a signed copy, let Mark know, markhmiller@att.net. He promises to respond once back from fishing.